THE PARK SERVICE

Book One of The Park Service Trilogy

By Ryan Winfield

The Park Service
Book One of The Park Service Trilogy
By Ryan Winfield

Please visit www.RyanWinfield.com

ISBN-13: 978-0988348202
ISBN-10: 0988348209

Cover art by Adam Mager

Cover image trees: Daryl Benson / Photodisc / Getty Images

Author photo: Sarah T. Skinner

Summary: In the distant, post-apocalyptic future, a fifteen-year-old boy stumbles on a paradise where humans are hunted by a mysterious Park Service and sets out to uncover who's behind the gruesome killings.

Printed in the United States of America.

BIRCH PAPER PRESS
Post Office Box 4252
Seattle, Washington 98194

Also by **Ryan Winfield**

Isle of Man
Book Two of The Park Service Trilogy

State of Nature
Book Three of The Park Service Trilogy

South of Bixby Bridge

Jane's Melody

For the misfits
Because misfits have big hearts

There is a pleasure in the pathless woods,
There is a rapture on the lonely shore,
There is society where none intrudes,
By the deep Sea, and music in its roar:
I love not Man the less, but Nature more . . .

— Lord Byron, from *Childe Harold's Pilgrimage*

THE PARK SERVICE

Book One of The Park Service Trilogy

Ho· lo· cene:

The current geological epoch dominated by the rise of human civilization; the age of man.

PROLOGUE
The End of the Holocene

Dead leaves scatter, caught and swirling in smoky exhaust.

Now the hiss of hydraulic brakes, the ticking blinker, the whine of straining gears as the bus disappears down the city hill like some mechanical land-whale sounding in a concrete sea.

A young soldier stands alone on the curb. She thumbs her earbuds in, cranks her music up, slings her service pack on and walks the empty morning sidewalk toward home.

Passing a pawnshop, she spots her reflection in the glass and stops to look—

Taller, broader, her hair shorter than before—she isn't sure who she is, who she has become. All she knows for sure is she isn't who she was when she left.

Nobody is, and nobody ever will be.

The streets are quiet, even for the early hour.

A digital clock on an unfinished bank building behind her blinks mindlessly, the red numbers reversed in the glass. She's turning to read the time when she's caught by the flash.

A bright magnesium burn in the corner of the gray sky.

Bright and then brighter.

Then the heat hits.

She stiffens, her skin crawling with searing pain.

Weightless now, she's floating above the blinding street, a garbage can suspended beside her, its contents already aflame. When she hits the pavement she feels the thunder of buildings collapsing around her, the tumbling stone, the falling glass.

All is black now, but black as only hell can be. She hears a distant fire bell. Then muffled screams. Shrieks of pain, moans of agony.

A voice calling softly—"Mother."

Another, more distant, mumbling some memorized prayer, strangely comforting in its innocence, despite the irony there. She smells sulfur, the dust of concrete, the pungent odor of cooking meat. She sits up and shrugs off her flaming pack. She strips free of her jacket, peels her shirt over her head, wincing as her skin tears away with it. Then the darkness lightens to a red haze that clears in a sweltering breeze. And from the haze a naked man stumbles toward her, his pale arms uplifted as if pleading to the burning sky, his quivering mouth agape in a silent scream. She watches with curious horror as he passes her by, his backside burned to muscle, to bone, the gushing blood running down his legs to leave a trail in the dusty street.

She closes her eyes for a minute, maybe two.

She opens them again.

Beneath the billowing mushroom cloud rising above the ruined city, the morning sunshine breaks through in beautiful beams of rainbow color down to where she sits in the middle of the street. She tries to stand but discovers her legs crushed beneath a giant granite cornerstone, the date carved on its face like a tombstone already on top of her—

ERECTED 2020.

Then her left earbud fades back in and her music plays on as before, the voice of some pop past echoing in her ear from a world already gone. She almost reaches to pull the bud free, but decides to leave it in. And so she sits, pinned and watching, with an oddly fitting soundtrack as the wild tornado of fire rips up the street toward her, setting everything it touches ablaze, melting light posts, incinerating corpses, cleaning the street and making way for the gathering clouds of black rain.

This street, every street—

The world will never be the same.

Part One

CHAPTER 1
Tomorrow's the Big Day

I stir awake.

I listen to the gentle waves lapping at the shore, smell the saltwater breeze, feel the sun on my closed eyelids, and I grasp at my daydreams as they drift like clouds across my mind.

A dark shadow flutters above, lands.

Something brushes my throat.

My eyes pop open.

The gull opens its beak and screeches in my face. I lift my arm to knock it away, but my arm won't budge. It's trapped, I'm trapped. Buried. A mound of sand rises above my chest, only my head and neck are free. The gull pecks at my throat again. Another gull lands and nips me with its beak, too. More gulls circle overhead. I struggle, I kick—nothing gives.

I'm frozen in the concrete grip of wet sand.

I open my mouth to scream, but stop when I hear them laughing. I can't show them I'm scared. I won't. I will myself to relax, to be calm and take whatever comes, and I lie there in my tomb feeling the weight of the sand above me and the sharp brush of beaks snatching crackers off my baited head.

The laughing stops. I hear their footsteps padding away on the wet sand. Then the gulls take flight, too. A moment later Bill's smiling face appears in the blue sky above me.

"I've never seen a beached seal," he says, laughing. "But I was sure they'd be better looking than you are."

"Stop making fun and dig me out."

"You need to learn to watch your back with those bullies," he says, dropping to his knees and scooping the sand away.

"Isn't that your job?" I reply, sarcastically.

"It's my job to make sure you don't drown."

I want to ask him who could drown in just a half meter of water, but I don't. Free of my confinement, I stand and brush the sand from my arms and chest, revealing my pale flesh. I'm self-conscious standing next to Bill with his olive skin and his electric-sun bleached hair. I smile nervously, buying time to come up with a self-deprecating joke, but before I can think of anything, the sun clicks off, the blue sky disappears.

"Looks like rec time's over," he says, his voice echoing in the sudden silence.

What were kilometers of sunny beach and blue horizon are now just a cavernous sand-filled room and a shallow, artificial reservoir gleaming gray in the overhead LED glow.

Bill walks me past the life-guard station to the locker room door. I smile up at him in silent thanks.

"Hey, isn't tomorrow the big day?" he asks.

I nod, not happy to be reminded.

"Boy, I'm sure glad I never have to go through that again," he says, shaking his head.

"That bad?"

He flashes me a smile. "Not for smart kids like you."

When he opens the door, I step into the shower room. He must see the worry written on my face because he lingers in the doorway before closing it. "You'll do fine," he says. "Just relax and follow directions. You don't want to end up like me, spending your career sifting sand for gull shit and buried boys."

Bill's smile disappears as the door seals shut.

I strip off my shorts and toss them in the hamper. When the hamper closes, the jets turn on, and I'm blasted from every angle with hot water. The water turns off just long enough for me to lather my body with a pump of soap before it turns on again and rinses me clean. I raise my arms for the blowers, then exit into the locker room.

I step onto the scale—no gain. Same as last week. I get identical food rations as every fifteen-year-old, but I can't seem to put on a gram. Two weeks ago Tuesday was my birthday. I'd asked for a weight set, I got a graphing calculator instead. My dad says my brain's the most important muscle anyway. I say nonsense. Besides, everyone knows the brain's not a muscle.

As I dress, I'm half hoping I do get sent to another level tomorrow, just so I can wear something different. The same gray jumpsuit every day gets old. I pull my hoody over my head and push from the bright locker room into the dim hall.

My steps echo off the polished-stone tunnel walls and the LED lights cast two eerie shadow twins on either side of me, so I imagine I'm actually a gang of three brothers heading to find that bully Red and teach him and his brainless buddies a lesson.

But I don't have any brothers, and I never will.

The tunnel widens as it joins with the others. Following it to the outlook, I stop and gaze over the parapet and admire the Valley, or what some of us sometimes affectionately refer to as the "Anthill." It's a seven story drop to the cavern floor and the buildings that make up Level 3 of Holocene II. The walls are lined with stacked housing units where we live, seven families on top of one another. Today is Sunday, so people are in their quarters and a thousand yellow windows glow against the dark rock. Maybe it's because of the unchanging view of laboratory rooftops, but I've spent at least a thousand hours looking out my bedroom window, and I've never seen another face looking back. Well, except maybe that bully Red when he sneaks out to go make-out with his sour-faced girlfriend, which is against the rules because we're not allowed to date until we test.

I look up at the cavern ceiling, the blue-glowing benitoite shining there like jewels embedded in the rocky sky. My dad says our ancestors used to look up and see the Milky Way—no ceiling, just four-hundred-billion stars twinkling in the endless night. It's never night or day here—just productive hours and rest hours, and the only difference are the levels of ultraviolet light that help us produce vitamin D. It's the UV lights that are sparking the blue benitoite on the cavern ceiling now.

I know from my lessons that our generators harness the Earth's electromagnetic field to power the lights and the fans that filter and condition our air. I asked my dad once why it's never warm here and he told me to just be happy I'm not on the surface, where the air is so thin and cold that my blood would boil then freeze in 60 seconds flat. But I think it would be worth it just to see the sky for a minute before I die.

I take the lift down to the Valley floor and weave my way through the deserted pathways toward our quarters. As I pass the food engineering lab, I get an idea. I check the door—it's open. My father works here to make our underground crops nutritious and visually appealing. Trying to remember where they keep the food coloring, I search the cabinets.

"Here it is. This should do the trick."

I stuff a bottle of green coloring dye in my jacket.

When I reach our quarters, I hear voices inside and stop

short of entering. My dad never has company. I put my ear to the metal door and listen to the muffled conversation inside:

"He's a smart boy," I hear my dad say. "I'm sure he'll be staying on here. I'm sure enough, I'm certain."

"You just never can tell anymore with these new tests, Mr. Van Houten. But I'm sure you're right."

It's strange to hear my dad addressed by our last name—Van Houten. He says it means "of the forest." I never thought of it before now, but I guess it's a little weird being named after something that's been extinct for over 900 years.

"Well, he's a smart boy, my son is."

Checking to make sure the dye isn't visible, I push open the door and enter our small quarters. My father sees me and smiles. He's sitting at the table across from a young man in a white lab coat, a man I recognize from around the Valley.

"There you are," my dad says. "At the beach again today? This is Mr. Zales. He's here to take a sample for tomorrow."

The man rises. "Just a quick draw. Won't take a minute."

I approach the table and sit in the vacated chair, pushing my sleeve up and exposing my arm. The man snaps open his black case, lifts out a needle and strips the plastic from its tip.

"Just a little sip, my good man, just a little sip," he says, his smile too big for the small room. A quick swab of iodine and then he plunges the needle into the crook of my arm and draws out a vial of my blood. My dad sees me wince and starts talking:

"You know, I can remember when you were testing age yourself, Bobby Zales. The boy whose parents earned their way up from Level 4. People were sure you'd be going down again, but I knew you'd make the grade. You're a smart boy, Bobby. I mean, Mr. Zales. A smart boy, just like my son."

"Thank you, sir," he says, removing the needle, capping it, and placing it back in his case before snapping it closed again. "Well, that's all we need for now. A few more 'fifteens' to prick yet, and I'll be getting on to quarters myself. Good luck tomorrow, Aubrey." He pauses at the door and looks back. "Could I ask you a favor, Mr. Van Houten?"

"Sure. Anything."

"You retire soon, don't you?"

Dad's face brightens. "Yes, I do. 123 days."

"Will you say hello to my folks for me?"

"I sure will, Bobby. I sure will."

The man smiles. A smaller smile, but a real smile this time. A smile that makes him appear young for a moment. Then he thanks my father and closes the door, leaving us alone.

My dad leans back and looks me over. "Nervous?"

I pull my sleeve down, covering the blood-specked spot of iodine. "Maybe a little."

"Well, it's nothing at all to worry about. Just remember what always works for me when I need to relax: breathe good energy in and breathe bad energy out."

I nod, taking a deep breath and letting it out.

"You've got good genes, Son, and a great work ethic. Plus, you've studied more than any boy in the Valley. All you can do is the best you can. And that's enough. I'm proud, no matter what happens. Darn proud. And your mother would be, too."

At his mention of my mother, my father's eyes get wet, and he stares off to some distant place only he can see. She left the same day I came. That's where I got my name—Aubrey. When I was young, my father said that even before he met her, he loved my mother's name. Said he loves it more now that it's my name, too. But we don't talk like that much these days.

"You think Mom will recognize you after all these years?" I ask. "I mean, she hasn't aged, but you have."

"I'm sure she will," he says, his gaze coming back to me. "And you can bet I'll tell her what a smart, wonderful young man you've become. I wish you'd known her, Son. I wish she'd known you. She was so beautiful. Almost too beautiful for this place. Maybe that's why she left us so early."

"Was it my fault, Dad?"

"Was what your fault?"

"Her leaving us."

"Why would you say that?""

I shrug. "Some of the kids say it was my fault. They say that I killed her coming out."

He reaches across the table and grips my hand. I notice the veins snaking across the back of his hand and running like ropes up his forearm.

"Now you listen to me," he says. "Your mother had an infected appendix. Had nothing to do with you. In the old days, above, they'd have fixed her up no problem. Like that!" He snaps his fingers with his free hand to make the point. "But things are different down here. The Foundation decided long ago that it doesn't make sense to invest in those costly medical treatments. When it's your time, it's your time—whether you make it to 35 or head for the horizon early." He squeezes my hand harder. "She's in a better place, anyway. You'll see. We'll all be together soon." Releasing my hand, he dismisses the conversation with a wave.

He reaches across the table for his trusty tea tin, pulls it to him, opens it, and lifts out his pipe—just as I've seen him do every Sunday since I can remember. Smoking is supposed to be prohibited in the Valley, but my dad's lab work in underground agriculture development allows him to always manage a steady supply of tobacco from Level 5, where they grow it for nicotine to use as an organic pesticide against the insects we cultivate to pollinate and manage the vast underground fields.

"Did I ever tell you about this pipe?" he asks, as he packs the stringy tobacco into the bowl with his thumb.

When I shake my head, he continues in his serious tone:

"It's from up there." He lifts his eyes to the ceiling. "From before the War. Your forty-third . . . no, must be your forty-fourth great-grandfather now, carved this pipe himself. Carved it under the actual sun. Look here. See that design."

He holds the pipe out to me and I take it in my hand. It's heavier than it looks; the carbon fiber stem cool on my fingers, the yellowed-stone bowl soft and warm in my palm.

"See the butterflies there?"

I look and notice for the first time the intricate detail work, worn thin by almost a thousand years of fingers and thumbs, but still visible. Beautiful butterflies. Butterflies beginning big at the base of the bowl then shrinking as they increase in number, creating the illusion of a rabble rising toward the pipe lip.

"The stem there's been replaced a few times, of course," he says, nodding, "but the soapstone bowl was quarried right in our family's backyard in a state called Georgia."

"I thought you said our ancestors came from a country called Holland? Not Georgia?"

"And they did, they did. Sailed to early America from Holland and migrated down south. But I never told you that generations later, one of your great-grandfathers grew up on a butterfly conservatory there. Real live butterflies, Son. Just like the ones you've studied in lessons. You know, they're the one thing I really wish I could see. Wish we had a few down in Agri. But not one, not a single butterfly survived . . ."

His voice trails off, his eyes on the pipe in my hand.

". . . I love the idea of butterflies," he continues after a pause. "I love their color, their metamorphosis, their freedom."

He shakes his head, as if waking from a daydream.

"Anyway, I guess it was the butterfly breeding that inspired your great-grandfather Eli's interest in genetics and led him to a career with the U.S. Department of Defense. He came west to work in the labs down here, forty-some generations ago now, and he brought his beloved father's butterfly pipe with him. It's been passed down to the eldest child ever since. Father to son, sometimes mother to daughter. But it was always passed down, passed at last on to me. I plan to pass it to you when I retire."

I notice the weight of the pipe, the centuries of history trapped like resin in its chambers, and I don't ever want it to be mine. I don't want my dad to retire, to render his body to the machine. I don't want him to leave me alone.

I hand the pipe back.

"Never too early to learn," he says, clicking the lighter and bringing it to the pipe. He puffs it lit, the flame illuminating the butterflies, shadows creating the illusion of fluttering wings—monarchs moving up the bowl. When he removes the flame, a coil of smoke rises from the pipe as if the tiny winged creatures have finally escaped their fossil prison and at last taken flight.

He hands me back the lit pipe. Unsure, I take it and look at the red-glowing ember smoking in the bed of tobacco.

"The other end, boy," he says, "the other end."

"I know it." I stick the stem between my teeth and breathe in, acrid tobacco smoke filling my lungs. Pulling the pipe away, I cough gray smoke across the table. "Ugh," I say, holding out the pipe to him. "It tastes nothing like it smells."

He laughs and peels the pipe from my hand. "I coughed, too," he says. "You'll get the hang of it when it's time. Now run on up to bed and get rested. Tomorrow's the big day."

My room feels smaller than it ever has. As if I'm just now noticing that I've outgrown it. Tiny dollhouse drawers built into the wall. My study desk too short. My bed a child's cot lying beneath the window.

I lean against the sill and look out on the Valley. The lights are dim, reducing the buildings to outline. It's quiet, everyone in their quarters for curfew, the only sound from the ventilation fans humming unseen. The Valley is the largest cavern in Holocene II, but tonight it closes in on me.

I think about the levels beneath us, the levels above. If I score well on tomorrow's test, I'll stay here to work in the labs, or in engineering, maybe. If I'm lucky, I'll even inherit these same living quarters when my dad retires. But if I don't score well, they'll send me down to manufacturing on Level 4, where I'll operate machinery building the unmanned exploration craft we send to the surface. Or worse, maybe Level 5 to work crops, where productive hours are twice as long. And if I really fail, they'll sterilize me and send me to Level 6, where I'll spend my days working the recycling and sewage plants, and my father's pipe will be left without an heir.

But I don't really care. Because regardless of how I score tomorrow, I only have to make it another 20 years and then I can retire, too. And when I do, I'll join my dad and meet my mom and spend an eternity in Eden. We know there's no such thing as heaven, but Eden is close—the Foundation's virtual world where anything can be had just for wishing—

Waterfront mansions for every family.

A blue-sky paradise filled with dreams.

All your friends, all your family, all your fantasies.

I imagine all of my ancestors gathered at a never-ending picnic, each of them 35, forever. I think of my father's pipe, about all of their fingerprints worn there. Would they share it? No. I guess they'd each call up their own replica pipe as real as the original just by thinking it—the butterflies worn a little less to match the memories of its earlier owners.

I can almost see it now: everyone sitting around visiting with their ancestral peers, grandparents indistinguishable from grandchildren, the men all puffing great clouds of smoke into the afternoon sky. How weird it will feel to be there with them. To listen to the grandmothers and granddaughters, all with the same tenor belonging to women of 35, except my mother—my mother who left us at 20. At 20! The same day I was born. She was only five years older than I am now. Dad says they got her up there just in time. Up to Eden. I wonder what it will be like to meet her. I bet it will be weird.

I imagine evening dropping on that digital picnic paradise, an endless feast appearing perfect to everyone's taste. I imagine stepping inside, looking into my mother's eyes. What will they look like, her eyes? I'll be fifteen years older than she is when I retire. A child grown meeting his mother still a child. It must be strange to be 20 in a place where everyone is always 35.

I feel the bottle of food dye pressing into my armpit. Red knows I'm testing tomorrow—he's testing, too. And he and his buddies buried me in the sand wanting to shake my nerves.

I climb out my window and onto the ledge, easing toward the plumbing junction. Once there, I scurry up to the catwalk that runs between the units. I peer into windows, checking to make sure it's clear before passing quickly, my steps short and careful. I spot an albino rat lumbering toward me, its white hair glowing in the low UV light. No room for both of us.

It's funny that of all the species that were lost in the War, rats managed to survive. Rats and gulls at our electric beach, of course. But Dad says they're just rats with wings. And I guess we do have some worms and insects working in agriculture on Level 5. Rumor is they used to house monkeys on much lower and forbidden floors, in the unmapped basements, but after so many generations they refused to reproduce down there. Maybe they're smarter than us, the monkeys—hard to say.

Without slowing, the rat steps on my foot, slides between my legs, and carries on with its brainless, tail-dragging march. I carry on toward Red's window. When I reach it, I remove the bottle of green food dye from my jacket and screw off the lid. The room is dark. Red must be downstairs, maybe getting his blood sample drawn by Mr. Zales. But I know he'll be sneaking out soon enough to go play grab and grope with his girl.

I set the open bottle of dye on the sill and tip it toward the window, resting it against the frame. I wish I could hang out, just to see his face, but I have no intention of getting beat to a pulp tonight. Tomorrow, maybe, but not tonight.

When I climb back in my window, my room seems normal size again. I wonder what was wrong with me earlier.

I pull the covers back and slide into bed.

My eyes close, my body sinks into the sheets.

I try to relax and think of anything except tomorrow's test. Anything. A rat sniffing its way through a never-ending maze in my brain. Blue benitoite hanging from the rocky sky of my skull. Warm sand, gentle waves. A single yellow butterfly, rising and falling and rising again, moves in a peaceful arc across a crimson sky. As I drift off, I inhale a sweet, familiar smell—rich and warm and safe.

My father's fathers' pipe.

CHAPTER 2
Good Thinking and Good Luck

It's finally here.

The day I've been dreading.

I throw open my window and look out on morning in the Valley. The benitoite no longer glows, the bright LED lights washing out the blue. The quiet rest-hour whir of fans is now overrun by the buzz of productive-hour conversation. Metal doors open and clang shut. Groups of giggling children wobble along toward their waiting classrooms, lunch rations and lesson slates tucked beneath their little arms. A pathway polisher halts his machine to let two women pass, tilting his head and raising his hand as if saluting, or tipping an invisible hat.

It's busy and bustling, and in a way funny, because everyone hurries through the same routine every day only to end up right back where they started. We're all just pacing well-worn paths in an underground cage. Sometimes I can't help but wonder if the ceiling were to disappear one day, if the walls just fell away, would everyone really rejoice, or would they go through the same old motions anyway?

My dad says I think too much; he's probably right.

I drop and force out 27 pushups—two more than yesterday. I roll over and do crunches until my stomach burns. I open my closet and curl my water jugs—each seven liters and seven kilograms—left and right, until I can't lift them anymore. Stripping off my shirt, I look at myself in the mirror. I hate what I see. I'm pale and thin, my chest sunken, my legs spindly, my bony arms dangling at my side. After forty plus generations of international scientists mixing their DNA down here, most people look about the same: average height, dark hair, dark eyes. But not me. I'm a misfit in the mix. Red calls me a little freak, although I've pointed out more than once that he looks more different than I do.

Downstairs, my father waits at the table, his eyes on his work slate propped in his lap, our cereal rations measured and waiting. I know he sees me but he doesn't look up when I slide the chair out and sit. I pour soymilk over my cereal and devour it without thinking, the taste as familiar as my own breath.

When I finish, he pushes his untouched bowl across the table to me. I push it back, but he slides it across again, so I pour more soymilk and eat his cereal, too.

With an expanding bellyful of soymilk and algaecrisps, I stand from the table and look down at my dad. He sets his slate on his lap and looks up at me. I think maybe there is more to say after our talk last night—about today's test, about us, about anything. I want to tell him how nervous I am, I want to hear him say everything will be alright. I want to hug him, to be little again and feel his arms embracing me.

He nods, I nod, but we say nothing. When he picks up his reader again from his lap, I grab my own lesson slate from its charger and head for the door without a word.

The metal door bangs shut behind me, and my ears are instantly bombarded with productive clatter as I pass through the Valley, following the same path I've taken every day for the decade I've been in school, heading for the last time to the gray, windowless Foundation education annex building.

Today, the elevator passes my usual stop and lifts me five stories to the testing room floor. The elevator door slides open and mean Mrs. Hightower stands before me guarding a plastic collection bin filled with the abandoned lesson slates recently belonging to the boys and girls already seated for the test.

She tilts her head toward the bin. I look at the slate in my hand. I've had it since I was five. Ten years, the same device. I remember the morning my first lesson blinked on the screen—a reading challenge titled Hear Tommy Talk. The lessons came fast then, a new lesson with each one completed. I graduated from reading and writing to linguistics. Then to social sciences, anthropology, even some pre-Holocene II history. The natural and applied science lessons came next—math, logic, chemistry, physics, geology, biology, engineering—all leading to lessons on the complex systems that support and maintain our life down here in Holocene II.

But it wasn't all work.

I read in my free time, too.

Poetry, novels, plays. Everything I could download about the old world above. By the time my last lesson blinked off the screen three days ago, I had nearly finished every title in the Foundation library. My dad says all that reading just makes me wish for things that no longer exist, but I cherish those hours spent dreaming. This slate has been my constant companion, my window into new worlds, my only escape.

I place it in the bin, where it joins the others, becoming just another indistinguishable LCD screen framed in stainless steel. Some kid had it before me—some kid will have it after.

Everyone's eyes are on me as I walk to an empty test chair. When I sit, their heads swivel again to stare at the blank screen at the front of the testing room. I recognize them all, even from the back of their heads, but I can't call any of them my friends. I just never fit into any of their cliques. Today I'm glad for that, though, because after this test, most will be staying here, but those who don't score well will be going down to new levels.

The mood is edgy. Everyone knows how serious today is. Not only is it a family disgrace to move down, but we're not allowed to visit other levels.

The elevator door slides open. I turn with everyone else to watch the latecomer enter. Red steps off, steaming. His chest is heaving, his fist clutching his slate, his face and neck stained a bright and shocking green. His eyes scan the room and bore straight into me. I don't know what to do, so I just smile. He chucks his slate into the bin and stomps to the only empty seat, one right behind me. I can feel his hot breath on my neck, hear his heart thumping. Recalling my father's advice, I breathe good energy in, breathe bad energy out, and force myself to forget Red for now and focus on the task ahead.

The lights dim. The screen fades from black to gray and the Foundation crest comes on: a shield of three interlocking triangles, a valknut of bound belief, a holy trinity of science representing nature above knowledge and humankind. It was one of my very first lessons, of course.

The crest fades and is replaced by our founder's face. The one, the only Dr. Radcliffe. His expression is stern but kind, his jaw well defined below a pointed nose, his bright blue eyes, his head of gray hair cut close and combed to the side. Of course, he's dead now. Or in Eden, I should say. I think he was around 60 when he retired. How long ago now? Forty-five generations, maybe. Almost 900 years. My dad says he could have served the

Foundation better by staying on until he died naturally, but the lessons say he didn't think it was fair to ask the other men to go to Eden unless he was willing to go first himself.

"Good morning, future citizens," he says. "I'm Doctor Robert Radcliffe, your Foundation President when this was recorded; your President Emeritus living on in Eden today."

He blinks three times and pauses. Even though I know I'm watching a recording from almost a millennium ago, something in his voice makes me sit up straight in my chair.

"If you're seeing this, you've achieved a great and noble accomplishment already by reaching near human adulthood. Let me sincerely wish you a happy belated fifteenth birthday, and, for today's undertaking, good thinking and good luck."

Blink, blink, blink—his blinking must be a tic.

He continues talking and blinking:

"We all must make sacrifices to keep our species alive and thriving here in Holocene II. With only so much space for us to live and yet so very much for us to do, we offer our productive years to the community in exchange for an eternity of bliss. And I'm proud to be the first of us to offer my space, as I am recording this message on the eve of my own retirement. The first to go to Eden. I want to assure you, there is nothing in biology that indicates the inevitability of our death beyond the limitations of these bodies that carry our brains."

He lifts a glass of water and sips before going on.

"I'm sure by the time you see this, you will all know what Eden is. Eden is a virtual heaven on Earth, an invented reality based on our once lush planet. Only it is better because nothing is ever used up in Eden. And not only does Eden provide us with an eternal human experience, it frees precious resources for Holocene II by reducing costly later-life medical treatments and consumption during non-productive years. You now need never die because when you each reach 35, you'll be rendered into retirement and live on in Eden, a thinking, lucid-dreaming consciousness forever. Your brain living beyond your flesh."

Blink, blink, blink.

"And it is this pact we make with one another here today, this dedication of our productive years to the community good before moving on, that ensures the survival of this great and enduring species we call humankind. We work for our ancestors as they have worked for us. We work for posterity as posterity will work for us. And so, this morning, you and your fellow fifteens will take the test you've been preparing for. Your blood has been drawn and tested, your genomes sequenced, your health and natural ability determined. And combined with the results of today's knowledge and aptitude assessments, this data will help us assign you to your most appropriate career.

"Many of you will engineer our foods; others will maintain our mechanical systems; some, with special skills, will be called on to design parts for the latest exploration drones. And, on rare occasions, a few exceptionally gifted among you may even be called up to a career at the Foundation here on Level 1."

He pauses to blink three times.

I watch the heads of my peers turning from side to side, calculating, predicting, wondering if they or any other will be called up to Level 1—something that hasn't happened, ever.

"Of course," he goes on, "we continue to build unmanned exploration crafts and send them topside with the hope of discovering habitable changes on the Earth's surface. And if we do discover a new home, our founding documents provide that every retired citizen will be reassigned a physical form."

Dr. Radcliffe pauses, consulting his notes. I look around at my test mates, their heads now frozen straight ahead, their eyes entranced. I wonder, as they must be wondering, what physical form each would receive if we ever discover a habitable zone. Mechanical hosts? Cloned bodies? Maybe I will be two meters tall and made of pure muscle, while Red, behind me and surely still seething, will be placed in the body of a pygmy. Why not?

"Here we are then," Dr. Radcliffe continues, with a flurry of fresh blinks, "embarking on the next phase of this puzzling life together. Please know that myself and many other men and women, generations of us by now, have gone before you and there is nothing at all to fear, not even fear itself. So, heads down, and do your very best for your sake, and for the sake of science." A subtle hint of a frown plays with the corners of his mouth, as if he's already seen our results and knows the score. "Thank you, and I'll see you all someday soon in Eden."

He disappears; the screen fades to black. The lights snap on and our desks slide open, exposing personal touchscreens glowing with the Foundation crest. Then Mrs. Hightower steps to the front of the class, sets a timer on the table, and says:

"You have eight hours to answer as many questions as you can. You must attempt an answer for each question to move on to the next. The system will not allow you to skip forward or go back. Don't even worry about finishing; no fifteen ever does. You may take up to four five-minute bathroom breaks and twenty minutes for lunch." She presses the timer, and the bright-red clock begins counting down. "You may begin."

I look down at my desk.

The Foundation crest disappears from my touchscreen and

an outline of a hand appears. I lay my palm on the cool glass.

NOW TESTING, AUBREY VAN HOUTEN scrolls across the screen and then the questions begin . . .

They come easy at first, almost in the same order as my early slate lessons. Simple, fill-in-the-blank language questions. Word definitions. Sentence comprehension. Short essays. Then moving on to history. The Big Bang. Humankind's rise. Our ever increasing population. Our overconsumption of resources, our rape of the rain forests. The agricultural revolution. The industrial revolution. The military revolution. War.

My eyes ache, and I pause to close them for a minute . . .

Images flash in my mind—explosions, fire, destruction. I see earth crumbling, passageways sealing never to be opened again. I rub the images away, open my eyes and power on.

Questions moving quickly now into science, the field where I'm most comfortable. Medical science. Germ theory. Bacteria and antibiotics. Mapping the genome. Understanding the brain. Algebra, calculus, trigonometry. A multitude of math equations with a graphing calculator on the screen—so easy. Incomplete chemistry formulas—multiple choice, simple.

Then the hard subjects begin to come. Screen after screen of geophysics questions. Difficult questions about our planet's internal systems, plate tectonics, atmosphere. Questions about the interrupted hydro cycles, about our frozen oceans, about the mile of radioactive ice choking our old surface home.

Faster now, more questions—

Trick questions about the Earth's electromagnetic waves that we harness for power. Timed multiple choice—pick the right growing soil produced from carbon extracted from oil. Surprise quizzes about the subsurface flow of water—how do we trap it, how do we treat it for potable use?

I move through them fast, almost without pause. Lessons learned and long forgotten now present themselves in my mind with vivid recall and perfect timing. I tap out a blur of answers, calculate enumerable equations, type a string of long essays, and then a strange question comes up and stops me cold. Not a science question, not language, not math—an ethical question, a moral dilemma. I read the hypothetical question again:

You've been placed in command of Holocene II and entrusted with protecting it. The basement level bio-testing lab has uncovered an airborne parasitic pathogen that kills almost every person it infects, and all or most of its citizens are infected. There is currently no cure for this infectious agent and you face an impossible choice—you can seal off the level, imprisoning its people to a terrible fate but saving the other levels from infection, or, you can continue to support the infected level in hopes that a cure might be discovered before it spreads into a pandemic that will destroy all of Holocene II and with it, our species. Please select your answer below.

A. Seal off the infected level and save Holocene II.

B. Render aid to those infected and risk total destruction.

I reread the question a third time. I've never seen an ethics lesson on my slate, and I'm unsure how to answer. These are the only options? Imprison and kill an entire level to save the rest of us, or take no action and possibly destroy humanity?

Not able to decide, I look to skip it. It won't let me. Then I remember Mrs. Hightower saying we must attempt an answer for each question. I shut my eyes, making a blind choice. When I open them again, the question is gone—replaced with bold red lettering that reads: TEST COMPLETE.

The desktop slides shut.

I lift my head and look past my calculating classmates at the timer—two hours and nineteen minutes left. And I'm already done? Can that be? I listen to the other testers sighing with confusion as the clock ticks off another minute.

I went too fast. Didn't take enough time. I begin second guessing my answers, thinking of other possibilities for each question. Whole sections of the test parade across my mind and now I'm sure I messed it up with overconfidence. And why is everyone else still tapping away at screen calculators, working out math problems from the first half of the exam? Did I miss an entire section? Did I miss two?

I grip the desktop, pull hard to open it again—it won't budge. I jerk it harder, grunting without realizing it.

"Is there a problem?" Mrs. Hightower asks.

Everyone stops working and turns in their seats, curious eyes looking at me, waiting for a response.

"I finished early," I say, "but I think I missed a few."

Red grunts behind me. Someone chuckles.

"I'm sorry," Mrs. Hightower says, "but your answers, right or wrong, are final. You're excused."

"I'm excused?"

"You may leave," she says. "You're disturbing the others."

As I get up and walk to the elevator, my legs are shaking, so I breathe good energy in and bad energy out. The door opens, I step on, and look back. Everyone's heads are bent over their tests again, except Red who's glaring at me.

CHAPTER 3
What Did I Do?

When I arrive at our living quarters, my father isn't there.

He's probably still at his lab.

With my lesson slate abandoned in Mrs. Hightower's bin, waiting to be rebooted and reassigned, I'm bored, with nothing to do. I head out, walking to the east side of the Valley where our social buildings cluster around the open square.

As I pass the public house, I hear the men and women laughing, and it hits me that I'm fifteen now and old enough to finally go inside, but the smell of the algae ethanol wafting out from the pub's open windows turns my stomach sour.

A few buildings farther down, I spot the green light above our theater door, signaling that an educational is about to begin. Stepping inside the lobby, I pass by the check-in kiosk without scanning my palm, and slip into the dark screening room unaccounted for. I'd rather not be on the grid tonight.

As soon as I plunk into my seat, I notice a mother and her daughter sitting in the front row, the only other people here. I watch as the mother plays with her daughter's hair, coiling it lightly in her fingers. I recognize the girl from the education annex where I think she's a couple of years behind me.

"Your hair is getting so thick," the mother says. "It must be the new oil rations you're taking."

They don't appear to have noticed my entrance, and I feel guilty eavesdropping on their conversation. I consider coughing to alert them, but before I do, the mother continues:

"Have you met any boys in your class yet?" she asks, still stroking her daughter's hair. "Anyone you like?"

The girl shrugs but says nothing.

Her mother continues: "I met a boy when I was your age."

"Daddy?" the girl asks.

"No, I met your father later. This was a different boy, a boy who sat next to me in main group."

"What kind of boy?"

"A handsome boy. Sometimes it was hard to focus because I kept wanting to sneak glances at him. He was very attractive. Thinking about him made me feel things in my body I hadn't felt before. Things, well, you know . . . down there."

"Ooh, gross, Mom," the girl says, turning her head away. "Why are you telling me this?"

"I'm telling you because you're at the age where things are changing fast. Too fast. And that's why I wanted you to see this educational. I want you to know those feelings are okay. That they're normal. Sex is as human as any other impulse is."

"But I already know all this, Mom," the girl says, huffing. "I'm not stupid, you know."

"Then you know that it's against regulation for you to date before you test, right?"

"I said I know."

"You have to wait for your test card," the mother says, her voice now filled with authority. "And even then, when you do meet someone, you have to check in with the health office to avoid genetic conflicts. Are you hearing me? Molly? I asked you a question. Are you hearing me?"

The girl folds her arms.

Her mother gives up.

They sit in their seats, both of them looking straight ahead, staring at the blank screen. A quiet eternity seems to pass. I'm aware of my own breathing, and I make an effort to be quiet, wanting to remain undiscovered. At last, the screen hums to life, glowing a dull silver, the mother and daughter silhouetted against its bottom edge.

Without taking her eyes off the screen, the daughter says, "What happened to him?"

"What happened to who, darling?"

"The boy."

"Oh, him . . .," she says, her response quiet and delayed, as if maybe traveling to her lips from the distant past. "He didn't test well. They sent him down to Level 6."

The educational begins with an image of a cell suspended like a Mylar balloon in a black sky. Music fades in. The cell divides into two daughter cells that grow and then themselves divide, making four. The tempo quickens. The cells divide again. Four into eight, eight into sixteen, and soon the entire screen is filled with thousands of cells nestled together like algae muffins on a baking sheet. The camera pulls back, revealing the cluster to be an egg. A hundred thousand sperm swim at it from every angle, bashing themselves against its outer walls.

Symbols clang.

Again and again the sperm push against the egg until one slips through and slithers into its center, coming to rest.

Quiet now.

Violins.

The black background changes to a deep red that gradually

lightens. A drum roll. The triumphant sperm combines with the egg, becoming a zygote, then the zygote dividing and folding and growing into an embryo. As the drums fade to silence, the embryo develops into an alien fetus floating in a soft pink sea.

Cut to: Ancient footage of gorillas in a zoo, before the War, before they were extinct. A silverback sitting on a rock, a female circling him, her behind pumping high in the air—one, two, three revolutions around his rock she turns, taunting, tempting. The silverback surrenders to the dance and rises from his rock as the female shrinks away, subservient, waiting. When he mounts her, she closes her eyes. He pumps fast, his head turned to gaze idly at something off screen. Almost before he's begun, the silverback is finished. He returns to his rock and sits while the female rolls away to lie on her back, cradling her hairy belly as if already expecting something there.

My eyes droop, the picture fades . . .

No longer in a theater five kilometers underground, I'm tucked away in my mother's arms. I see her face, the face I imagine from my father's descriptions, her hair brown and soft and straight. She smiles down at me and rocks me, and for the first time I feel safe.

I look up and watch her fade away.

When I wake from my dream, the theatre is dark. Nothing on the screen, no lights except the soft LED glow of the aisle markers. The mother and daughter are gone.

Stepping from the theater into the dark square, it appears to be long after curfew because nobody is out. Even the public house is shuttered and dark. Now I'm in trouble. Not from the police—we have very few, and they don't enforce curfew—but from my dad. The last time I came in this late he grounded me. There seems no point in hurrying back to my punishment, so I take my time walking through the dim Valley.

In the breezeways between dark buildings, I catch glimpses of lit doorways, seeing something strange that I've only seen once before when I was young: neighbors visiting neighbors.

I stop and lean against a building to watch. On every floor, people are coming from their housing units onto the walks and knocking on doors to either side, passing some news. The last time I saw this happen was when Joel Limpkin tested so poorly that he was sent down to Level 6, despite his parents' protests.

Suddenly, my father's waiting punishment seems silly.

What if it's me this time? What if I flunked?

The visiting slows, moving away like a wave, and by the time I reach our unit, only a few distant doors bang shut on the other side of the Valley.

I breathe good energy in, breathe bad energy out, pull back my shoulders, and prepare for my father's anger.

When I open the door, my heart skips a beat—

A dozen different voices scream: "Congratulations!"

They're all crowded into our small room—our neighbors and a few of my father's coworkers and friends.

My father steps to the front of the crowd, his posture tall and proud, and instead of sending me upstairs and grounding me, he wraps me in his arms and lifts me into the air.

"You did it, Son."

"What did I do?" I squeak, my feet dangling, my breath caught in my father's embrace.

"You've made us all proud."

"But what did I do?"

"Perfect score, Son—an absolutely perfect score," he says, setting me down again and gripping my shoulders.

I look up at him, confused. "You're not mad?"

"Mad? Why would I be mad?"

"Because I missed curfew."

"Didn't you just hear me, Son?" He gives me a little shake. "You're going up. Up! You've been selected as a fellow at the Foundation. Nobody's gone up before. You're the first, Son. You'll be making a real difference now. You'll be helping the best and the brightest up there figure out a way to get us back above ground someday. Free men again. I knew it would be you. Maybe you'll make a discovery to reverse the ice age, eh? Return our atmosphere? Maybe even terraform Mars?"

Someone clears their throat. Everyone's staring.

Still gripping my shoulders, he stops and looks around the room, caught off guard and embarrassed by his outburst of enthusiasm. His posture wilts slightly. Releasing my shoulders, he brushes them off as if clearing away some invisible lint.

"Sorry. I get a little excited sometimes," he says, looking at me but talking to them. "Of course, we'll all be retired by the time you get your fellowship anyway."

After several quiet, uncomfortable seconds, someone says:

"Let's have a toast. To Aubrey."

"Yes," someone else says. "After all, he is a fifteen now."

Smiling with relief at the suggestion, he leaves me standing before the group to go retrieve his ration of algae ethanol. Now the visitors stare at me with a mix of pride and something else that might be envy, or even pity covered up.

CHAPTER 4
I Love You, Son

The week passes fast.

Before the test nobody wanted to talk to me. Now, I can't leave the house without being stopped and congratulated. But as annoying as their new friendliness is, they're the only thing saving me from Red.

I see him lurking everywhere I go, his green face fading by the day but still shocking against his red hair. But every time he approaches me, he's interrupted by some well-wishing Valley resident clasping my palm and smiling. And I'm glad because I don't want to go up to the Foundation with a black eye.

Without a lesson slate now to distract me, and with classes at the education annex over for fifteens, I spend most of the week hiding out in the theater, watching educationals.

I'm nervous now about going. My father's work has taken him up to the Transfer Station on Level 2, even once or twice down to the crops and algae refineries on Level 5, but nobody has ever been up to the Foundation headquarters on Level 1. Nobody. At least not from here. Everyone goes up that way to retire, of course, but nobody can come back from Eden.

Besides managing Eden, the Foundation has the important job of guarding the surface exchange chambers, of making sure that no toxic material makes its way down to Holocene II. Plus, they launch our unmanned exploration craft and analyze the data that returns. And that's maybe the only thing I am excited about—getting closer to the surface and seeing images of the outer world, no matter how desolate and depressing they are.

It's already Sunday again, and I'm back at the beach.

As I sit on the sand watching the mechanical waves roll in, I see past the illusion for the first time. It's remarkably real. Or at least it's how I'd imagine a real beach must be. But when I gaze at the horizon and let my eyes drift, focusing on nothing in particular, I see a line where the pool ends and the projection screen begins. And now I notice the sky is a little too blue, the clouds a little too perfect. Then there are the gulls. They scatter on the shore, making short flights between perfectly bleached pieces of driftwood, but they never fly off into the horizon to join the other gulls forever flapping in the virtual sky.

"Hey, look—the pride of Holocene II," Bill calls, jogging over from his guard tower, his bare feet kicking up sand.

Stopping, he rests his hands on his hips, breathing heavily.

"I'm getting too old for this job," he says, smiling. "When I come up to retire in a few years, you better remember me."

Retire? It hits me then that I don't even know how old Bill is. Never asked him. Never asked him anything, really. All these Sundays here and not once did I have the courage to start up a conversation. Maybe because of how everyone's been treating me this last week, or maybe from desperation because I leave tomorrow, but today I stand up and run to Bill and hug him.

"Hey, there," he says. "Okay, kid. We'll miss you, too."

As we walk toward the locker room, I look left to soak up one last view of the familiar fake horizon. It's hard to believe only a week has passed since Red and his buddies buried me in the sand. It's even harder to believe that I'll never see any of them again. When I get to the door, I look up to say goodbye, but Bill didn't follow me this time and he's back at the guard tower with his head bent over a flotation device and some impossible lifeguard knot he's tying. I lift my hand to wave goodbye, but Bill doesn't look up.

I step into the shower and close the door.

Clean and dressed again, I stop on the outlook platform and take in the Valley one last time. All these years I've dreamt about leaving, but still, I'm going to miss this view.

It's strange to think of the other levels buried beneath us—people living out their lives so close but yet worlds away. Maybe there's a boy down there just like me, looking up just as I look down. Maybe he's on his way here to replace me. I wonder if he's nervous too. I gaze up at the sparkling benitoite and think of five kilometers of rock and earth pressing down on the cavern ceiling. I wonder just how far up it is to Level 1.

Back at our housing unit, I say goodbye to my things. My instructions said there's no need to bring anything, only what I wear. I empty my water-jug weights down the bathroom drain and leave them standing outside the bedroom door. I lay out a clean jumpsuit for the morning. Fresh socks. My newest pair of shoes. Everything else I fold away neat in the drawers. Even my favorite hoodie, too worn and threadbare to wear up to Level 1. Shutting the closet door, I wonder what other boy or girl they'll assign to my room once my father retires? Will they look out my window, and will they see anyone looking back?

There's a tap on the door and then it opens.

"May I come in?" my father asks, his shadow filling the small doorway. When I nod yes, he steps into the light.

I've never thought of my father as big, but seeing him now in my tiny room, he seems to be a giant. He sits on my bed, the mattress sagging beneath his weight, and he pats the space next to him and I sit, too. We both look at our feet, his stretched out almost touching the wall, mine barely reaching the floor.

The silence is heavy, and after a few minutes, I can hear the soft whir of the ventilation fans humming in the Valley outside my closed window.

My father reaches over and rests his hand on my knee. I look up and see his eyes are wet, the same as they get whenever he talks about Mom. I feel a lump in my own throat, then my eyes get wet, too. I look back down at my feet.

He pats my knee and stands, and then I hear my door shut softly behind him as he leaves.

The next morning, I eat breakfast alone.

I know my dad's no good with things like this, but did he really need to leave for work early? Today? Oh, well, maybe it's easier if we don't say goodbye anyway.

I just hope they have better food on Level 1.

When I finish, I stand to leave but stop in the doorway and look back at our living quarters one final time. We don't call them homes because they belong to Holocene II and are often reassigned as people retire and others have children. We were lucky to get to stay here this whole time. It's small and cramped and lacking anything too personal, but still, I can see imprints of our life here everywhere. Ghosts of my father and me. My height marks notched into the corner wall. Our matching elbow indentations worn into the table's surface where we sat across from one another and ate five thousand silent breakfasts. My father's faded tea tin of tobacco sitting on the counter, waiting for his ritual Sunday smoke. I guess this was a home after all.

Closing my eyes, I picture the room to make sure I have a

snapshot memorized. It's there all right, perfectly preserved in my mind's eye. In that way, I'll take it with me wherever I go.

The metal door bangs shut behind me one final time.

Unless someone is retiring, the platform usually sits empty and ignored. But today is a very big day: the great exchange of genetics and brains. Today, the platform is crowded.

They've all gathered to say goodbye. Mothers combing hair and pestering departing sons with last-minute instructions on hygiene and manners. Father's issuing stern and final warnings to departing daughters about lower-level boys lurking in wait to take advantage of them. Promises from scared and embarrassed fifteens that they'll raise their own kids to study better than they themselves did; promises that the next generation will return the family name to Level 3. Best friends clinging to one another, crying, waiting to be pulled apart, knowing they'll never see one another again until retirement, when we're all reunited in Eden.

It's all a wild flurry of nervous energy, leading up to those of us who are leaving being herded into the waiting elevators destined for our new levels. And once we're all gone from here, the waiting will begin—waiting for the arrivals. I know because I've been here to see it myself in prior years. I've seen the families double-checking the names on their slips and wondering about the new boy or girl assigned to them. I've seen lab managers and engineering leaders eagerly expecting a new crop of capable young apprentices that they can train to replace themselves when they retire. And, of course, I've seen the most excited group of the bunch—the lucky fifteens who've tested and are staying here at Level 3, the girls and boys now free to date and dying to lay first eyes on any cute newbies stepping off when the elevators arrive from other floors.

I feel a tap on my shoulder and turn around . . .

Red is standing over me. The green dye has faded to just a birthmark-like shadow running from his forehead down to his neck. I close my eyes and brace for the blow. It doesn't come. When, I open my eyes again, Red is turned away, staring down. He kicks an invisible stone and then sighs.

"Guess this is goodbye," he says.

"You mean you're not gonna hit me?"

He shakes his head. "Nah . . . not this time."

"I'm sorry about your face," I say.

He shrugs. "Sorry about treating you so mean."

"Well, why did you?"

"Maybe I just didn't think you'd like me," he says, kicking another invisible stone. "Guess I'm not so smart."

All this time he's been knocking me down, pushing me around, burying me in sand, and he's been doing it because he didn't think I'd like him? People are funny.

"Is that why you were trying to corner me alone all week?" I ask. "Not to beat me up, but to tell me you were sorry?"

"I guess so, yeah."

I'm not sure what to say. I stick out my hand: "Friends?"

He reaches over and clasps my hand in his and we shake. My first real friend, I think. Releasing my hand, he walks away and joins the small crowd of fifteens waiting by the elevator that will take them down to Level 5.

All the elevator doors open at once . . .

No warning, no fanfare—they just slide open, revealing sterile, empty cars big enough to transport an entire class of fifteens if necessary. The sobbing begins. Quiet here, hushed there, but with a sort of repressed dignity. Then, as if being counted down by an invisible clock, the fifteens hurry onto the elevators despite their obvious desires to linger with their loved ones in farewell. The few low-testing fifteens going down to Level 6 step boldly into their car, not smart enough to understand what lies ahead. I see the back of Red's head, tall above the others, as the fifteens going to Level 5 crowd into their waiting car. Then the elevator to Level 4 fills with a handful of fifteens heading down to work as welders and riveters in the plants that build parts for the exploration drones. And because Level 2 above is not a full living level, but just a Transfer Station worked by the shipping and receiving teams moving supplies, I step alone into the only car going up.

Inside, I turn and look out—

The elevator is big and empty and its steel walls and LED lights create the illusion of me floating in empty space. The open door in front of me looks like a disappearing window into an already distant Level 3. Waiting for the doors to seal, I scan the crowded platform. Last week I was the talk of the Valley, but now everyone's attention is on their own family and friends, loaded into the other cars and about to leave forever.

I hear him before I see him.

"Aubrey!" he calls out, his voice strained and breathless.

Then he bursts from the crowd onto the platform and rushes toward the elevator. I step forward to meet him just as the door begins to slide shut between us. He reaches into the shrinking opening and presses his pipe into my hand. He pulls his arm back out, and as the door seals shut, I swear I hear him say it for the very first time—

"I love you, Son."

CHAPTER 5
I've Died and Gone to Eden

Closed inside, the elevator is quiet.

Too quiet.

I'm used to the constant hum of Level 3 ventilation fans. My ears search for something to ground me, to set my balance. Any sound. Nope—complete silence. With nothing to listen to, my ear goes inward and I hear my heart beating, my pulse throbbing in my head, and the echo of my father's last words—

"I love you, Son."

I wish I'd had time to say it back.

Wiping my eyes with my sleeve, I slip my father's pipe in my pocket and stand in the center of the elevator and brace for the ride. My stomach drops and I know the ascent has begun. After my guts settle, the silent elevator moves without vibration or sound and there is no way to gauge how quickly I'm rising or how far. A minute goes by. Two, maybe three. And just when I'm sure the I'm not moving after all, my stomach bounces and settles again—the elevator has stopped.

I wait for the door to open. Nothing happens. Maybe it's stuck? There's no call button, no floor indicator.

Hearing a metallic sound, I look up. A ceiling vent slides open and a cloud of gas blasts into the elevator. I drop to the floor and crawl away from the gas, crouching in the corner and managing one last clear breath as the gas covers the floor and covers me. Why are they doing this, I wonder, my breath held, my heart racing. Why? I panic and crawl to the door, pounding against the metal, but nothing gives. Air. Please. Now. I gasp out my expired breath and suck the gas into my lungs . . .

The door slides open and I fall out onto the ground.

"Sorry about that," a deep voice says above me, its owner hidden in the cloud of gas billowing from the open elevator. "First time's never fun."

The gas clears and I see his face. Thick dark hair, blue eyes, maybe 30. He reaches out a hand to help me up. I take it and scramble to my feet, coughing to clear my lungs.

"We do it too, if it helps to hear," he says. "Disinfect, I mean. Every time we move between levels. Clothes, skin . . . lungs, too. Hope I didn't scare you too bad. Gotta make sure you take a breath. Average man panics his first time—holds it about 55 seconds. Second time they hold it longer. Us pros, we just suck it right in and take our medicine. I'm Dorian."

Dorian waves his electronic clipboard, indicating for me to follow, and then he heads off into the Transfer Station.

It's a large warehouse with concrete ceilings supported by steel girders, and we weave our way through stacks of metal crates, dodging busy electric lifts carrying supplies.

Dorian walks through the machines as if anticipating their movement, following a path visible only to him. I stay close on his heels and out of harm's way. As he walks, he marks things off on his clipboard and talks, half to himself: "Finally, some iron ore. You'd think those damn tunnelrats could dig a little quicker. Don't see my soybeans yet. Haveta send another ton of damn algaecrisps." Then he points his clipboard in the air, raising his voice. "You know what that is there, young man? That's a brand new fuselage for a PZ-51 Ranger drone. I'd give my retirement to see one actually fly."

I do recognize the drone body because they're designed by our engineers on Level 3, but they're built on Level 4, so it's amazing to see one in person. Long and black and angled, its wings detached, the Foundation's interlocking Valknut shield on its nose as it hangs from a crane being loaded on the back of a waiting train . . . train?

"I didn't know we had a rail system," I say, surprised.

Dorian laughs. "No rails, youngster. This sexy beast here slides along on magnetic fields," he says with a level of pride as if he'd built it himself.

"Well, where does it go?"

"Mostly services the deep mines down south. But don't worry," he adds, seeing my confused look, "we don't send fifteens there. Tunnelrats is tunnelrats and they always will be. You see, Levels 2 through 6 are stacked like one big algaecrisp layer cake, but the mines are spread out south. Anyway, today she's going up, up, up. And so, my young man, are you."

Having arrived at the end of the train, he stops beside a steel-walled windowless passenger car.

"I'm getting on the train?"

"Unless you want to stay here and load supplies with me."

"But isn't Level 1 above us?" I ask.

"Above us? And here I thought you scientists down there knew everything. Level 1's closer to the surface, sure. But it's north, young man, north. Sweet, sweet north."

"I'm going north?"

"Sure are. And every man in Holocene II would give his left nut to be getting on this train today and going north. Eden, my man. Eden! Of course, in a way, you're being taunted more than treated. You'll be near enough to taste it, I tell you. Sweet Eden. Those lucky folks there get to go."

He nods toward another car hitched several ahead where a guide who could be Dorian's twin, with a matching clipboard too, ushers two smiling women and one anxious man through the open car door. Before stepping in, one of the retiring women looks back, and for a moment we lock eyes. Then the door shuts and seals and the guide walks off with his clipboard.

"In you go," Dorian says, sliding the door open.

I hesitate, remembering the elevator. "No windows?"

He shakes his head. "Nothing to see."

Grabbing the handrail, I step up into the car.

I turn, but before I can thank him, he shuts the door.

The car is dim, a rail of pale LED lights running along the ceiling. Down the center, an aisle cuts through rows of metal seats facing forward and pointing toward a projector screen at the front of the car. Sitting on a seat in the front row is a water and lunch ration. I scoop them up and sit. It's quiet, but at least I can hear a soft clanging as the lifts do their work outside.

I glance around nervously, looking for more gas vents. The empty car makes me uneasy, so I keep looking behind me at the vacant seats. Finally, I get up and carry my lunch ration down the aisle and plunk into the farthest seat in the last row.

I'm bored so I open my lunch—soy crackers, tofu paste, and, of course, algaecrisps. I open the crackers and snack on a few. Taking a sip of water, I realize I have to pee already. I go to the door to ask about a bathroom, but the door's locked. No handle on the inside, no call button.

"Great," I mutter. "Guess I have to hold it."

The train jerks forward and stops. I catch my balance and

head back to my seat in the rear. Another jerk, another stop. Then a steady acceleration that pushes me hard into the seat before leveling off and gliding along silent and smooth.

Almost immediately the lights cut out, leaving the car in total blackness. The projection screen glows. A sepia flicker, a run of antique film counting down, 10 to 1. Then I'm barreling down an old iron track with snow-covered trees rushing past and a glorious alpenglow peak rising ahead as the train charges full steam into a mountain pass.

This is a nice touch. It must be old film from a camera mounted on the front of an actual train. I've seen educationals showing footage from planes, and even satellites, but never anything this old. It must be really ancient footage, from before roads and cars and freeways replaced the trains, from before fighter jets and drones cruised through our polluted skies, from long, long before the War.

I settle into my seat and pretend I'm the engineer guiding the silent train as it winds its way up, plowing through drifts of snow, snaking around bends in the tracks, crossing a trestle over a deep and rocky gorge, up, up, up—

A single lighted headlamp boring into the past like an eye, sweeping across the landscape, the trees, the fast approaching night, following the tracks toward the bright northern star.

The seat is cold and hard when I wake, its edges cutting into my thighs—certainly not designed by our engineers. The screen is dead now, the dim lights back on. I stand and stretch, walking to the front and checking the door again. I consider peeing on the floor, just to ease the pressure on my bladder, but decide instead to sit and wait. I feel the force of the train arcing left, and I stare at the blank screen and try to imagine the cars ahead, sliding along the tunnel, rushing like a giant worm deep underground.

It happens so fast there's no time to prepare—

A vibration running along the metal floor and tickling my feet, a metallic warble followed by a screech, the sound of steel tearing open. And then I'm weightless for one quiet, suspended moment before my head slams against the metal seatback in front of me and the lights go out . . .

. . . I come to in pitch-black confusion.

What just happened? The cold metal floor presses against my cheek; something hard is crushing my hip. My fingers move, searching—my face, my chest, my legs. Wet pants. Is it blood? No, it's urine. I've wet myself. I wiggle my toes, bend my knee. Throbbing pain. My hands find a lump on my forehead, but no blood. My foot finds a surface, I push my hip free from where it's wedged. When I sit up, the entire blind Earth seems to spin fast and in the wrong direction.

Hearing a soft whistle coming from the front of the dark car, I shimmy free and crawl toward it. The car must be on its side because the seat backs now hang from the side wall, and I grab them one by one and pull myself along. The whistle grows louder as I move forward, and I feel a cold blast of air against my face. Must be a ventilation fan. I grab for another seatback and my hand lands on stone. Hard, cold stone. I turn my face toward the rush of air and see a gash in the car illuminated by sparkling benitoite outside. Must be a cavern out there.

I scramble to my feet and use the seatbacks to climb the wall toward the opening. Easing my head out, I look out on an immense darkness, cold and crisp, the blue-jewel cavern ceiling glinting on the metal surface of the tipped train.

"Hello!"

Hello, hello, hello . . . my voice comes echoing back.

Carefully, I hoist myself from the crippled car and stand outside. A cold blast hits my face, and I look away, blinking to clear my watering eyes. When I look back, I see the shadowed cavern spread out before me.

It's gorgeous! Like nothing I've ever seen before. I can feel the size of it. The emptiness, the space. The ceiling is high, its blackness punctuated by a million luminescent jewels. It's cold here. And it smells funny, too. Or maybe it just seems like it because it doesn't smell—at least not like conditioned air.

From somewhere out of the blackness below, a strange but beautiful song erupts. A high and tiny warbled kind of birdsong like I've heard in educationals. Another joins in. And another. A whole chorus now of pitch-perfect birds singing in the dark below. Then, as if responding to the singing, an orange glow fades slowly brighter on my right. A light unlike any light I've ever seen. Not the dead white glare of light-emitting diodes, not the blue-black flicker of ultraviolet, but a soft golden glow.

The birdsong rises, and the orange glow comes on fast, the fading sky-hung jewels shrinking from the advancing orange into a deep, deep blue, a blue like I've never dreamed.

Then, from between two jagged peaks in the wall, a yellow fireball climbs into view, blinding me. I turn away and face the fresh breeze, looking out on the twinkling stars of forgotten constellations sinking in the deep-blue horizon, sent back into the blackness of space by the sun rising over the world.

I've died and gone to Eden.

Part Two

CHAPTER 6
What in the World Happened?

Sunlight on my face . . .

For the first time ever in my life.

I'm standing on top of the wrecked train car, its front half pinned beneath a rockslide at the entrance of a tunnel, its back half lying free on a steel trestle spanning a deep canyon.

The trestle connects two mountainside tunnels, the one caved in ahead, and one lower behind. I feel bad for those few retirees ahead of me, crushed beneath the stones, but I feel lucky that I moved seats and survived.

I look out and devour the view—

The canyon leads down to a pine forest. A real forest, just like my name—Van Houten. The sky is full blue now and the singing birds have ceased, the only sound that of the wind whipping up the mountain slope. Cool wind on my cheeks, warm sun on my neck—so unlike anything I ever imagined.

I'm seeing everything I've read about for the first time. A distant bird circling above the trees, its flapless wings riding an invisible current. A green valley below the forest, a silver river snaking through its center. And beyond the valley, far beyond, I can just make out white lines of surf on the blue ocean.

For a moment, I fear it's another virtual reality scene like our beach. But I search the sky for any sign of a screen and can't find one. It's real! The world is real. All those lessons, all those educationals, all teaching me that there was nothing on the surface—but here it is, in living color.

Does no one know?

I don't understand: the surface is uninhabitable, has been for almost a thousand years, they told us. Lingering radiation, disappearing atmosphere, walls of advancing ice.

Where am I and how did I get here?

Then I see a column of smoke against the distant horizon, near the ocean shore, black and straight in windless skies until it catches a high draft and is whisked away in a hazy smear.

If there are fires, there are people.

Something near catches my eye—a small white butterfly rising in the gusts and then falling again as it flits blindly across my view in wild little arcs. A real live butterfly! My hand jumps to my pocket and I breathe with relief when I feel my father's pipe. I pull it out and look at it in the sunlight. It looks smaller, more ancient somehow. As if it were an artifact sifted from the ground, a mined relic remained long after its entombed owner had gone to dust. I remember my father rushing to the elevator, and thrusting the pipe into my hand, and I can hear his parting words again as the door sealed shut:

"I love you, Son."

I wish he were here to see this.

A great rumbling stirs somewhere above, followed by a crunch of stone, a peel of metal. I turn and see rocks tumbling down the slope and slamming into the overturned car and have to dodge left to avoid being brained by one.

Stuffing the pipe back in my pocket, I lower myself onto the trestle, hustling along the tracks away from the falling rocks. When I reach the steel doors standing open on massive hinges, I peer down into the tunnel descending into the mountain like some throat thirsty to swallow me again.

No way am I going back in there. I'll take my chances out here with whoever's fire that was I saw.

I shimmy away from the tunnel and step from the trestle onto a ledge in the canyon wall. It looks impossible to climb at first, but I find handholds in the stone, and every few meters there are trestle braces to use as steps on my slow climb down.

No sooner do my feet touch the ground when a hollow, mechanical knocking comes rattling out from the tunnel above. Clack, clack, clack—some persistent machine working, maybe some tunnelrat crew coming to repair the tracks. Not wanting to find out, I race, slipping and sliding, down the canyon slope.

I'm not sure what I'm running from, but I run for my life anyway. I run toward the trees, the forest, my only chance. Free now of my underground prison, I won't go back. Ever! My toe catches a stone, sending me flying headfirst down the slope and the only thing that saves my face are my hands. The rock grates the skin off my palms, chips of rock wedged in the meat. I wipe my bloody hands on my jumpsuit, and keep moving.

Down, down, down.

The trees grow tall, blocking out the view beyond, and I run for them even faster now. A bee buzzes by, grazing my ear. I leap over shrubs, clearing them easily with the slope on my side, and with one last push, I'm safe in the shade of the trees.

Spent, I throw my arms around a mossy tree and hug it as I catch my breath—my chest heaving, my heart pounding, my neck dripping with sweat. But I feel alive.

I look back up the canyon at the trestle and I'm shocked at how far I just ran. I shiver at the thought of how close I was to missing all of this. Had it not been for a chance rockslide, the windowless train might have slipped through these mountains with me sealed inside. Going where, I wonder. But who knows? Who cares? I'm here now—I'm here and I'm free.

It's magical. The colors, the smells. All the things I've read about but thought I'd never see are animated around me.

As I start into the forest, the trees grow thicker with every step, sunlight filtering down through the pine canopy, dropping in freckled shafts at my feet. I scoop up pine needles in my raw hands and hold them to my nose. Something furry scurries up a tree, stopping halfway and turning to peek down on me before chittering and continuing to the safety of the bows. A squirrel, maybe. The forest is quiet. But it's an alive kind of quiet, as if you could sit and listen all day and hear the trees grow.

I drop to my knees and inspect a caterpillar crawling across my path. These are supposed to be extinct, too. But here it is, a real would-be moth living in a real forest. When I pet its fuzzy back, the caterpillar drops on its side and curls into a ball. I scoop it up and inspect its black and orange stripes.

"I won't hurt you," I promise, poking it in my hand.

It rolls itself tighter in response.

"Okay, fine," I say, slipping the caterpillar into my breast pocket. "We'll talk later." A pinecone drops, landing beside me. I look up and see a gray bird perched on a limb, taking me in as if I'm as foreign to it as this new world is to me. "You see," I say to my pocket as I get up to walk on again, "I probably just saved you from being that bird's lunch."

The bird flits from tree to tree following me, its curious head twisting as if listening to hear some whisper on the wind. And the wind does whisper, too. High in the treetops it passes in swooshing waves, rustling the canopy and then disappearing.

When you listen, the forest is far from quiet.

Coming to a fallen tree across my path, I sit down to rest and take stock of my situation.

Basically, I'm a mess. My jumpsuit is torn and dirt-covered from my fall, bloody handprints smeared on its legs. My hands are caked with drying blood, and when I wiggle my fingers they crack open and ooze again. Other than the clothes on my back, I have nothing. No water, no food—just my father's pipe. I remember my uneaten lunch ration on the train, but it's way up there and I wouldn't go back for it even if I could.

My mind races with questions that need answers:

Who lives up here?

Why have we been lied to?

What in the world happened?

Still, as bad as things appear, and despite these questions running through my head, nothing can dampen my mood. I'm here in the open air, no longer trapped underground. And if I find that fire, I'll bet I find people too. Maybe they'll have some answers. But I know it's water I'll need first.

Remembering the river I saw in the valley below the forest, I set off moving again toward lower elevations.

First water, then the fire.

CHAPTER 7
The Boy Who Sits on Water

Grass.

Brushing against my legs, rising to my chest.

No, not just grass—wheat gone wild.

Here we're eating algaecrisps by the kilo and there's wheat growing up here like weeds. Why don't we know about this? Why are we still underground?

Threshing through the wheat, I grab handfuls of it as I go, ignoring the pain it causes my bleeding palms, sliding my fist up and stuffing seeds into my pockets.

I burst without warning onto the sandy riverbank, freezing in mid-stride when I see it—

There, not more than a few meters away, in shallow water with the current parting around its enormous body, is a grizzly bear staring straight at me. No surprise, no fear—just the cold, calculating curiosity of a predator sizing up prey.

It lifts its muzzle, nostrils dilating as it breathes me in. My pulse races, my pits sweat, my legs vibrate with terror telling me to run. But I can't move—I'm frozen with fear. I've read very little about bears, except that they're supposed to be extinct, along with everything else. Yet somewhere deep in my DNA a little voice whispers for me to remain very, very still.

A long time passes. Me standing statue still, the grizzly an unmovable mountain in the current, our eyes locked in some timeless standoff between man and beast. The river bubbles by.

A gust of wind carries its musty scent to my nose, then passes by rustling the wheat on the bank behind me. My mouth is dry, my saliva metallic with fear, and when I swallow, I can feel my Adam's apple lift and then drop again.

A splash at the grizzly's feet.

It breaks the stare and looks down.

In a brown-blur flash of power and speed, it plunges its jaws into the river and pulls out a huge silver salmon, flailing, helpless now in the iron-grip of its teeth. With great sloshing strides, the grizzly carries its catch several meters downstream and climbs dripping onto the bank where it holds it still with its claws and rips out mouthfuls of meat.

Overtaken by thirst, I inch toward the river and sink to my knees, keeping my eyes on the bear as I lower my mouth to the current and drink great gulps of clean, cool water.

When I stand, my belly is weighted with river water and the grizzly is picking at the salmon head, now attached to a rack of near translucent bones. Before it can turn its attention back to me, I step backward and disappear quietly into the wheat.

The sun moves west; I move west.

Using the treeline as a guide, I walk through the valley in the direction of the river's flow. Hydrated, I feel my energy return and my steps lighten—like I'm walking in a daydream. All my life reading about the world of old, curled up nights with my lesson slate, imagining myself living in another time when everything wasn't doom above. And now here I am on a pristine planet as if it were up here all the while.

Shadows lengthen, pines stir restlessly in blue skies. Soon, the valley widens, the forest recedes, and I'm walking on near barren rock as the river fans out to cover the entire valley floor, its shallow progress dotted with humps of sun-dried boulders here, pierced by gnarled tree trunks washed downriver there. Before long, mist rises in a rainbow before me, carried on an almost deafening roar, and I come to the edge of a falls where the river spills over the lip of the valley a hundred meters or more to froth and foam in the water-cut pools far below.

When the beauty of it wears off, I realize the hopelessness of my situation. The waterfall is an impossible obstacle, and even if I weren't stuck up here, I'm not even sure where I'm headed except down. Down in search of food and shelter. Down toward the spire of smoke still visible in the distance.

For a moment, just a quick and jarring moment, I wish the train hadn't crashed. I wish I hadn't discovered the surface here thriving on, hidden from us below. I miss my father already. Mostly, I miss his face across the breakfast table, my fondness for algaecrisps already improving. I miss our housing unit. I miss my routine. I even miss Red. I long to hear the metal door bang behind me as I head to the education annex with my lesson slate in my hands once again, the lesson slate that was my only friend, the very lesson slate that taught me everything about the world and then lied to me about it being gone.

I'm about to turn back and find another way down when a faraway flash of silver catches my eye. Training my gaze to the edge of the waterfall, I see another flash. A sort of silver leap followed by a splash. Salmon. Lots of them. Climbing the falls in steps at its edges where the water tumbles down into tiers of swirling pools. An indicator species the lessons called them—nearly extinct even before the War. But here they are thriving.

I notice the slope on the far side of the falls is less severe, tufts of grass and stringy roots dangling from the rocky face where they stretch to catch the mist from the tumbling water. I strip off my shoes, tie the laces together, and hang them around my neck. Then, with my jumpsuit legs rolled up, I wade across the river at the edge of the falls. The water is cold, the current strong, but it's shallow enough that I make quick progress.

Safe on the other side, I lower myself onto the slope and climb down, gripping the rock with my bare feet, ignoring the pain in my hands as I stick them into cracks or grab onto roots, searching for suitable handholds. Halfway down, something tickles my neck. I reach up and cut off the caterpillar's escape.

"Making a run for it, were you?"

He coils up again in my palm.

I look up at the water plunging over the falls. One wrong step crossing, and I would have been cut to pieces by rocks on my way down. And I'm still not safely passed.

Dropping the caterpillar back into my pocket, I climb on without looking down—down past pools of leaping salmon, down past the cool spray on my face, down until the rumbling water is thundering in my ears, down until my feet land on solid ground. I stand on the lower bank and look back up at the falls.

"We did it," I say, peeking into my pocket, not really sure why I'm talking to a caterpillar. "We did it, little fella."

I sit on a boulder at the riverbank and rest in the afternoon sun. Stretching out my tired legs, I dip my bare feet in an eddy of cool water swirling past. And I feel really, really good.

Night comes on fast

The darkness begins behind me and stretches toward the shrinking light ahead, bringing with it cold gusts of wind racing upriver and chilling me to the bone. I'm starving. Not hungry like I've been in Holocene II, but famished to the point of pain.

It's as if the soft ache I've always carried in my guts has spread to every cell of my body. My stomach, my limbs, my tongue—even my eyes are hungry, if that's possible.

I search the dark riverbank for shelter. Finding a tall and sturdy thicket, I crawl beneath it until I come to a hollow that will hold me and there I sit protected from the wind, plucking the thorns and sucking the scratches on my skin.

Exhaustion overcomes hunger and I lie back and pray to science that the dense shrubs will protect me as I curl up on the soft ground and fall fast asleep . . .

I dream I'm in the testing center again and everyone's heads are bent over their desks. I'm sitting, staring, not understanding any questions. Mrs. Hightower appears before me and asks if there's a problem. I jump up and turn my desk over, racing to the bin of lesson slates and I smash them one by one against the wall.

"Lies!" I shout, "Lies!"

Then someone knocks me down. I feel a knee on my neck, another on my back. I'm suffocating and screaming but my scream is muffled by the bodies piling on, and I'm crushed and buried beneath Mrs. Hightower and the entire class and five kilometers of rock and dirt and lies.

It's freezing when I wake, shivering and wet with sweat.

In my delirium I drift off again, back to that wrecked train car, and everything since then seems only a dream. But the cold and lumpy ground presses hard into my sore back, making sleep impossible, my dream morphing into a waking nightmare as I roll onto my side and puke into the brush.

"Ah, man, am I ever sick."

It's mostly just water, really. An acid spume of river water filled with whatever vile microbes are multiplying like mad and leeching on my intestines. I unzip my jumpsuit, pull it down, and vacate the foreign intruders from the other end, too. When I zip it up, I notice a moist lump in my pocket and reach in and find a black and orange mush of hairy guts.

"I'm sorry, little fella. I really am."

Leaving the crushed caterpillar behind with the contents of my stomach, I crawl from the thicket into the cold dawn.

The ground is damp, the air crisp, the pink sky pulling a fog up from the river's surface. Appearing from the fog, at first no more than an apparition seen through the misty gray, an eagle glides upriver, its flapless wings spread from nearly shore to shore, talons tucked and ready, pale head swiveling silent and pendulum-like less than a meter above the water. I watch as it passes me by, so close the wind from its cupped feathers tickles my ear, one yellow-piercing eye taking me in without interest. It tips a wing and disappears around the bend, following the river up toward the salmon falls down which I came.

The sight of that majestic bird leaves me feeling small and useless and pathetic as I turn and vomit again.

The morning drags on forever as I drag myself downriver. I forget why I'm even heading down, but I'm consumed with a desperate need to reach the ocean. Maybe to see for myself that it isn't frozen over, or black with tar, or boiling in an unfiltered sun. Or perhaps it's the call of some distant past that wants me to plunge into it and cool my fever, one last human returning to where it all began. All I know for sure is that I need salt. I'm dehydrated and sick, but my body is craving salt.

I collect small stones and bits of dried river weed and suck them for their salt as I continue stumbling downriver, catching myself on beached logs, climbing carelessly down banks, hanging onto exposed roots. My hands bleed. My Level 3 shoes prove themselves no match for the real world, one sole flapping lose, the other somewhere kilometers behind lying limp on the riverbank like a solitary clue to mark my passing.

Morning turns to afternoon, afternoon to evening, and like the hand of a giant planetary clock, the sun arcs in its sky and beats down on me where I walk. I wish I could wish it away—send it barreling down into the depths from which I came. I'm sunburnt. My nose, my ears, my neck, even my scalp beneath my hair, are all radiating a kind of flesh-on-fire pain. And when the sun finally does lower, my skin seems to burn with a heat of its own against the quick and coming cold.

I shiver with fever. The fish are fine, the grizzly, too. It's not some deadly radiation killing me—it's my years of isolation down below, my immature immune system. It seems as if the surface is punishing me for daring to climb upon it uninvited, or maybe for all those years of denying its existence.

I think these rambling thoughts as I lurch on into the setting sun, my shadow cast a mile behind me, staggering and nameless, broken and small, mumbling to myself about the lies I've been told, I'm angry, my face is lifted, my steps defiant, my hand held before me pushing the giant sun away where it sinks, now enormous and orange, into the shimmering sea.

End of land relief.

Nowhere to walk now.

I drop to my knees and flail my useless arms into the sky, but when I open my mouth for a victory scream, my tongue is cotton dry, my throat swollen, and not even the faintest sound comes out. I fall forward and press my cheek to the cool, salty mud, and with one eye open, I see a vision just beyond the surf.

Twenty meters offshore, he crouches on a coral rock, his

toes arched, his butt resting on his heels. His long arms wrap his shoulders, and he stares out to sea as if he were sending the sun to bed with his gaze. His hair is thick and dark and long, falling down around his elbows in curly, sun-kissed waves. His tan skin is smooth and glistening wet, and he looks like the sun himself fallen into the ocean and just now having climbed out.

I'm reminded of Bill watching from his lifeguard tower in Holocene II. Bill, buried somewhere beneath me now, just a faded remembrance of some other life.

I continue watching.

His pose is still and calm, grounded in the sea. So much time passes that I wonder if he's not just some illusion invented by my delirium; firm and wishful thinking chiseled by my mind from some striking outcropping of rock.

The rising waves lap at his feet. Soon, the rock disappears giving him the look of a bronzed effigy cast after some godly boy who sits on water. And then he rises and dives forward and disappears headfirst into the orange, sun-dappled water with hardly a splash. The ripples move away and diminish, the rock now completely covered by the tide, and no evidence remains of his ever having been there at all.

I surrender to exhaustion and close my eyes and beg the universe to give the liars what they deserve. I beg it to save my father from his prison, to save my mother wherever she is. And I beg it for my own easy and painless death.

CHAPTER 8
Jimmy

I can't see them, but I can hear them.

I'm lying on something soft in a dark room, my waking eyes watching shadows play on what appears to be an opaque and glowing canvas wall. Busy shadows moving back and forth, tall and thin, hunched and fat. Shadows belonging, I assume, to the women's voices. They speak my language, but in a different way—an accent of stunted consonants and drawn out vowels. It's hard to catch anything more than a word here, or a phrase there, because they're talking fast, each to more than just one other, and sometimes at the same time.

"Are ya sure?"

"Nah, but did ya look at his skin?"

"Poor fella."

"Gets what it deserves."

"Camille!"

"She jus' bitter."

"Oh, hush and let 'em rest."

"Here, hold this while I check on 'em."

"Pass the stitch there."

"It ain't worth the mend."

A flap opens in the wall and a triangle of light lands on the dirt floor. The opening darkens, clears, and then the flap closes again. I flinch when I feel her hand on my forehead.

"Shh . . . relax now," she says.

A cool cloth replaces her hand on my brow and then I feel her smearing something on my face and neck. My hands sting when she peels the bandages away, but they're quickly soothed again by a layer of cooling gel. She hovers over me working, her silhouette immense against the backlit canvas wall, and when she begins to hum, I let myself relax and surrender to her care. Her voice is light, as if the air itself were singing. Her hands are coarse but gentle. Her smell is of fern and fire and earth.

She props my head in her strong hand and brings a cup to my mouth—warm liquid that tastes of honey, a bite of bitter. It seeps into my belly and salves the pain. I try to thank her, but she holds her fingers to my lips. She lays my head back, and her humming fades away in the flash of the flap and she's gone.

Days pass this way . . .

With every visit, I know her more and more. Changing my bandages, feeding me broth and tea, emptying my bedpan. She sometimes sits in the dark and hums me to sleep and if I waken in a feverish panic thinking I'm alone, her quiet breathing there comforts me. Now, when the women chatter nightly beyond the canvas wall, I can tell her voice with just a word.

Once, in the feverish thrashings of a terrible dream, I'm in Eden and everything is burning and I run to my mother and cling to her waist and when I wake, she's holding me, humming in the darkness, her gentle rocking lulling me back to sleep.

Then one day she doesn't come.

Nobody comes. No food, no humming, no voices beyond the wall. My hands are unwrapped, my skin no longer on fire. My stomach even feels right again. I sit up—careful, easy, not too fast. Finding my jumpsuit folded beside the bed, I pull it on in the dark. Then I crawl toward the flap in the wall.

The flap opens to another room. Larger, sunlight filtering in through holes high in the outer wall. A small charcoal fire pit lined with stones. A crude chimney made of tree bark running up the wall and turning out. Indentations worn in the red-clay floor where the women must have sat and done their work.

I duck beneath the flap and stand full height in the outer room. I see I'm in a cave. I see that my burnt skin has peeled to reveal a light tan. My palms are still red and somewhat scarred, but finely healed with new flesh. I'm thinner than I was, but I feel virile and vibrant and strong. My jumpsuit is clean, even mended with patches over the tears. Then I notice my shoes parked next to the thatched exterior door, the soles replaced with layers of thick leather. Next to the shoes I find a canteen of water made from some sort of gourd and a leather pouch containing nuts and dried fruits and salty red flakes of meat that I'm assuming to be smoked fish.

I wonder where I am? I open the door to look out and pull back just in time to keep from falling to my death—

The cave door opens to a narrow ledge fifty meters above a treacherous span of shore where waves heave high, lashing themselves against jagged rocks.

I retreat back into the cave and sit, wondering what to do, wondering if the women will return. I watch a beam of sun poke through the smoke-hole and pool on the floor. It rises up the far wall, then moves onto the ceiling before disappearing. No one comes. I drink from the gourd and nibble on nuts. Late in the night, I crawl back to the inner room and sleep.

When I wake all is as before—the beam of light again on the floor, the cave quiet and empty. I slip on my shoes, sling the canteen over my shoulder, and step out from the cave.

The narrow ledge, steep switchbacks.

I flatten myself against the cliff and inch my way, sliding my feet and trying not to look down.

When I scramble over the lip, the sound of crashing waves fades, and I scan the barren plateau for any sign of the people. In the quiet sunlight, I realize how totally alone I am, and just how ill-equipped my lesson slate reading made me for surviving here. Across the plateau, snowcapped mountains loom in the distance, reminding me of the trip down from that train crash.

I'm not going back that way, so I guess it's either north or south. Deciding to leave it to chance, I pick up a broken stick and toss it twirling into the air, committing myself to setting off in whatever direction its broken end indicates. I'm disappointed when it lands pointing north. I remember Dorian loading me into the train at the Transfer Station and saying that Eden was north. "Sweet, sweet north," he said. I'm not sure what's going on, but until I get some answers, Eden or Holocene II are the last places I want to go right now.

I kick the stick off the cliff edge and watch it tumble and bounce, landing in the surf a hundred meters below.

Then I set off walking south.

I walk the day into dusk, exhaustion and darkness catching up with me just as I come upon an enormous burned out fire. Kicking over black coals, the white clumps of ash, I uncover a blackened jaw bone—molars, a wisdom tooth still attached.

Too creeped out to eat anything, too tired to move away, I lie down within spitting distance of the fire and sleep beneath the stars with my head on a tuft of prairie grass.

I'm cold and bug bitten when I wake.

The food these mystery people left for me touches parts of

my tongue never reached by our rations down in Holocene II. The fish is very salty—at least I hope it's fish—and the dried fruit is chewy and sweet. I finish my breakfast, wash it down with water from my canteen, and I set off again, walking until I come to a red-rock caldera dropping like a bowl in the plateau.

The caldera is alive with color. Tufts of green shrubs, fields of purple wildflowers, a distant lake reflecting the blue sky, its shore ringed by oak trees. Despite my fear of getting sick again, I need to fill my canteen. Finding a natural path, I descend.

The caldera floor is full of life. Not just flowers, but animal life, too. Grasshoppers leap in front of me, their clicking wings carrying them off above the flowers. A snake slithers from my path, freezing me in my tracks. Lizards sunning themselves on rocks, independent eyes rolling in their sockets, following me out of sight. Then, without warning, the ground darkens and a wild smell wafts down on a warm, fluttering breeze. I look up; the entire sky above the caldera is blacked out by a billion birds. They move like a living sky, flying wing to wing, flying belly to back, stirring the humid air as they spill together and roll with an aquatic rhythm, moving on without break for what seems like half an hour as I stand watching in awe.

When they finally pass, my eyes are blinded for a moment by the return of unfiltered sun and when they adjust again, I'm standing face to face with him—

I recognize him right away. I had convinced myself he was a hallucination, but here he is, dropped from the sky. His dark hair cascading over his shoulders, his chest bronzed, his waist narrow. It's him, I'm sure—the boy who sits on water. I would have guessed he stood three meters tall, but his piercing gray eyes are almost level with mine. And he's young, too. Maybe not much older than I am. He wears some kind of loin cloth stitched from animal skin. Slung over his shoulder he carries a large netted bag containing several dead birds.

After looking me over, he passes me by and continues on walking toward the lake. He walks quick and easy, loose on his feet, and I have to jog to keep up.

"Hey, what's your name?"

He ignores me, walking faster. I've never seen anyone like him before. His skin seems to fit him perfectly and the way he walks suggests that the very ground is there only for him to cross. He's long and lean, his arms already ripped with muscle, and I can't imagine him ever being afraid of anyone.

"Hey, slow down."

I trot along behind him, dodging left and right, desperate to get his attention. He ignores me, his eyes focused, the netted bag of birds bouncing against his naked back.

"Was it you who found me?"

When he reaches the grove of trees at the edge of the lake, he stops. I stand in the leafy shade and watch as he opens his bag and tosses birds onto the grass, bending over to artfully fluff them up, or tuck their wings. Five, six, seven dead birds spread out. Then he breaks a narrow limb from a sapling and strips it of leaves. He pulls a string from his belt and lashes his last bird to the stripped limb. Then he buries the free end of the limb into the ground, pumping it back and forth to make a sort of hinge before lowering it onto the grass.

"What are you doing with those birds?"

He squats and ties a coil of rope to the stick just beneath where he tied the bird, then he uncoils the rope over to me.

"Pigeons," he says, stuffing the end of the rope into my

hand. "They's pigeons."

So he can speak. His voice is higher-pitched and more like mine than I expected it to be.

"What do I do with this?" I ask, holding the rope.

"On my signal," he says, "pull fast an' bring 'em up."

"Bring what up?"

"The stick pigeon."

"What's the signal?" I ask, but he's already walked off.

He unfolds the pigeon sack into a large circular net edged with small stone weights, looping it together with well-practiced folds and climbing with it up the nearest tree.

Several minutes pass and I stand there, feeling stupid with the rope in my hand. He conceals himself in the overhanging branches so well that I have to keep refocusing to even see him there. I want to ask what we're doing, but with every passing minute the silence grows heavier until I give up the idea of ever speaking again. So I stand, rope in hand.

"Now," he hisses, "now."

I pull the rope hard and stand the stick up in the grass, its dead-tethered display flapping lifeless and limp on its end.

Now what, I wonder.

They come twisting out of the sky fast—a much smaller flock of the pigeons that passed earlier—and within seconds the ground is covered with them pecking and cooing, chasing one another in circles, no idea yet that they've been duped.

The net comes down in a gorgeous spiral, hovering for a moment in a whoosh of air spun by its stony edges, and then it drops on the confused birds, and he drops from the branches after it. He quickly scoops up the drawstring, sweeps the net around the stunned birds, heaves it up and holds it closed—

closed and writhing with fifty flapping pigeons.

He wrestles the sack to the lake's edge and I follow.

Before I can say no, he has me breaking their necks. We take turns reaching in and drawing out the panicked pigeons, flipping them backwards with quick jerks, their necks giving with thin cracks, their fluttering hearts stuttering then ceasing to beat as they go limp in our hands.

"It's all in the wrist," he says.

At first it takes me several attempts each, but as the pile grows, I get to where I'm almost as quick as he is.

With the net now empty and a pile of dead pigeons at our feet, he produces a tiny ivory knife from some hidden pocket in his waist. He snatches up a pigeon and cuts a ring just below the tail. Then, in one slick motion, he strips the bird clean of feathers and all, tossing the skin onto the ground where it lays deflated and slimy, wrong side out, perhaps closer resembling some feathered salamander ancestor of a bird. Next, he slides his blade up the rib cage, reaches in and pulls out a handful of slippery guts, tossing them onto the pile, too. I gag a little.

"This is disgusting," I say, looking at the pile of parts.

"It's called field dressin'," he says.

"Well, it looks a lot more like field undressing to me."

He chuckles and hands me the dressed bird, pointing to the water. I look at him, confused, the slimy bird cradled like a venomous slug in my palms. He takes the pigeon back and dips it in the lake and runs his fingers inside its disemboweled breast rinsing it clean. Then he rips free a handful of grass and stuffs the grass inside the bird and puts the bird in the bag.

He nods. I nod.

Then he strips another. Skin, guts, head—the pile grows.

He hands the bird to me and I rinse it clean, fill it with grass, and slip it into the sack, just like he showed me.

He smiles. "It's Jimmy, by the way."

"What's that?"

"Jimmy," he says. "My name's Jimmy."

"I'm Aubrey."

"Sounds jus' like a girl's name."

"Well, Jimmy sounds like slang for a pecker."

"What's a pecker?"

"Never mind. Aubrey's a boy's name, too."

We work this way for half an hour, faster and faster, until it takes us less than half a minute to complete a bird. When we finish, the netted sack is bursting with pink approximations of pigeons and three separate piles lie at our feet—feathers, guts, and blank staring pigeon heads looking up into the sky where three red-headed vultures now circle, waiting for us to leave.

"How ya gonna carry yers?" he asks.

"Carry my what?"

"Yer half," he says, nodding toward the pigeons.

"I don't want any."

"Suit yerself," he says, hefting the sack over his shoulder, leaning under its weight, and walking off without another word.

I chase after.

"Wait! I want to come with you."

"You's cain't."

"I don't have anywhere to go," I say, running ahead of him and blocking his path. "You can't just leave me out here alone."

"Sure can," he says, moving around me and walking again.

"I'm coming anyway."

"I told ya no," he says. "They dun' voted already."

"Who voted?"

"Ever-one."

"Voted about me?"

"Well, who else?"

"You voted to leave me?" I shout, my voice louder than I expected and echoing back to us from the caldera walls.

"I ain't voted."

"Well, why not?"

"'Cause I ain't been born yet."

"You talk funny," I say.

"So do you's."

"Well, I don't like you."

"I don't like you's neither," he says.

I fall in behind and follow anyway. After a few minutes, he glances over his shoulder and scowls at me.

"How come you's followin' me if ya dun' like me?"

"Why do you keep talking to me if you don't like me?"

He laughs and walks on.

CHAPTER 9
Thank You, Robert Frost

He walks fast.

Even with the pigeons weighing him down.

It's hard for me to keep up, following his shadow across the caldera, climbing out behind him, trailing him south.

When the plateau rejoins the ocean, he follows its edge as it wears away and drops in natural steps down to rolling dunes of sand. He never breaks for food or water. It's hot and I sweat my jumpsuit through and then drink from my canteen and sweat it through again. He never looks back, not once. But I know that he knows I'm here. He must be hoping I'll give up and fall away. I won't. I'll match him step for step if he walks the world round. I don't care who they are or what they voted, I'm not going to give up and die out here alone. If they want me dead, they'll have to kill me.

Evening arrives as he leads me into a canyon, inland along some dry riverbed littered with boulders the size of buildings down in Holocene II. He weaves his way expertly around the mammoth rocks, never once halting or checking his direction. Dragging with fatigue, but still committed, I follow behind him slipping and stumbling over lose stones.

Darkness descends fast in the canyon and before long, the boulders become giant black shadows looming overhead in the night. Suddenly, I realize I've lost him. I'm not sure how long I've been walking without seeing him ahead, but I've lost him. I stop, my path blocked by an enormous boulder. I must go left or right, and in the pitch-black night I don't know which to choose, or if it even matters anymore. I choose left. Another boulder. Another left. Another. All but a slice of starlit sky is blocked by the towering canyon walls, and I walk blind with my hands stretched before me in the blackness.

At first, I only see a spark. A tiny red ember climbing on the wind ahead. I round another boulder—yes, there, I'm sure that's fire I see, the orange glow against the canyon wall. I creep forward. A block of stone sits beneath an overhang and from its other side, the fire casts their shadows on the canyon wall. Tall, elongated shadows. Ten-meter shadow-men painted on the glowing wall, alive and gesturing wildly as if some ancient cave painting from my lesson slate history had animated itself from the night. Then I hear them, their quiet, throaty voices carried with the fire's embers on the wind.

"How'd he get here anyways?"

"Yeah, thought we left 'em at the caves."

"I'll tell ya how? Jimmy here went to find 'em."

"Is that true, Son?"

"I's followin' pigeons. Ain't my fault I run into 'em."

"Yeah, right."

"Well, he cain't stay with us, Son, he's one of them."

"Papa!" Jimmy pleads. "He'll die out there alone."

"It's decided already."

"He'll lead 'em right to us."

"Ah, let the Park Service have 'em," another shadow says, tossing a log onto the sparking fire.

Listening to them, I feel my pulse quicken, the blood rush to my cheeks. Fine then—if they don't want me, I don't want them either.

"I'll take my half now," I say, stepping around the boulder and into the firelight.

They all turn to look at me—Jimmy and five other men. They're circled around the fire facing me. Behind them, against the canyon wall, animal pelts hang dripping from crude stands made of sticks lashed together. Next to the men, some meters off, glows a cooking fire dug into the ground and reduced to coals. An old gray man kneels there, turning one of the pelt's former occupants on a spit. He looks up momentarily from his roast without expression and then resumes turning it again.

"Half of what?"

The man speaking looks like Jimmy's father. Jimmy nods to the sack of pigeons lying next to the pelts.

"Well, stake 'em his claim and let 'em scat," his father says.

"Cain't he jus' stay till morning?" Jimmy says. "Please."

I stand just outside the warmth of the fire and watch the flames dancing on the men's bearded leather faces. Strong men, practical men, resolved men. The fire brightens in a gust, settles again. The old man turns the roast, glistening above the cook fire embers. I've never eaten meat before, but the smell sets my mouth watering. A cold wind whips at my back, knocking my empty canteen against the boulder.

"I can help around camp," I say.

"We dun' need no help."

"Everyone needs help."

"Not yers."

"I can entertain you, then."

"Entertain us how?" the father asks.

"What if I sing for you?"

"We dun' need no songs neither."

"How about poetry then? I can recite poetry."

"What kinda poetry?"

I step closer into the firelight, buying time to remember a poem from my lesson slate.

"Okay, how about this?" I clear my throat and recite the only poem I can remember on the spot:

A voice said, Look me in the stars / And tell me truly, men of earth, / If all the soul-and-body scars / Were not too much to pay for birth.

When I finish, the men all stare at me.

"You's jus' made that up now?" one of them asks.

"No," I say, laughing. "I read it. That's Robert Frost."

"Go camp with this Frost fella then," another says.

"That's impossible. He's been dead a thousand years."

"That's too bad," the father says, "'cause you cain't stay."

The old man looks up from his roast. "He can stay."

"What?"

"Said he can stay."

"I heard ya, but . . ."

"Cain't you see this here boy can read?"

"Well, so what if he can?"

"Dun' ya think that mightn't be some value to us?" the old man asks. "Specially seein' cain't none of you's do it? I'd like my grandbabies to read and write. Sides that, I liked his poem."

The old man raises an eyebrow and waits. When there's no further response from the boy's father, he signals the end of the discussion by turning back to his roast at the coals.

"Fine," the father says, glaring at me. "But jus' tonight."

Jimmy grins and takes me by the hand and pulls me into the circle around the fire. The men go about inspecting their pelts and setting up beds. We hang the birds from a river stick and prop them between two large rocks. The stick bows with the weight of them, fifty little shadows twisting in the wind just outside the firelight, as if trying to remember how to fly.

When the roast is finished, we sit around the fire and gnaw on greasy handfuls of meat. It's the most amazing thing I've ever tasted. The fattiest parts almost melt in my mouth, and I can feel the protein seeping already into my tired legs. Nobody talks at all. They just stare into the fire and eat. The flames are mesmerizing. They rise and fall and rise again, lapping at the night in some strange fire dance, as if trying to tell some ancient story in a language forgotten long ago.

The men finish eating and leave the fire one by one, each of them rustling around in the dark as they lie down on beds of fur, or bits of brush, falling quietly asleep almost right away.

Now only Jimmy sits across from me, his arms wrapped around his knees as he stares into the flames. I strip the last bit of meat off my last bone and toss it into the fire.

A long time passes with neither of us saying anything as we sit across the fire from one another. I watch his face glowing in the shadows, his gray eyes sparkling as they reflect back the red embers. He seems to be looking into the coals and beyond to the very center of the Earth.

"You's come from below," he says, "dun' ya?"

It's been quiet for so long that his question catches me by surprise. That, and it's a strange question.

"How'd you know?"

"Look at ya. I ain't dumb."

"No, I wouldn't imagine you are."

Must be my outfit, I think. That and my sunburn maybe. It

seems like a lifetime ago already. The train crash, the elevator goodbye, the test—all of Holocene II, really. And something one of the other men said earlier is bothering me, too. He said something about letting the Park Service have me.

"Why'd that man say to let the Park Service have me?"

"Oh, dun' mind that. That's jus' Uncle John talkin'," he says, tossing a pebble into the coals.

"But what is the Park Service? Why would they want me?"

"Ya really dun' know?" he asks, looking up from the coals and searching my face.

"Know what?"

"All this is parkland," he says, unfolding his arms from his knees and spreading them out wide, as if to take in the world.

"So?" I say, shrugging.

"So, they'll kill ya if they find ya here."

"Who will kill me?"

"The Park Service, ya dummy," he says, shaking his head. "They'll kill ya dead. Kill me, kill ever last one of us. And they do it, too. Do it all the time."

"Well, why don't we just leave the park then?"

"Because we cain't leave," he laughs.

"I don't see why not."

"Ya cain't ever leave the park," he says, shaking his head. "It's all park. The whole damn surface belongs to 'em."

"Who is them?" I ask, more confused than ever.

"The Park Service."

"Well, who on Earth is the Park Service?"

He stands and brushes himself off and looks down at me.

"You's are," he says, walking off toward the sleeping men.

I sit alone beside the fire and think about what he said. I'm not sure what this Park Service he's talking about is, or why it hunts these poor people, but I do know that my people down in Holocene II have nothing to do with it. No way.

Something is going on, though, and I wonder what. Where was that train headed? Why was it crossing those mountains? And why is the surface not covered in ice? And not just that, but who are these people up here?

The fire burns down until only a few coals glow from the bed of dark ash, pulsing there like some buried heart throbbing against the coming cold death of night. I curl up close, catching its lingering heat, and thank Robert Frost as I drift off to sleep.

CHAPTER 10
Welcome to the Cove

The fire is nothing but ash.

The ground is hard and cold.

In the dim light of dawn I see that the men are gone from where they slept, and so are the pelts, and so are the birds. Fully awake, I jump to my feet to set out and find them. When I turn around, Jimmy thrusts a pack at me.

"Try to keep up," he says.

The pack is lashed together from sticks strung with animal skin and it's piled high with pelts and dangling with naked birds now shriveled in the open air. I heave it on and nearly topple over backwards. Jimmy straps his pack on, pausing to show me how to stand straight and let my legs take the weight. With our towering packs, we walk side by side like two strange and furry beetles crawling out of the canyon.

Jimmy doesn't mention our fireside conversation last night and neither do I. We walk south again following the coast at a distance, and soon the landscape changes from scrub brush and dunes to fields of short grass rustling in the ocean breeze. After several hours walking, we enter a solemn redwood forest where the trees reach more than a hundred meters each into the sky. It's quiet, a mist still rising off the moss on the forest floor.

Coming to an enormous tree, its trunk ten meters across, Jimmy slips off his pack and lies down on his back in a beam of sunlight filtering through the branches. I slip my pack off, too, and stand there marveling at the majestic giants all around.

"Number one rule of packin'," Jimmy says, his head resting in his hands, "we dun' stand when we can sit, and we dun' sit when we can lie down."

I drop down beside him, looking up at the redwood rising to a distant green point piercing the blue sky above. I feel as though we've been shrunken—two brother ants reclining on the forest floor, our chests rising and falling together, breathing fresh forest air in, breathing our differences out.

"Ain't it beautiful?" he says.

"You have no idea," I reply, marveling at the ancient tree and remembering reading in my lesson slate about them. About how we cut them down to near nothing, then wiped the rest out in the dark years of the War.

"How old do you think they are?" I ask.

"Oh, I dunno exactly," he says, biting his lip and thinking. "My pa says one tall as this'n is near two thousand years old."

And then it hits me, what I was thinking, why I asked—two-thousand-year old trees right in front of me. The War that drove us underground was not even a thousand years ago, which means this tree must predate it. The lessons lied. Some things did survive. I want to ask Jimmy about his people, about his family. I want to ask him how long they've been on the run from this Park Service they talk about. I want to ask him what he meant when he said that I was one of them.

"There's no way my people have anything to do with this Park Service," I say. "We don't even know this is up here."

Jimmy stands, heaves his pack on, and walks off.

"Best be gettin' on," he says over his shoulder.

Guess that means he doesn't want to talk about it. I sling

my pack over my shoulders, adjust it, and run after him.

It's a strange camp we arrive at later that afternoon.

"Welcome to the cove," Jimmy says.

We stand on the bluff and look down on a protected cove, hidden until we're nearly on top of it. With a narrow inlet to the sea and high cliffs on all sides, it's a perfect hideaway.

Children play in the water below—big ones, little ones—dark ones, light ones—all thrashing about noisily in the surf. Small ones being picked up by waves and tossed ashore, then running back out into the water, laughing again. Bigger ones skating the wet sand on skimboards made from bark.

Several yards beyond, unseen by the children, two giant sea turtles almost mimic their behavior riding the waves, feeding on whatever small stirred up things turtles eat.

Onshore, past the high tide line, sun-bleached animal skin tents flap idly in the wind. Smoke rises from a fire. Women pad about camp with children on their hips, others sit in the shade with toddlers clamped onto their breasts. The men cluster in groups. One group breaking firewood from tree limbs, another working pelts, yet another gutting fish. They're a misfit mix of people, too—some black as coal, some dark with tan, a few red ones with white sun blotches on their skin and blond hair.

During a break in the surf below, I hear a familiar tune—a humming carried to the bluff on the breeze. I follow the sound and spot her right away, her silhouette rocking beside the fire as she mends a skin in her lap.

"There's the woman who cared for me," I say, pointing.

"That's my mum," Jimmy says. "Come on."

"You sure it's okay?" I ask, hesitating. "What about what your dad said last night?"

"That was out there," he says, jerking a thumb behind us. "Not here. Here, if mum wants ya to stay, then ya stay."

I follow him down a well-concealed path to the camp. He drops his pack near a tent, and I drop mine next to it.

His mother looks up at me and smiles. Not just her mouth, but her entire face crinkles up in a happy grin. Her eyes twinkle.

"Ya must be starved," she says, setting aside her stitching. "Come gets ya some stew while it's hot."

I look at Jimmy and smile.

"Guess this means I can stay."

Jimmy and I sit on a log and watch the kids play while we eat our stew. It's the most amazing thing I've ever tasted, even better than last night's meat. It's warm and salty, thick with soft starchy vegetables and chunks of seafood that Jimmy tells me are scallops and butter clams. I could eat a thousand bowls of it every day forever and never eat anything else again.

"Is this your permanent home?" I ask, licking my bowl.

Jimmy swallows a mouthful of stew and wipes his dripping chin with the back of his hand before answering.

"We move lots," he says. "We's headin' down the coast fer the summer runs when I's found you's."

"What about that cave where you left me?"

"Stayed longer'n usual this time so's mum could nurse to you's. But then they's took the vote and we moved on."

"Do you move because of the Park Service?"

"Yep," he says, draining his stew and hopping off the log.

He returns our empty bowls to the tents, leaving me alone. I watch the children play. Three boys communicating only with hand gestures, floating a beach log raft, but it rolls on them every time. Four girls sitting on the shore talking, one of them scrawling pictures in the sand. So innocent, so pure.

Who would hurt them? Who could?

Jimmy has it all wrong—Holocene II and the Foundation have nothing to do with the Park Service. They can't. Last week I didn't even know this existed up here. Still, something doesn't feel right. And I have no idea why we've been lied to. I need to find a way to talk with my dad, to tell him about all of this.

But first I need to go see about another bowl of stew.

CHAPTER 11
You'll See Soon Enough

The days roll in and out with the tides in the quiet cove.

I'm ashamed of myself because although I think about my father and my people down in Holocene II, I'm having too much fun to do anything about it. I push the thoughts away.

I share a small tent with Jimmy, and every morning when I wake, he's already out swimming. I stand on the shore and watch him cutting through the water, disappearing beneath the waves and then surfacing again surprisingly far away and in another direction entirely from where I was looking.

I spend afternoons walking the cove collecting shells and investigating things I've read about but thought I'd never see. Sand dollars and starfish and crabs that scuttle from overturned rocks. I wear my shoes only rarely, the soles of my feet growing thick and calloused. A steady diet of protein is putting weight on my bones, and I can do fifty pushups without breaking a sweat. My jumpsuit gets tighter by the day and I tear the sleeves free because my arms are filling out. On hot days, I wear it unzipped with my chest bare, and although not nearly as dark as Jimmy is, I'm becoming bronzed in the sun.

Everything here is about food—finding food, preparing food, eating food—which takes some getting used to because in Holocene II rations arrived automatically every week. They have boats here hidden in the cave at the back of the cove, and on the days they cast them off, the men are gone until sunset, returning with the boats low in the water, the hulls piled high with fish. On days Jimmy goes out with them, I'm on my own to investigate the cove.

There are kids everywhere. Baby's crying for milk, toddlers being chased by their mothers, boys and girls always organizing some new game or intently watching the adults work. I ask Jimmy why so many kids and he tells me that most are orphans whose parents have been killed.

"Besides," he says, "we needs lots of 'em jus' so a few can survive the Park Service."

"That doesn't seem right," I say.

"It's jus' the way it is."

"Still, it doesn't seem right."

Jimmy shakes his head. "Right ain't got nothin' at all to do with it," he says. "You'll see soon enough."

Today, when the boats return, Uncle John grabs me and walks me to where they clean the fish. I'm nervous because he's the one who said to let the Park Service have me.

He stares down at me, his eyes the color of honey, his face as black as night.

"You's jest ain't gonna go away, is ye?"

"No, sir," I say, shaking my head.

"Well then," he says, "you's better get learnt on helpin'."

He slaps a stone knife in my hand, the black blade polished so smooth I can see my reflection in it. Then he hooks a fish through the gills and hefts it onto the pine-log cleaning table.

"Stick 'em in the arse, and cut up to his gills."

Even the idea of it grosses me out, but I don't dare argue. Slipping the knife point into the hole he pointed out, I slide the blade up the belly and slit it open, the skin parting in a red gash.

"Now," he says, pointing, "slice into his jaw flap there and cut his tongue loose. Good. Now put yer thumb in his mouth, pull it free, and every bit of his plumbin'll come clear with it."

I push my thumb into the mouth, its bony lip sharp against my hand, and pull down toward the slit in its belly. Its tongue rips free, then the pink gills, now the ribbed throat trailing its guts in gray and purple coils as they suck free of the slit belly.

Uncle John slaps me on the back.

"There now. That's how ya do it, boy. Two cuts is all ya need. Now wash 'em out good and finish the rest." He turns to go, then turns back, smiling at me with his honey eyes. "The knife's yours."

I look down at the knife in my hand and I smile, too.

Waking first for once, I lie next to Jimmy and listen to him breathing. His sleeping face in the morning tent-glow is young and free of worry and I wonder what dreams he dreams, what he allows himself to wish in that private world of sleep.

His face tightens, his eyes open.

"I'm gonna start sleepin' with my knife if ya keep starin' at me," he says. Then he sits up and rubs the sleep from his eyes, pulling his knuckles away and blinking at me. "You's wanna learn to swim today?"

"I don't know." I try to sound bored rather than scared.

"Come on," he says, gripping my wrist and pulling me from the tent. "It's easy as breathin' once ya get it down."

There's just a hint of morning blue above the cove, and I sit on a dark log by the shore and roll up jumpsuit legs.

"What're ya doin'?" Jimmy asks, stripping naked. "You's like to drown in that damn thing. Take it off."

I look around. The boats are already gone, the men gone

with them. The women and children are still sleeping. Still, I'm nervous to be naked in front of Jimmy. I stand and unzip my suit and let it fall to the ground. When I step out of it and look back, it lays on the shadowed beach like a shed skin. Even with my tan, I look pale and infant-like compared to Jimmy. I hurry into the cold water to cover up my nakedness in the waves.

Jimmy walks me out until the water's up to my chest, but I stop there, not wanting to go any farther. A wave comes in and knocks me backwards. I cough and spit and wipe my eyes.

"Dun' be a damn wimp," Jimmy says.

"I'm not a wimp."

"You's actin' like you's is."

I dive headfirst into the next wave and paddle my arms like I've watched him do. And it works—I'm swimming!

Excited now, I paddle into deeper water. Then I sink. Fast. The water closes over my head and everything gets quiet and dark. I'm back in that silent elevator again—panicked, holding my breath, flailing against an invisible door.

A shadow darkens my eyes, strong arms wrap around me from behind, Jimmy's bare chest pressing against my back, and then I'm rising toward the pale light. My head breaks free and I gasp in lungfuls of cold air. Jimmy cradles me, laughing.

"It's not funny," I say, shaking with fear.

"I know it ain't."

"Then why are you laughing?"

"'Cause I cain't help it."

"Well, I was swimming for a second."

"Ya did good, buddy," he says, "ya did good."

When he calls me buddy, I smile, even laugh a little, too.

First, he teaches me to tread water. Then we work on the

breast stroke. Before long I'm gliding easily across the cove—back and forth and back again. I even learn to dive, carrying up small rocks to prove to Jimmy that I touched bottom.

We swim until I'm too exhausted to go on. Then we float together on our backs and watch the sun rise over the bluff, the saltwater carrying us on gently rocking waves. I feel cradled by the ocean, my insignificance absorbed by the Earth, suspended and weightless in the blue-morning peace. I think of everyone down in Holocene II, doing their daily routine, having no idea that this heaven is just five kilometers above their heads.

I have to find a way to tell them.

We scamper dripping onto the shore and quickly pull on our clothes just as the waking children come scrambling down the beach, screaming. We share a silent smile above their heads and then head up to camp for breakfast.

Jimmy says I take to the water like a baby seal.

He gradually leads me from the cove and into deeper water where we spend mornings diving for mollusks. When the sea is calm and the water clear, I can see an entire underworld—jellies rising and falling on invisible currents, colorful fish patrolling reefs, beautiful plants waving from rocky shelves.

We drag nets of oysters onto shore and shuck them in the sun, sucking them from their shells and swallowing them raw. Afternoons, I float on the surface with my head underwater and watch as Jimmy holds his breath and walks on the sea floor with a spear gun he's carved from ash wood and stretched with sinewy tendons stripped from a deer. He's a dead-on shot, too. He hands the speared fish off to me, and I hook them through the gills and swim them to shore, carrying them into camp to clean them, their panicked hearts still beating in my hand.

My skin is almost as dark as Jimmy's now, and I'm filling out more every week. I do my daily pushups and Jimmy shows me how to do pullups from a tree limb. I cut the legs off my jumpsuit, making them little more than a patched pair of zip-up shorts, the Foundation crest so faded you can hardly see it.

One afternoon while the men are inland hunting, Jimmy takes me out in one of the boats. Keeping the cove in sight, we row into deep water and drop nets. Then we lie on our backs in the bottom of the boat, rocking gently, listening to the waves lap against the wooden hull.

I remember lying on the beach that Sunday before my test, I remember dreaming about escaping that life down there. I've come a long way from five kilometers underground. I feel a pang of guilt about my father, about not making an effort to get news to him, but I do my best to push the thoughts away, pushing the guilt away with them.

A gull arcs across the blue dome of sky above. Then I see a flock of much larger birds silhouetted against the sun. But as they approach overhead it becomes clear they're no birds made of feather and flesh. They're too perfect, too smooth, too slick. They come rushing in on silent wing in perfect formation.

"What are those?" I ask, pointing.

Jimmy lifts his hand to shade the sun, following my finger with his eyes. Without a word he grips the edge of the boat and throws his weight into the sidewall and tips us over. When I emerge from the water, coughing, everything is dark.

"What happened? Why'd you tip the boat?"

Jimmy clamps his hand on my mouth.

We tread water beneath the boat, rising and falling on the waves. After a minute, Jimmy peers out. Without saying a word, he slips beneath the capsized boat and swims fast for shore.

He's much too fast to keep up with.

When I finally get to shore and race into camp, I find him hustling the women and children to the back of the cove and into the cave where they store the boats.

"What is it?" I ask, stopping at the cave entrance to catch my breath. Two dozen staring eyes blink back from the dark. Jimmy grabs my arm and pulls me into the shadows.

"Drones," is all he says.

And that's enough.

Later that afternoon, the men come stumbling into camp carrying a body on a makeshift stretcher. What remains is not much more than a mangled pile of charred flesh, and I have to look at the pallbearers faces and count them off by name to see who it is they carry. The only one missing is Uncle John.

Nobody talks that evening as we work to gather wood. We disperse in silent groups of twos and threes, carrying back what dry driftwood we can find and dragging it up the path, out of the cove, and stacking it two meters high at the top of the bluff.

If anyone is worried about the fire betraying our location to the Park Service, nobody shows it. We lie outside our tents and watch the flames high on the bluff, burning white-hot in the breeze, like some lighthouse warning to any lonely traveler lost on the dark and starless seas. With no Eden here, it must be sad to say goodbye forever. I expect a prayer of some kind, or maybe a eulogy like I've read about in lessons, but nobody says a word, and the only sound besides the flames crackling in the breeze is the stifled sobbing of Uncle John's pregnant wife.

In the morning, we use turtle shells to scoop the ashes and toss them into the wind.

CHAPTER 12
Idols from the Past

John Jr. is born three weeks later.

The night before a full moon.

In the morning, Jimmy leads me along the bluff south out of the cove. He's hardly asked me anything about my people, so today it catches me by surprise when he says:

"Tell me about where you's from."

I watch him for a moment, trying to guess why the sudden curiosity, but he seems preoccupied, staring ahead as we walk, swaggering loose and easy the way he does. It hits me how he's perfectly adapted to his environment, surviving off the land.

"Please tell me," he says.

"Well, we don't have anything to do with the Park Service, if that's why you're asking."

"I ain't sayin' they's did."

"Good," I say, relieved. "I don't know what to say, really. My people are just people. No different than yours. Except we live underground and we didn't even know this was up here."

"What's it like down there?"

So I tell him about Holocene II. About my mother dying when I was born, about my father raising me. I tell him about turning fifteen and taking the test. About being called up and getting on the train and the train crashing and my climbing out. I tell him how we're taught that the surface is uninhabitable and has been for nearly a thousand years.

He nods, listening without interrupting me once. The only sound he makes is a kind of grunt when I tell him about retiring at thirty-five and living forever in Eden.

"Who'd wanna live forever?"

"I don't know," I say. "Don't you?"

He shakes his head and spits in the dirt.

"We return to the Earth when we's gone."

"You mean from ashes to ashes, and all that?"

"Where'd ya hear that?" he asks.

"Hear what?"

"Ashes to ashes."

"I don't know—I probably read it. Why?"

"I like it," he says.

We walk in silence for a while, our feet kicking loose rocks, our eyes trained on the coastline ahead.

"Now you tell me about your people."

"You already know 'em," he says.

"No," I say, "I mean tell me about how you got here."

"We've jus' always been here."

"You have?"

"Yeah, we's Americans."

"Native Americans?"

"I dunno. Jus' Americans, I guess."

"Well, tell me about the Park Service then."

He sighs. "All I know is stories they pass down."

"Okay. Tell me those then."

So he tells me about his people surviving a great war and migrating to the coast in search of food. He tells me they came to vast cities, destroyed and empty. He says they settled there and began to rebuild. And then the Park Service came.

"There was no safety," he says. "No place for us to hide. Machines, ships, flyers. Even the stars was shadowed by drones killin' our people. Least that's what they tells me."

"What did they do?"

"Went on the run," he says. "Hunting and hunted."

"Who are they?"

"The Park Service?"

"Yeah, the Park Service."

"I dunno. Nobody knows."

"Well, why'd you think I was one of them?"

He points to the faded Foundation crest on my jumpsuit.

"It's no connection to them," I say.

He shrugs. "What's it matter fer anyhow?"

"Don't you want to fight back? Change things?"

"Change things? It's how things is. It's how they's always been far back as stories tell. Many, many moons now," he says, "and will be fer many more to come."

Then he stops and turns to me.

"Ya remember that thing ya did that nigh by the fire?"

"What night?"

"The first night," he says. "The poem."

"Yeah, I remember."

"Can ya really read?"

"Sure, I can read."

"Good," he says, smiling. "Follow me."

He leads me up a narrow path into the red-rock cliffs. We climb high, passing exposed bulkheads of rock with shells and fossils peeking out from their weathered faces and I wonder at the strange fact that all this was once under sea. He stops when we arrive at the opening of a cave.

"Ya dun' mind goin' in, do ya?

"No, I don't mind. Really. I'm fine."

Stepping inside, he uses his flint and stone to light one of several torches waiting there. He offers one to me, but I wave it away and follow him into the cave. The opening fades behind us and our world shrinks to the ball of light cast by the torch. The flame flickers in the musty air, sometimes almost touching the ceiling of low passageways, sometimes casting a faint glow on stalactites hanging high above like teeth ready to close down and swallow us forever into the belly of the Earth.

I feel panic creeping on, a familiar feeling of being closed in, trapped with no escape, the way I felt the first fifteen years of my life. I breathe in, breathe out, and follow Jimmy deeper.

Reaching a small circular cavern, he touches his torch to others waiting propped in the cracked walls, and with each new flame, the cave's contents come more clearly into view.

It's an underground junkyard, a hoarder's heaven—but to Jimmy it might as well be Tutankhamun's tomb.

He leads me around the room, touching everything once as if to make sure it's still there. Strange, leftover things. Things I recognize from lessons and educationals, things that must be a mystery to Jimmy. A rusty manifold from some ancient internal combustion engine. Two warped wheels without tires. A boat propeller with a broken blade. An iron post. Bits of glass. Antique transistors. A green-plastic circuit board from some twenty-first century computer.

When he finishes touching everything, he leads me to an old rusted oil drum resting in the farthest corner. Propping his torch up, he reaches his arm inside and removes something heavy, wrapped in oil-soaked leather. He stands holding it in his arms, caressing it as if it were a pet.

"This is a big, big treasure," he says, his eyes both excited and solemn at the same time. "It was recovered from the city before we left. My people keep it hidden here many centuries now. This here . . .," he pauses to hold up his covered treasure, "This is our foundin' father."

"One of the first presidents?"

"Maybe even a god," he says. "My grandpapa was named after him, my papa. Even me. My son I will name fer him, too. And then maybe even he has a son to name James."

He pauses, staring into my eyes, the torch flame reflecting on his black pupils. Then he continues:

"My pa says it is our duty to multiply, to carry on the race. He says we're seeds. He says we must survive until a golden time comes again. It is our duty, our right. You understand?"

I nod that I do.

"Good," he says, nodding, too. "I need a favor from ya."

"Sure," I say. "Anything."

"None of us can read. Well, not much anyways. I hoped ya could read me this writin' here."

He holds the heavy treasure out in his trembling hand, and with the other he pulls the leather cover free, revealing a bronze sculpture of a man's head. A gleaming bust, worn and polished by a thousand years, a hundred hands, but an unmistakable and boyish face with thick wavy hair and perfect features—features I recognize immediately from lessons on American culture.

He twists it so I can see all sides in the torchlight, then he points to a plaque at its base. The plaque is etched with dates, the name, an inscription honoring the man and his short career.

"What's it say?" he asks, excited, pushing it closer to me, turning it gently under the light.

I study the writing long enough to read it three times.

"Can ya read it?"

"Just the name," I say. "James—just like you."

"Nothin' else, though?"

I shake my head no.

"No? Ya sure?"

"Listen, it's a beautiful bust, and I'm sure you're right—he must have been some kind of idol from the past."

He sighs. Frowns. Runs his fingers over the plaque and the text etched there, as alien and as dead to him as Latin would be to me. Maybe more so. Then he accepts it and nods. Covering the bust again, he returns it back to the bottom of its barrel. He stands and collects his torch and snuffs the others out and leads me from the cavern out the way we came.

I look back once at the darkness swallowing the room, our shadows stretched long and quivering on the torch-lit floor as if lingering behind to stay there forever with the past, and I have the strange premonition that no soul will ever see it again.

I feel bad about myself for having lied to Jimmy—but I just couldn't tell him that James Dean was just a movie star.

CHAPTER 13
Rites of Passage

Three times the conch shell blasts.

As if answering the call, a super moon rises above the bluff and casts its silver spotlight down on the cove.

"I'm nervous," Jimmy whispers.

"Me too," I say, my hands covering my nakedness.

Aunt Salinas blows the shell again, the men begin dancing around the fire, their twisted shadows cast onto the sand. They howl and scream, clouds of breath rising like ghosts against the dark sky. Then they stop. In the sudden silence, I can hear the children giggling from their tent flaps behind us.

"You's better go to sleep," Jimmy hisses at them. Then he turns back to me. "Sure ya wanna do this? Ya dun' have to."

"I know, but if you're doing it, I'm doing it."

The men stand at the fire, waiting. Their heads hung, their arms crossed. The women circle around them. Then they begin to wail, their arms flailing about, their voices riding the night. When they finish, they kneel on the ground, creating a pathway between us and the men at the fire.

Jimmy and I step up, stripped and trembling.

The women reach across the path they've made and grip one another's arms, creating a tunnel, a human arch, writhing, waving, inviting us in. Jimmy ducks beneath them and crawls through the tunnel toward the fire. When he comes out the other side, the men pull him into their circle, his father forcing him to the ground and sitting on his chest. The knife glints like a fish in the firelight as he lowers the blade to Jimmy's waist. I watch with horror as he tugs and saws, his head bent and focused on his work. Jimmy doesn't even make a sound. His father finishes, holding up the bloody knife in one hand and the results of his work hanging lifeless and limp in the other.

My legs go wobbly. I think I might faint.

Jimmy's father pulls him up to his feet and embraces him. Someone paints charcoal on his cheek. Then they circle the fire again, dancing and howling, Jimmy with them now, until they come to rest and stand still, waiting for me.

I drop to my knees, and crawl beneath the arch of arms. They press down against me and I'm trapped in a living canal, forced to my belly, squirming, crawling along the tunnel toward the fire. They press closer, smothering me with their bosoms. My breath quickens and I push forward, harder, faster. They close tight around me and just when I think I'll surely suffocate, I burst free into the firelight and the circle of waiting men.

Jimmy's father forces me to the ground and sits on my chest. I smell his sweat, feel the weight of him pressing me into the sand. I see the blade's shadow as he bends to his work, but I feel nothing. Then he releases me. I lift my head with horror, but other than my nakedness, there's not much to see.

"What's wrong?" I ask, feebly, uncomfortable and nervous with everyone's eyes on me.

"You's cut already."

"I don't see it."

Jimmy points. "Da cirkemsizhen."

"Circumcision? They do that when we're babies."

"Babies?" he says, looking confused. "That's barbaric."

"Is okay," the eldest man says. "Jest finish the rites."

Jimmy clasps my hand and pulls me up. Someone paints charcoal on my cheeks. Then I'm swept into the circle, dancing and howling around the fire. Faster now. Everyone. All taut muscle and hot sweat and charcoal dripping. The women skip, turning in the opposite direction, mixing in and out of the men. The moon shines down and the night hangs heavy with joy, the cool air infused with the scents of bodies and salt and fire.

Aunt Salinas blows the conch and everyone stops.

We fall exhausted where we stand into piles and heaps on the ground, everyone laughing and relaxed.

I lean into Jimmy and he pushes my sweaty hair away from my brow. I look up at him and he smiles. I smile. We don't say it, but we both know that things will never be the same again—never after this night, because after this night we're men.

We lie beneath the moon and let the fire burn down. A gourd passes filled with some kind of sweet milk. A basket of fruit appears. We eat and drink and breathe, but nobody says a word. When Aunt Salinas blows the conch again, people begin to rise. One by one we all get up and drift away to our tents and retire to reflect in solitude and then drift off into whatever wild dreams might visit us each on this free and uninhibited night.

CHAPTER 14
The Butterfly Waits

Kids crying all night.

In the morning, they crawl tired from their tents itching and scratching their raw scalps.

Jimmy's mother orders everyone to leave camp so she can turn out our tents and treat the bedding. Jimmy piles with the men into boats and they shove off to drop nets. The mothers take their children to collect crabs for stew, and they march off down the beach, a dozen little arms raised and scratching at a dozen little heads. I stand around wondering what I should do.

"Maybe ya won't mind collectin' some poppies?" Jimmy's mother says, handing me a leather pouch.

"Poppies? You mean the little yellow flowers?"

"Them's the ones," she says.

"What for?"

"We grind 'em up and dry 'em," she says. "Makes a paste to kill the lice."

With a canteen around my neck and my pockets filled with dried fish, I head out from the cove carrying the poppy pouch.

The bluff above the cove is rocky, the only plants being scrub brush and sawgrass, but farther inland the bluff drops down into a lush valley where I stroll beneath a shaded canopy of trees, on the lookout for the little yellow flowers.

Soon the path turns into a thick tangle of thorny bushes and I use a stick to beat them back. I walk east, knowing that if

I lose my way I can follow the setting sun back to the coast and the cove. Tearing through a thick patch of brush, I step into a small, circular clearing where the grass has been bedded down. There, staring at me with large, dewy eyes, is a mother elk with her baby attached to her tit. Her eyes are the deepest black of any I've ever seen and my reflection stands there in each one, my stick upheld as if to murder her with it. I'm surprised by her calm and steady gaze, devoid of any fear. A feeling of embarrassment comes over me, as if I've interrupted something sacred. I back from the clearing and take another path around.

I find the poppies in the shade of a big oak. They grow in a ring around the trunk, so yellow and bright that they cast a warm glow upward onto the dark bark. It feels almost a shame to pick them, but I quickly fill the pouch.

It doesn't take me long to realize that I'm lost. The thick canopy hides the sun, and I can only guess which way is west. Every time I think I've got it right, the sun peeks through in the wrong place, forcing me to correct course. Around stumps, over the gnarled roots of rotting trees, bypassing impossible blackberry vines covered in thorns, I move on and on and on. After hours of going nowhere, I know I'm walking in circles.

When the rain comes, it comes without warning.

One moment the warm forest is filled with chirping birds, an instant later it's silent and dark, the rain gushing down all around me. It falls in heavy drops, thrashing leaves overhead, leaning plants, dripping to the forest floor. I'm soaked in sixty seconds. The ground grows muddy. Puddles appear. I splash through them and walk toward what I hope is still west.

The water brings new life up from the forest floor. Frogs croaking, slugs slithering, a giant salamander sliding across my feet in a stream that only a moment ago wasn't even there. The rain keeps coming until I can hardly remember a time before. A bog sucks my shoes from my feet, the tattered material finally tearing when I try to retrieve them, so I leave them sticking in the mud like abandoned oyster shells and walk on barefoot.

It rains and it rains and it rains.

And then it stops.

As quickly as it began, the rain ceases and the golden light returns to the canopy. Great droplets of water hang from leaves like heavy crystals just waiting to be plucked, dripping onto the forest floor and then growing again. The frogs fade, the birds sing. I push on, whacking drenched growth with my stick, the rainwater bursting into little rainbow showers as I hack them down, and then I step into the most amazing view.

Before me, a strange field of leafy vines stretches almost as far as I can see, dotted everywhere with alien pods. A hundred, a thousand, a million glistening melons, golden in the stormy light of an enormous rainbow arching over the field with the retreating storm clouds piling up behind it.

I inch into the field, not wanting to disturb the moment. Reaching down, I pick a melon and weigh it in my hand—the thick skin pocked and coarse, the melon heavy and cool. I cut it open with Uncle John's knife and bury my teeth in the fruit. The flavor explodes in my mouth, sweeter than anything I've ever tasted. Within minutes, I'm standing with juice dripping down my chin and holding an empty rind. I eat another, and another after that. The rainbow fades.

When I'm stuffed so far beyond full that it hurts, I pick through the vines, collecting the best melons and piling them at the edge of the patch. Some are too green, others too ripe, a few cracked open and rotting with splotches of mold covering them like green fur. But most are just right. It would take six hundred people six months to pick them all, and I quit only a few meters into the patch when I realize my pyramid of fruit is already too tall for me to carry.

I gather them in my arms and start off west into the setting sun, feeling like some loaded lunatic melon juggler walking off in search of an audience to entertain. Every few steps I drop a melon, and when I stop to collect it again, I drop more. My dad would have called it an idiot load. I carry on like this until so many melons have dashed themselves open on the ground that the stack is reduced to a manageable size. I look back once from a hill and see a trail of mangled melons marking my path.

When I get to the cove, Jimmy's mother is yelling at him.

The camp is swept clean, the tents open and airing out, and everyone mills about listening to Jimmy get admonished in his mother's tent. She's telling him about honor, about being a man. About integrity and respecting personal property. And when her voice finally fades I hear Jimmy whimpering in soft apology. Then they step out from the tent and everyone averts their eyes and pretends not to be listening.

Now that the drama is over, the children see me and rush to take the melons from my arms, jumping in little circles and begging to eat them while aunts and uncles warn them to wait until after supper. I hand the pouch of poppies to Jimmy's mother and she thanks me. Jimmy stands beside her with his head hung. She nudges him in the ribs with an elbow. He looks up and he has tears in his eyes.

"I owe's ya an apology," he says.

Then, after another nudge in the ribs, he reaches into his

pocket and hands me my father's pipe.

My father's pipe!

I'd forgotten all about it these last few months in the cove, hadn't even missed it. I look at the pipe in my palm and I'm back in Holocene II, sitting at the table with my father, hearing him tell me about how proud he is of me and how my mother would be, too. I look back up at Jimmy and we're both crying.

He runs off, leaving me alone with his mother.

She takes my arm then, leading me down to the beach and the log where I sat and ate her stew my first night in the cove. We sit side by side and stare off into the setting sun.

"He only took it 'cause he likes ya," she says. "He likes ya and maybe he jealous some, too."

"Jimmy?" I ask. "Jealous of me?"

She nods. "He jealous when I care for you while you's sick. There's time in a boy's life when he becomes a man, to become this man he must let his mother go. I've had to push my son away more than it feels good to push . . . done it for his own sake and that's been hard for me, see? When Jimmy brought ya to us, you's in bad shape. Boy, you's bad off. I wasn't sure ya'd make it. My time was all yers, see?

I nod, understanding. I want to tell her how much it meant to wake and hear her humming, to feel her arms protecting me in that cave. I want to tell her that I never had a mother for real and that she's as close a thing to it as I can imagine.

"Thank you," is all I say.

She smiles and puts her arm around me as if she'd heard all my thoughts anyway in just those two words.

"Pipe was yer father's?" she asks, after a long pause.

I look at it and nod.

"Ya know," she says, taking it from my hand and looking at its carving in the fading light, "butterflies are spirit symbols. Many say butterflies represent the change, the stages of a life."

"Like the chrysalis breaking open and taking flight."

"The chrysalis?"

"You know, the cocoon."

"Yes, yes. The second egg. But even more than that, see? The rebirth. Caterpillar dun' become butterfly—caterpillar die so butterfly can be. A new thing. We all must let ourselves die to be what we will be. But we cling to what we know."

"Is that why Jimmy clings to you?"

"Yes. And you's too now. But there'll be time soon when you's must be strong, Aubrey. You's a special boy."

"People keep telling me that, but I don't see why."

"That's 'cause you's still a boy. A special one, but still a boy. Trust the heart, child. Always listen and trust. The answer is inside, since the beginning of all time. The butterfly waits."

When she finishes talking, she squeezes me close, and for a moment, one lingering sweet moment, the world is clear to me, and perfect, and I feel safe and wanting for nothing except to sit here beside her forever in the twilight. Then she releases me and walks back to camp, leaving me alone on our log. A black moth flits by and lands briefly where she sat, and then it too takes flight. I sit looking at my father's pipe, trying to recapture the moment, trying to absorb the meaning of what she said. But all I feel is the summer warmth leaching from the fall air.

I sit until I hear the call to supper.

CHAPTER 15
The Slaughter

"Whale!"

The cry comes echoing up the cove.

"Whale!"

The camp comes alive. Tents fly open, waking faces blink into the morning sun. The men dash to the cave and drag forth the boats. The women whirl around camp collecting supplies, thrusting things into pouches and draping the pouches over the men's necks. Jimmy jumps from our tent and races to the high cliffs and disappears into a crack, reappearing moments later carrying an armful of lethal-looking harpoons, their barbed-antler tips wrapped in blubber-soaked skins.

I follow him to the water's edge and watch as he loads the harpoons onto the waiting boats.

"Can I come?"

Jimmy ignores me, boarding the last boat as it shoves off.

"Watch from up there," he calls, pointing to the bluff as they row away from me. "It's my first time at the harpoon."

I clamber up the path and by the time I get to the bluff, the men are rowing clear of the cove and out to sea. I shade my eyes and look in the direction they're heading and catch sight of their goal a hundred meters offshore.

Massive gray crescents rising from the still water, barnacle-crusted and splotchy, spouting great plumes of mist and rolling before disappearing beneath the splash of their gigantic flukes.

The water stills, the mist fades, the boats advance. They surface again farther off, at least a dozen gray whales all moving south along the shelf just past the reefs, where the deep water looks black in the dawn light. Big whales, small whales, mothers leading young—they rise and roll and splash, the loaded boats rowing toward them like slowly approaching arrows launched from the cove. I run along the bluff to keep them in my sight.

Jimmy's boat reaches the pod first, intercepting a large cow and cutting her off from her calf. She's fifteen meters long if she's a foot, and half again as round. Her huge flippers slap at the water as she spins, and then sensing the boat behind her, she dives and smacks her huge fluke, showering the men with spray. They shake themselves dry and row on.

Jimmy hoists up a harpoon that's twice as long as he is tall and carries it to the front of the boat. His father ties a coil of rope to the harpoon, the other end to the boat. Then he slaps Jimmy on the back to let him know he's ready. Jimmy climbs onto the bow and balances there, holding the harpoon.

He looks magnificent!

Standing proud at the very tip of the boat, long and lean, harpoon clutched in his hand, he has the look of some wood-carved Viking ship warrior I might have dreamed about seeing.

The whale surfaces not far away. Jimmy points, the men dip their oars faster. The boat advances, the others following behind, and they encircle the whale and turn her out, cutting her completely off from the pod.

She rolls and slaps her fluke and rolls again.

Jimmy lifts the harpoon above his head, and as the boat closes on the whale, he steps onto one leg and crouches, knee-bent and ready, as taut as the string on his spear-gun bow.

And then he leaps—

He leaps high into the air, out over the sea, and he hovers there a moment, suspended, harpoon in hand, looking down upon the whale, and then he falls like lightning onto its back and drives the harpoon home with all his weight.

He releases the harpoon and dives free of the speared and angry animal and swims toward the boats. The whale hits the end of the line, jerking the boat around and towing it behind her as she runs. She blows and her plume is pink with blood.

I feel sick watching the slaughter, and now I'm glad they didn't let me on the boat. I remember these gray whales from educationals and I know we nearly hunted them extinct. And here they are back in force, and we're doing it all again.

Jimmy climbs aboard a trailing boat, hefts another harpoon and steps again into the bow. The rowers dip their oars, dip and pull and dip again, passing the tethered boat and chasing down the whale. Jimmy leaps again, and again he drives the harpoon home, the whale now tethered from two sides and Jimmy being flung wildly above the water, clinging to one of the ropes, as the angry whale thrashes and turns. The third boat approaches and another man leaps with another harpoon and now there are three taut lines and three tugging boats and the whale rolls and slaps its fluke and the water turns red all around it.

A wind comes up, rifling across the water, hitting the bluff and kicking sand into my eyes. I look away and see the other whales escaping farther down the coast, the calf bringing up the rear, either not knowing or knowing and having abandoned its captured mother to her fate.

Then I see the ship.

It comes cutting through the black water like an enormous

gray mechanical whale hewn of carbon fiber angles and molded steel. It moves fast and silent. The hull rises sleek and tall, and if the ship were closer to shore, the alien wind meters and radar dishes turning slowly from its riggings would be eye level with me where I lie on the edge of the bluff.

I open my mouth to scream, to warn the men about the approaching ship, but stop when I notice the emblem displayed on its side—the green interlocking Foundation Valknut.

Feeling sudden relief, I sigh—it must be a research vessel.

My scream comes when the slots slide open and the guns push out. I scream loud and long and useless into the wind as the ship barrels down on the men tethered to their catch. It's nearly on top of them when they see it.

And then it fires.

The cannons cut like thunder over the water, and several men explode into red mist and rain down on the already bloody sea. The sun darkens momentarily, brightens again as drones go racing by overhead. Helpless, I watch as the men scramble to make an escape. The ropes cut, the oars turned out—too late, the big cannons fire, this time blasting an entire boat to pieces and blasting Jimmy's dad to pieces with it. Another boat turns over, flipped by the men now hiding beneath it, just like Jimmy and I did that day the drones flew overhead.

"No!" I shout. "Swim! Get away!"

A shell pierces the upturned hull, detonating in a bloody blast of splintered wood. Men dive from the remaining boats and swim for their lives toward shore. The loud rat-a-tat-tat of machine guns sawing them to pieces, water rising in showers like tracers behind the slugs.

My heart hammers in my chest.

I'm soaked through with sudden sweat.

And I scream again, but if any sound comes I can't hear it for the ringing in my ears.

Then the ship stops firing and comes about and floats still, its guns swinging in their turrets, slow over the bloody water—looking, waiting, looking.

A splash there.

The gun moves, sights itself, fires.

The water is calm again except for the slow rolling of quiet waves glowing red with blood where the sun shines through.

I lie flat against the bluff and hold my breath.

The ships stands off for minutes and the minutes seem like hours. Waves lap against its side at the waterline, bumping flesh and body parts and blubber wooden-like against its hull.

Still I hold my breath.

The ship turns, and as if powered by the same silent force of gravity that moves the tides, it glides swift and sure back the way it came and disappears down the coastline out of sight.

I gasp out my breath—

And the long scream of horror that it held.

CHAPTER 16
Horror in the Cove

I race down the bluff to the water's edge.

By the time I arrive, pieces of wood and parts of bodies are already washing ashore. I wade into the gory surf and sift through the floating debris, desperate to find Jimmy. A corpse that looks like Jimmy's floats up beside me, face down. I turn it over, and his father's head lolls on his half-severed neck, his staring eyes milky and lifeless, glazed with death. The bottom half of his body is gone. I turn and retch in the water.

More bodies, more blood.

A sudden wave surges past me, an oar smashes me in the head, and I nearly drown and join the rest of them floating there all dead. I cough up saltwater and shake off the blow.

I'm sloshing back to shore when I see what's left of the whale floating several yards farther out. She's cut in half, and white blubber spills like curdled milk from her amputated body. Her entrails float out red and purple and bloated among the wreckage in the bloody surf.

I see movement in the tangled guts.

Yes—there. An arm wrapped around a hunk of blubber.

Diving in without hesitating, I swim to the floating whale, cautious of its bulk being tossed in the waves. I paddle through the mess, kicking intestines free from my feet, pushing a chunk of blood-soaked baleen away from my face. When I seize the arm and turn him over, Jimmy stares up at me, blurry-eyed but alive. I wrap my arms around him and kick with everything I have toward shore, making slow progress through the corpse-littered surf. We pass another man also alive and moaning, but unrecognizable with half his face and all of his shoulder gone. He won't make it, and even if he might, I can't save them both.

In shallow water, I get my feet beneath me and drag Jimmy onto the sand and flop down, spent and exhausted with him in my lap. He's breathing. Barely, but breathing. His cut forehead is bleeding, his leg is worse. A nasty gash in his thigh spreads open, his flesh filleted from the bone. I need to get him back to the cove, back to his mother and her healing hands.

I try pulling him along the shore, but his feet drag in the sand, stretching the thigh wound open, blood pulsing out with every heartbeat. I yank a piece of rope free from the wreckage and tie it around his thigh above the wound. I stand him up, hoist him off the ground, and with a new adrenaline-fueled strength, I stagger off with him draped and dangling over my shoulder as I lurch up the shore toward the cove.

The cove is awash with blood—

More blood and more bodies.

I stand stunned, Jimmy still on my shoulder, and watch as the gentle tide washes its crimson waves up onto the shore, the blood-soaked sand deep red as they retreat, fading as the water drains, only to have another bloody wave darken it again.

The women and the children are scattered, pieces of them everywhere—floating in the water, washed up on shore, lying outside of tents in bloody patches of soil. The shot-up tents are collapsed, a few with the bodies still inside, red-splotched and humped like some pale and bloated beasts bleeding out in the sun. Then I remember the drones flying overhead. Drones like the one on the train that was bringing me up from Holocene II. Drones designed on Level 3, built on Level 4. Drones that we ship to the Foundation on Level 1. Not exploration drones like I was told, but drones that murder women and children.

I carry Jimmy across the cove, stepping around the bodies, and take him into the cool dark shade of the cave and lean him against the wall. His bleeding has slowed, so has his pulse.

I tear through wrecked tents, ignoring the corpses there, frantic to find the sewing kit Jimmy's mother used to mend our clothes. When I find it, my frenzied pace fades, and I carry the small wooden box back to the cave, out held like an offering, in no hurry to do what I know I need to do.

Kneeling beside Jimmy, I open the box. The curved-bone needle sits on a pile of sinewy thread, its ivory surface polished as smooth as soap from years of use. Jimmy fades in and out of consciousness while I stitch his wound, and several times nearly so do I. His thigh is cut through skin, fat, muscle—all the way down to yellow bone. I know it should be stitched in several layers, but he's bleeding, and I'm scared, and it's all I can do to squeeze the wound closed and thrust the needle deep, hooking it out the other side and cinching it tight, then tying it off every quarter inch the long length of the gruesome gash. Three more shallow stitches close the cut in his forehead.

When I finish, Jimmy is passed out, either from blood loss or from pain. He lies slumped against the cave wall with his leg in a pool of blood, already swelling against my crude sutures. He looks so helpless and so young, like an exhausted boy tired from a long day in the sun. I kiss him on the forehead.

I start a fire and boil water in the salvaged cook pot, using it to clean his wound as best I can. Next, I gather bedding and make him a place farther inside the cave, close enough to the opening for fresh air to circulate, far enough away to stay in the shade. I slide him to it, careful of the new stitches, and lay him down and elevate his leg.

Then I sit in the mouth of the cave and watch the sun set on the blood-red waters painting horror in the cove.

CHAPTER 17

The Funeral Pyre

Sunrise.

Same as any other day.

Except I know I'll have to gather the bodies.

I clean Jimmy's wound, the dried blood wiping clear and revealing angry flesh swelling badly now against the stitches. He wakes, wincing with pain. I make him drink water and choke down some stew. He doesn't say anything, he doesn't have to. He just points to the bluff where we cremated Uncle John.

There's no way I can carry them up to the bluff by myself, so I settle on a spot between the beach and the cave, just above the high-tide line.

I start with the nearest bodies.

Cutting a piece of tent free, I use it to drag them to the spot and I lay them out on the sand. I scoop them in pieces onto the tent skin and pull them to the pile and dump them there. Others are intact but with gaping wounds and things never meant to see the light of day hanging out. The children are the worst. Their small faces frozen, twisted with confusion, their tiny hands clenched in agony. Their little limbs are already stiff with rigor and unbending as wood. Most are drained of blood and waxy cold even in the sun. Others are beginning to bloat and look as though they might pop if poked with a point.

My stomach coils up; I vomit several times.

"They're just seals," I mumble. "Just dead seals."

I keep telling myself that as I work. Just seals or sharks or fish—anything but the people I've grown to love.

There is one small blessing in that I can't find Jimmy's mother. Or if I do, she's so unrecognizable as to allow me to pretend she made it safe away. But I know she didn't.

I move next out of the cove and south down the beach. The tide has come in and gone out again and the shoreline is scattered with body parts and debris the entire length of a mile. I wear the tent skin through and have to fetch another. I chase ravens away from the corpses, their bloody beaks pulled up, their evil heads cocked in confusion as I drag their lunch away. I find a torso and turn it and a dozen small crabs covered in slime scurry away. Farther down, I find what's left of the whale washed ashore in an enormous gray and stinking hulk already torn apart by things in the night and being slowly returned to the sea from which it came.

By the time I've gathered all I can find or am willing to see, the bodies and pieces of bodies line nearly half the cove, and I've become numb to the horror of it, moving mechanical-like as if it were just some dirty job I'm meant to do.

Next I gather wood.

I know it will take hours and lots of heat to render all this flesh into ash and I labor fast and frantic, dragging great pieces of dry driftwood and broken branches into a tall pile that looks already like so many bleached bones. I drag over the log that I sat on with Jimmy's mother, and I cry for five minutes straight while I tug and pull and roll it end over end toward the growing pile. I add bedding to the stack. Tent skins, brush-brooms—anything that might help the fire burn.

With the funeral pyre complete, I begin stacking the bodies

on, layering pieces in, leaving room for the fire to breath. The work is messy and hard, the bodies slippery and smooth, the hunks of flesh surprisingly heavy with the weight of death.

I finish and stand back and look.

The pyre is three meters across and two meters deep, the bloated limbs and heads poking out from the stack. I begin to sob uncontrollably, stomping around camp, snatching personal effects off the ground and adding them to the pile. Necklaces, clothing, children's toys. A little seashell comb. An apron that belonged to Jimmy's mother. Then I use Jimmy's strike-a-light and start several small fires around the base.

Exhausted and drained and covered in blood and sweat, I turn and see Jimmy propped up in the cave watching me, and he's crying, too. We sit inside the cave with arms around one another and watch it burn.

It starts slow, but as the sky darkens, the fire spreads. It works its way up the pyre in little advances and short runs of flame and soon flesh begins to sizzle and fat begins to burn. By the time the sky is fully dark, the pyre is completely engulfed and burning so bright and hot that we shield our eyes and sweat rises on our brows and we scoot farther into the cave to escape the heat. Three, five, maybe ten meters the flames rise lashing into the night, and the cove is lit on all sides with an eerie glow of flame and shadow. The dark water is unusually calm and a second fire burns on its mirror-like surface, stretching to the cove mouth and out into the open ocean. The fire hisses and pops, and caves in on itself as it burns. I watch shadows and outlines of bodies fall together in sweet embrace as their flesh evaporates and drifts away like departing smoke-colored souls turning a slow and final dance high into the night.

Jimmy leans into me and I caress his hair.

I sit with him sleeping in my arms and watch the fire burn down, casting its flickering orange ghosts onto the cove walls. I think about my people down in Holocene II loading up into train cars at thirty-five and heading off to Eden, and I wonder what they do with the bodies there. Burn them, bury them, grind them up to fertilize our food? I wouldn't be surprised. Nothing seems impossible now in this new nightmare world.

Jimmy's eyes open, blink away tears, shutter, then close again. My eyes droop, and fight though I do, they close, too.

CHAPTER 18
The Storm Passes

Black smoke.

Burnt flesh.

The fire is smoldering when morning breaks on the cove. Jimmy is smoldering, too. He's hot to touch and dripping with sweat, and when I pull the makeshift bandage away to look at his wound, it's bright-red and puffy with yellow pus leaking from between the stitches.

I drag him farther into the cool shade of the cave. I fetch clear water from the stream and kick up hot coals at the edge of the fire and set the water to boil. The fire is horror to look at, the bodies not completely burned. The charred, eternal grins of fleshless faces smile at me from the ashes.

I spend a solid hour cleaning Jimmy's wound. Then I make him drink what water's left. He's hardly conscious, and I worry about water leaking into his lungs, but his throat moves and I assume he's swallowing. I collect the few remaining shreds of prized cotton clothing, tear them in strips and dress Jimmy's leg. Then I drape damp cloths over his burning forehead. It's clear he has an infection, and it's clear he's going to die. He needs medicine, and he needs it now.

I search the collapsed remains of the supply tent, but find nothing except some herbs and pouches of dried roots. I have no idea what they are or how to use them, and I doubt they'd help even if I did. What he needs are antibiotics. I rouse Jimmy to ask if they have any, but he just stares at me, delirious, as if he can't understand my words. Then it occurs to me that he's never even heard of antibiotics, doesn't know they exist.

My mind races for a solution.

"Think, Aubrey, think."

I'm back in Holocene II now, sitting in my testing seat, the questions coming fast. Twenty-first century medicine—I have to know this, I have to. Then an image pops into my head: the melon field. In my mind I'm there again, and I see the cracked and rotten melons I passed over, melons covered in furry mold.

It takes me all morning to find the field again, but when I do I scour the patch, ignoring the ripe and almost ripe, picking only the rotten melons and gathering them in Jimmy's netted sack. I sling the sack over my shoulder and run with it back to the cove where I find Jimmy freezing and covered in sweat.

I swaddle him in furs and heat more water, boiling dried fish into a brine and making him drink it. Then I set up my lab and go to work. I lay a square of tent skin just inside the cave where the sun will hit it but the wind won't. Then I shave mold off the rotten melons with Uncle John's knife and spread it out on the skin to dry, piling the scraped melons in a shady nook and sprinkling them with water, hoping they'll mold again.

By afternoon the mold is dry. I shave it loose and fold it in the skin, setting the skin against a rock and pounding it with a stone. I pour half the powdered mold into boiling water, being careful not to let it blow away, and when the tea cools, I feed it to Jimmy. It smells awful, but he swallows it down. I make a paste with the remaining mold, drain the puss from his wound, clean it, and smear the paste on. I can't be sure there are even any active antibiotics in the mold I'm using, and even if there are, it won't be very concentrated. But it's the only hope I have and I cling to it all night as Jimmy moans with fever.

In the morning, the melons are molded over again, but it's not enough. I race back to the patch and pick another sack full and carry them back and repeat the process.

Days pass like this. Scraping melons, drying mold. Making broth and making paste. I create an assembly line in the mouth of the cave. Five sheets of drying mold, melons piled high in the shade. I make Jimmy a bed from furs and wash him twice a day, turning him every few hours so he doesn't develop sores. I feed him nothing but fish brine and mold. His tongue turns green. He stinks of spoiled bedding and sweat. I fashion him a diaper from found clothing, changing it several times a day and washing it in the surf.

I can't stand the bony faces grinning at us from the ashes so I pile the fire with fresh fuel and burn it again. I add to the fire all night, the crackling flames my only companion, and in the morning I scoop sand over the few bones that remain.

On the fifth morning, Jimmy's fever finally breaks. He's still not talking, but he seems more alert, sipping brine on his own and even trying to refuse my mold tea.

That night the storm comes . . .

At dusk, dark clouds gather offshore and rain drops like black fingers on the horizon, white combers rising on the surf. A cold wind races in from the sea and rips howling through the cove. The tide comes on fast, swells of seawater funneling into the cove, waves stretching high onto shore. In the pitch dark of night, the water comes crashing into the cave, and I drag Jimmy back to the farthest wall to keep dry. Outside, the tempest rages on in the dark, and I huddle beneath the skins with Jimmy as we're blasted with cold spray, and for the first time in my life I pray. I pray to anything that might listen to deliver us from this bloody hell. I pray for the storm to stop, for Jimmy to be better, for all of this to be just a nightmare from which we'll wake. And as if in mocking answer, the storm intensifies, the waves surging, heaving logs into the cave where they crash against the walls, the bang and clatter jolting me where I sit, peering over the skins, the cold sea-spray stinging my face.

During a break in the barrage, an enormous bird flutters into the cave and perches a mere meter from where we huddle. Its magnificent silhouette is visible only when a retreating wave reflects a tiny bit of starlight into the cave, and when it spreads its huge wings to shake them dry, they stretch out in front of me and I can smell the musty odor of its plumage.

"You leave us alone, we'll leave you alone," I say.

Jimmy stirs in my lap. The bird turns its shadow head away as if agreeing to my terms, and together we watch the storm.

Come morning, the bird is gone. No feather, no print—nothing to mark its ever having been. I check on Jimmy in my lap. He's sleeping. Not delirious with fever, not passed out with fatigue, but really sleeping, his face relaxed and even content in the low gray light. I slide from beneath him, get up and stretch. Then I step to the cave entrance and look out.

It's gone.

They're gone.

Everything is gone.

The storm waters have retreated, taking everything with them. The fire, the ashes, the bones. The tents and cookware. The blood. Everything. No boats, no men, no mothers—no children laughing in the surf. There is no evidence left of our life here. No record of the horror that happened. The cove is as pristine and new as if the Earth itself were called out of the storm and created just last night.

The beach is clean and smooth, the wet sand undisturbed, glistening like a blank canvas waiting for some new life to make its mark. The giant sea turtles rise again on gentle waves, silent witnesses, their sad, unblinking eyes staring out from ancient and leathery heads, their beaked mouths open as they feed.

CHAPTER 19
There's Nowhere to Go

Jimmy limps.

The crutch helps some, but not much.

"I dun' wanna go," he says, breaking his sullen silence.

"Me either," I say, "but we can't stay in the cove."

I lead us north up the coast, retracing our journey.

We stop often to rest Jimmy's swollen leg, nibbling on the little bit of dried fish we stuffed in our pockets before leaving the cove. I carry bedding bundled in Jimmy's netted bag; he carries the canteen around his neck. We have our packs stuffed with furs but little else. I bring two melons, hoping to continue culturing mold, but they quickly dry out in the sun and I leave them lying baked and useless on the ground behind us.

We pass through the quiet redwood forest, somehow less impressive to me now. Reaching the boulder-strewn riverbed where I first joined the men and ate meat around their fire, we stop and make camp. We have no energy to build a fire tonight, and nothing to cook even if we did, so we lie huddled together beneath the furs and sleep beneath the cold, clear stars.

Late the next morning we come to the caldera where I met Jimmy and where we netted pigeons. His leg is too injured still for him to descend, so I leave him at the caldera lip and head down alone. I see no pigeons this time, and I have nothing to bait them with even if I did. I climb back out an hour later with only the canteen filled from the lake.

Another cold and hungry night beneath the stars, another day of Jimmy limping beside me on his crutch, and we arrive again at the cliffside caves where Jimmy's mother nursed me.

It takes us several hours to shimmy down the path, the ledge being too narrow for Jimmy's crutch, and him crying out in pain every time his weight hits his wounded leg. The cave is exactly as I left it, seemingly a lifetime ago. I make a bed inside the inner room and lay Jimmy on it just as I once lay.

I set about caring for him and the days bleed together until I lose track of them entirely. I spend mornings hunting food, or carving spears and catching fish. I collect water from streams and boil it, cleaning Jimmy's wound. I find another gourd and make a second canteen. I drop my threadbare jumpsuit shorts, fashioning a kilt from skins. I tie a strip of leather into a thong and I hang my father's pipe around my neck.

In the evenings, I squat in the cave doorway and watch the sun slide down into the ocean, the horizon burning itself into night. I can see the curve of the Earth, and I imagine our planet hurling through the deep void of space, a lucky accident circling a dying star, nothing but the net effect of some random chaos set in motion by chance, before even space or time began to expand. I used to believe in science, maybe even some cosmic wisdom behind it. I used to stare out my bedroom window in Holocene II, looking down on that Level 3 Valley, and I would tell myself that something out there, something above, knew of my existence and would not deny me.

Now I believe in nothing.

At night, I sit in the dark humming to Jimmy his mother's song, sometimes holding him the way she held me.

One morning walking, a rabbit stops to consider me and to

my surprise, it sits there looking confused while I snatch it up and break its neck. Must have never seen a human. Hanging it from a branch, I clean it with Uncle John's knife. There isn't much to it once the fur is off. We cook it that night over our fire, and the next day I dry the skin and cut it into thin strips and braid the strips into a thick thread that I use together with a worn leather pouch to make Jimmy and me shoes.

Jimmy's leg heals.

He sleeps less and eats more.

He even starts telling me which herbs and spices to hunt for, making the food I cook taste better, and that's how I know he's better even though he says he isn't. That, and he refuses to let me see his leg anymore when I come to empty his bedpan.

He's physically healed but emotionally wrecked. As long as he stays tucked away in the dark, he seems able to blot out the memory of all that happened in the cove. We never talk about it. He grows weak from inactivity, turns pale from a lack of sun, and I stop bringing him food, making him eat instead with me in the outer cave just to get a spot of sunshine on his skin.

One night, after watching the sun sink beneath the waves, and after watching the sky burn red long after, I crawl into the inner cave with Jimmy and tell him what I've decided.

"I'm leaving in the morning."

"Why would ya leave?" he asks.

"It's just time to go."

"Go where?"

"I don't know."

"You dun' know 'cause there's nowhere to go."

"Maybe I'll go back to where that train crashed," I tell him. "Back to where I first climbed out into all this mess."

"And what then?"

"Then I'm gonna follow it wherever it was headed and get some questions answered."

"Follow the train?"

"Yeah."

"Why?"

"I don't know. Find out who's responsible for all this."

"For all what?"

"You know for all what—the Park Service."

He drops his head. "Who's gonna take care of me?"

"Aren't you coming?"

"No, I ain't comin'."

"Why not?"

"'Cause it's stupid."

"Stupid?"

"Yeah, way stupid."

"Fine. You're on your own," I say, heading for the flap to the outer cave. "I'm out of here."

"What'll ya do if ya find 'em?"

"Uh, well . . .," I stammer, pausing to turn back and wondering the same thing myself. "I'm not sure."

"Sounds like a great plan."

"Anything beats rotting in here with you."

"Suit yerself," he says, flopping back on his bed.

"I'm leaving at sunrise," I say. "And not one minute after."

"Good luck," I hear him reply as I shut the flap.

I storm into the outer cave and sit in the doorway to watch the stars and wait for morning.

Part Three

CHAPTER 20
Just Passing Through

Jimmy nudges me awake with his foot.

"Sun rose an hour ago," he says, looking down at me, the hint of a smile playing on his face. I scramble up from the cave floor where I fell asleep and brush myself off.

With everything we own strapped to our backs, we set off together north toward the delta where I first saw him squatting on that rock and sending the sun to bed. We have the crude kilts we're wearing, our fur-stuffed packs, the shoes I fashioned together, and two full water gourds. Jimmy has his knife, I have Uncle John's, and we each have a spear carved from red alder.

Even though Jimmy's leg is fully healed, he walks with a limp, and we use our spears as walking sticks to lighten the load. The days have grown shorter, the morning air crisp with the coming fall. When we reach the delta and turn east to follow the river, the trees have already turned and their orange leaves catch the setting sun and cast the hills in a painter's light.

We walk until dark and we make a fireless camp on a sandy shoal beside the river. We lie there beneath the clear night sky and listen to the soft ripple of water rolling over stones.

"Aubrey?" Jimmy says softly, just before we drift off.

"Yeah, Jimmy."

"Thanks."

"Thanks for what?"

"Thanks for ever-thin'."

"Even for making us leave?"

"Yeah," he says. "That too."

In the morning we bath in the river, wading in the cold water, spearing trout. I gut them while Jimmy builds a fire. The fish make a light breakfast and we're both still hungry, but we lick our fingers, kick sand over the fire, fill our canteens, and set off following the river up.

The river runs lower than before, and when we reach the falls, they look like no big deal so I don't even bother bragging about climbing down them myself. Above the falls, the fields of wheat have been trampled and eaten down to the nubs by some grazing beasts, leaving the river fully exposed, its banks littered with the gray carcasses of rotting fish everywhere. Nothing left but bony heads with hooked snouts and hollow-picked eyes. I poke one with my spear and a cloud of flies rises into the air, revealing the inner framework of a fish, the intricate woven basket of tiny translucent bones, and then the flies settle again. The whole river reeks with a rotten odor that reminds me of the cove, and we leave our canteens unfilled and move into the quiet alpine forest, heading higher.

By late afternoon, we come to the edge of the treeline and stand looking up the canyon at the trestle where I stood and watched the sunrise on my first day in the world.

"So that's it, eh?" Jimmy asks.

"That's it."

It's much slower going up loaded with our packs than it was coming down running for my life. We work our way up the canyon in long switchbacks, using our spears for balance and keeping the trestle above us in sight. When we reach the foot of the trestle, Jimmy looks up and sighs.

"No way I'm climbin' that," he says.

"Wait here, I'll go check it out."

I've grown much stronger, and this time I climb the trestle with little effort and not once do I fear I might fall.

Scrambling over the edge, I stand and look at the tunnels. They're closed. Iron doors sealed shut on either side. The track glints in the sunlight, its electromagnetic plates smooth as glass. No rocks, no wreckage, everything has been put right again.

I look out over the landscape. The treeline, the rolling hills, the river running through the valley. The late sun is orange on the horizon and it lights the world below me in soft pastels so that if I didn't know the evil that happens here, I'd think it a paradise still. But I know what horrors lurk beneath the beauty, and I almost wish I'd never seen it at all.

I climb down and rejoin Jimmy.

"No going that way anyway," I say. "It's all sealed up."

He nods. "What now?"

"Well, at least we know what direction it was headed."

"Where's that?"

"Northeast there," I say, pointing toward the jagged peaks now dark and distant in the setting sun.

"Oh, great," Jimmy says, shaking his head. "It would be over the damn mountains."

"I'm not happy about it either."

Neither of us says another word—we just poke around the base of the trestle inspecting the steel joints.

Jimmy whistles; I throw stones.

The sun sets the rim of the world afire, and we drift to the trestle and sit together on a beam looking down the canyon, watching it burn out. The heat drains away with the color, the stars blink on one by one, and cold creeps into the canyon.

We lie down and cover ourselves with our furs, tossing and turning on the hard ground, and finally falling asleep.

I dream I'm underground again, standing at the train platform and a thousand blank faces stand beside me, their features melted away or not yet cast, and the train slides in from the tunnel and the doors slide open and we file into the cars and sit facing the movie screen ahead. The train glides off, and the screen blinks on and shows us a movie—the slaughter in the cove. Screaming men diving from boats, cannons tearing them to shreds, bodies drifting in bloody tides. All the faceless people begin to laugh, as if it were all some great joke, and I scream at them from my seat to be quiet, to turn the horror show off, but they only turn their heads and laugh at me, every one of them with my father's face.

Something wakes me in the cold blackness of night.

I sit up and see Jimmy's sleeping silhouette, and all around us is quiet and dark. Even the stars seem far away and only half lit now. I lay back and search for sleep again.

Just as I'm drifting off, I hear a metallic knocking echoing softly through the trestle beams, as if some deep and sleepless machine were bent already to its mindless work.

The next day, the mountains seem farther away.

We climb higher and higher, cresting ridges and dropping into low saddles between them, up again, over again, and the mountains in the distance never seem to grow any closer at all.

The few animals we drive out ahead of us are skittish and we never get within spear's reach of anything. Jimmy spends an afternoon whittling a pine bow while we walk, but the wood is too soft for shooting arrows, and we have nothing to string it with besides. As our smoked fish reserves run low, I realize just how dependent we were on the sea for our protein. The river streams we cross are shallow; the tiny trout are impossible to spear and hardly worth the energy to catch.

On the third day, we crest a high ridge and get a good look at the mountains we're headed for. They run north and south, rising before us like a jagged snow-covered wall, piercing clouds that gather and form around their summits.

I shiver with cold just to look at them.

"Maybe we're going in the wrong direction?"

"Nah," Jimmy says. "The flyin' drones always come over the mountains. Had an uncle set out to find 'em once."

"Did he make it?"

"No."

We make camp on level ground near the top of a ridge and the wind comes howling up from below, whistling through the canyons all night so we hardly sleep at all. Moving on in the gray light of dawn, we crest the ridge and stand looking down on a swath of charred spires poking out of a thick fog.

We descend into the fog and make our way over the rocky, charcoal ground in near zero visibility. The burnt trees seem to grow out of the fog itself as we pass, materializing like eerie ghosts holding their black, skeletal arms aloft. We come upon a single green tree in that fog, a tree untouched by the fire, and on a low limb sits a large white owl, an owl as pure as snow in all that black. Its red eyes glow with some inner fire, or perhaps still reflecting the fire that passed, and it looks as if it's been perched there forever and will be forever perched, waiting for the forest to regrow and then burn again. I lift my spear to take a try at him, but Jimmy grabs my arm and shakes his head. The owl follows our crossing with the slow turn of its head and then its red eyes blink and disappear into the fog again.

Hours later, we pass through the fog and stand looking down a V-shaped valley at a raging river in our path. We walk several kilometers north to find a shallow crossing where we strip naked and stuff our clothing in our packs and hold our packs up over our heads and wade into the freezing current. Jimmy slips once and nearly sets off downriver, but I catch his arm until he finds his footing and we both climb onto the far bank, shivering with steam rising off our naked backs.

The bluff above the river is steep, only one narrow path made by some migratory animal crossing, or maybe just carved by chance of nature. Halfway up it, we see two figures coming down the path toward us.

"Maybe we should go back," I say.

"They's already seen us."

"All the more reason to turn around."

"Makes us look chicken," Jimmy says, pulling his shoulders back and walking on with stiff strides to hide his limp.

The sun has risen behind the approaching figures and we can't make them out until they stop, a meter ahead and slightly above us, no room on either side to go around them.

The lead man is a massive bundle of filthy furs, his knotted dreadlocks hanging like tentacles from his greasy head, thick as rope and nearly dragging on the ground behind him. He has a long wooden bow and a quiver of red-feather fletched arrows hanging around his chest, a gnarled staff in one hand, and the end of a leash in the other. At the other end of his leash dances a strange little man collared at the neck. He might be fifteen, he might be fifty. He's naked save for a filthy cloth at his groin, his ribs showing beneath gray skin, his bare feet as big and flat as seal flippers. A hideous pink tumor grows from the side of his neck like a second aborted head, and he leans his ear into it as if listening to something it might be whispering to him as he hops from flat foot to flat foot and sucks his few remaining teeth.

The big man holds his leash and takes us in with squinted eyes but says nothing. After several moments standing off like this, he slides the looped end of the leash over his staff, gathers up his mop of dreadlocks with his freed hand, sweeps the hair around, sits down on a rock, and lays the hair across his lap. A bone knife handle shows from his belt and he sits with his hand just inches from it, twisting the nappy locks of his hair between his filthy fat fingers. He opens a hole in his beard and spits a mouthful of brown juice into the path and says:

"Where ye boys headed?"

"We prefer keepin' to us own selves," Jimmy says.

"Wise more times than not," the man says, spitting again. "But I's jest askin' where you's all headed."

"We's headed yonder to the ocean," Jimmy says, a layer of sarcasm in his voice. "Goin' for a swim."

The man nods the way we came up. "Ocean's thataway."

"Maybe we's headed to the other one," Jimmy says.

The man laughs, his huge belly shaking, the freak dancing faster on his leash. Then his laugh cuts off abruptly and he spits another mouthful of juice on the ground.

"Ye got any women with ya?"

"Where would they be," Jimmy says, "in our packs?"

"Yer friend's got his self a smart mouth to go with that limp of his," the man says, turning to search my face.

Right away I recognize the look of a bully in him. I know he's testing me for weakness, calculating my resolve, so I lean on my spear and tilt it just enough in his direction that it could be taken as either natural adjustment or a threat. He's above us on the trail, and that gives him an advantage, but coming down against two grounded spears gives us an edge. He eyes my spear and taps his finger on the bone handle of his knife. He smiles; his leashed man-boy hops from foot to foot.

I nod to the path beyond.

"We don't want to hold you two up any longer. We're just passing through."

"Passin' through, eh?"

"That's right, passing through."

"Ain't ever last one of us?" he says.

Then he looks past us to where we came up, as if to see if any others are following.

"Jest curious if y'all travelin' with any women," he says. "You's pretty young yet, the both of ye is, and I'd bet my son here ya didn't nurse one another takin' turns at the other's dry little tits. Or did ya now, boy?" He spits again.

"No women," I say. "Just us two crossing the mountains."

"Shit. Over there? You know what's over there, boy?"

"No. What's over there?"

"Ain't nobody know 'cause ain't nobody never crossed them mountains," he says, looking back and shaking his head.

"Well, you's musta come over 'em," Jimmy says.

"Nah," he replies. "I was trackin' something sure, but had to quit the trail or we'd all be dead on the mountain by dusk."

"Well, whatever you's trackin' seemed to prefer its odds up there better'n down here with you," Jimmy says, spitting on top of the man's brown stain.

"As she oughta," the man says, tagging the spot again and grinning as if enjoying the contest. "As she oughta. But evens if ye could cross, there's evil over there, boy. Evil for sure."

"We'll take our chances," Jimmy says.

"Isn't there a pass?" I ask.

The dreads slide across his lap as he turns to look up at the mountain, as if searching it for a pass he might have missed.

"Nope," he says, simply. "Not for a hundred miles either way. Only way over's straight across the summit itself."

"Ain't no mountain cain't be climbed," Jimmy says.

"You's way wrong there, young fella," he says. "Ain't no mountain that can be climbed. Mountain decides whether she'll let ye pass or not. She either lifts ye over or she swallows ye up. This'n here's hungry." His shifty eyes train again on me. "How about coffee?" he says. "Ye got any coffee?"

"Ain't never drank no coffee," Jimmy says, spitting.

The man nods, as if he'd expected not. He spits again on top of where Jimmy spat. "Got any tobacca?"

"Ain't no settlin' nowheres long enough to grow none," Jimmy says, "And besides, we dun' smoke."

"Then how come he's got a pipe hangin' round his neck?"

My hand jumps to my neck and my father's pipe.

"Family keepsake," I say.

"Ah, family," he sighs. "Family's all a man's got. Man with no children disappears when he's dead, but a man with a family, well, that man lives on in his kin." His eyes tear up sentimental like, and he grabs the leash and jerks it, pulling the dancing freak onto his lap. We stand for a minute watching as he pets its head, the freak closing its eyes and moaning with pleasure, and just when I'm beginning to think he's forgotten that we're here, he looks up.

"Sure there ain't no lady folk down there yonder? From

where y'all come from?'

"Everyone's dead," I say.

Jimmy pushes me aside and steps up.

"That's more'n enough talk now," he says. "We ain't come all this way to sit and visit with you's. Now good luck to ya, sir. Damn good luck to both of you's."

That said, Jimmy steps forward and turns, squeezing past them on the path. I hesitate long enough to watch the man's shocked expression turn to acceptance and then almost to an expression of sadness. Then I step forward and squeeze past him too, and I can smell his sweat and mildewed fur, his freaky son in his lap looking up at me wide-eyed, head resting on his tumor, and I step clear of them and follow Jimmy up the path.

I look back once from high above, before we turn and lose them from our sight, and I see them sitting as before, the man cradling his son in his lap and watching after us as we go.

CHAPTER 21

One Foot In Front of the Other, and Don't Slip

Snow appears in shady patches.

Nooks and crevices.

Places where the sun doesn't penetrate.

Miniature icefalls melting into tiny streams where we stop and drink and fill our canteens.

We crest a ridge, the air suddenly cold, and snow stretches beyond the shadows and comes together in a vast snowfield up which we climb. The snowfield is dirty and littered with dead insects, and when we step our feet crunch through and reveal perfect white powder hidden beneath the crust. I look back and see our two sets of white footprints trailing behind us, glowing in the shadows as if they had a light of their own.

With the sun high now in blue skies, the icy crust begins to melt, and we slosh through it soaking our tattered shoes, finally taking them off and walking barefoot. The air thins, Jimmy wheezing beside me. I breathe better up here, which is strange because I grew up at much lower elevations than Jimmy did.

Arriving at a swath of sun-dried boulders cutting across the wet snowfield, we sit down to rest and drink, admiring the fine lichen that swirls gray and green across the stone surface like ancient writing. A curious marmot pokes its head over a nearby rock and stands still against the blue sky taking us in, but neither of us have the energy to make a move to kill it. When we start up again, I look back and see the marmot on its toes, inspecting our urine stains on the rock.

"Is yer vision blurry?" Jimmy asks, hours later.

Trudging the clean upper snowfield now, I pause to rest my weary legs, looking behind us and then ahead again.

"Yeah, but it's probably just the glare from the snow."

Jimmy strips off his pack where he stands.

"Shit, we'll be lucky if we dun' lose our sight."

"What's that mean?"

"Snow blindness."

"Where'd you hear that?"

"That uncle tried to cross once. He come down blind as a mole, all bloodied from trippin'. Never did see nothin' again."

We tear strips of skin from our packs, stretch them over our faces, and mark the location of our eyes with smudges of charcoal. Then we poke holes there and tie them around our heads. Jimmy looks like a cartoon bandit from some old story I read on my slate and I must look just as silly to him.

We pause to look up at the summit high in the hazy blue sky, smoking like some windblown and frozen other world.

"What do ya figure we'll find?" Jimmy asks.

"On the other side?"

"Yeah, if we make it."

"Think positive," I say. "We'll make it."

"Well, when we make it then."

"I don't know. Probably nothing."

"Then why's we goin'?"

"We gotta do something."

Jimmy laughs, shakes his head, and we start up again.

After a while we come up on a strange set of tracks in the snow, and Jimmy stops and squats to inspect them. He brushes the edges clear, looking them over for a long time.

"Bear," he says.

I want nothing to do with another bear, but Jimmy sets off again following the tracks and I fall in line behind him.

"What do you think a bear's doing way up here?"

"Prob'ly same as us," he says, smirking over his shoulder. "Tryin' to get to the other side."

The man was right: Jimmy does have a smart mouth.

When the snowfield steepens, we switchback our way up, crossing the bear tracks, and then crossing them again. The sun beats down and we pant and drip with sweat, but when we stop to sip from our canteens, I go from hot to freezing fast.

Another half hour climbing and we crest the snowfield and stand on a windblown saddle of rock, looking back through our pinhole bandito masks at the way we came up. We've climbed much higher than I thought. The snowfield drops away beneath us, and the fading ridges we crossed roll away into the distance like rock waves on an endless sea, puffs of white cloud floating through the valleys there. A gust of wind rises up the snowfield and tickles my hair. Time seems to stand still up here.

"We better find shelter for the night," Jimmy says.

"Okay, just a little higher."

We spot a horizontal cut of recessed rock, enough of an overhang to protect us from the wind. We drop our packs and settle in. Jimmy sits watching the sunset with his feet dangling off the ledge, and I lie down and look at the darkening sky and one single point of light that must be a planet.

"First rule of packing," I say, "don't stand when you can sit, and don't sit when you can lie down."

Jimmy laughs and lies down beside me. We fish the furs

from our packs and bundle up together to share our body heat.

"What planet do you think that is?" I ask.

"There's more planets than jus' ours?"

"Yeah, there are lots of planets."

"I though those were stars."

"Well some are," I say, "but some are planets."

"Ya think there's some other boys up there lookin' back and wonderin' about us?"

"Maybe," I say.

"Yeah, maybe," Jimmy says.

The sky darkens, a few stars appear.

"Maybe there's jus' planets goin' on forever," Jimmy says. "Boys lookin' up at boys lookin' up at boys as far as any eye could ever see."

"Yeah, maybe so," I say. "Maybe so."

"It still dun' make a fella feel less alone, though."

"No, it sure doesn't."

The sky fades blue to purple to black, and one by one stars punch through it until the whole royal canvas above is littered with stars swirling in clusters and constellations.

"You really believe anyone is out there watching?"

Jimmy doesn't answer.

"Guess I'm asking if you think we're really alone. I mean, do you believe there's any God or anything?"

A gust of wind whistles past our ledge, dies down again.

"Jimmy?" I nudge him, but he's fast asleep.

When we set off, the sky is still dark and hung with stars.

The sky turns gray and then blue, but the stars never do leave it in this high and barren twilight landscape. The air bites cold and we wrap ours furs tight, climbing over cleaves of rock and steep snowpack until we come to the foot of the glacier.

It comes down the mountainside like a giant frozen river, a treacherous incline cracked with crevasses and hemmed in on either side by impossible cliffs. On its low side, it turns down a thousand meter drop where huge seracs hang precariously from its edge like ice houses perched to fall off a cliff. The glacier chews up the mountain as it grinds on slow as time itself, and huge boulders sit, spit like crumbs at our feet.

"There's no goin' around less we go back."

"We can't climb it," I say. "We'll both end up in a crevasse and a hundred years from now somebody'll be standing right here looking at us spit out the bottom instead of these rocks."

Jimmy points up. I look, but the sun's reflection on the ice blinds me so I strap on my mask and look again. Very high on the upper glacier a figure moves. I shield my eyes with my hand and squint through the mask and look harder. Sniffing its way around the crevasses and lumbering toward the summit, climbs the bear whose tracks we've been following. It's little more than a speck from this distance, but we stand and watch as it shrinks into the altitude, climbing ever higher, until with one burst of energy and a sort of leap, it disappears over the crater rim.

Jimmy ties our rope around his waist and then pays out the slack and hands me the other end. I copy his knot as best I can and follow him up onto the glacier. There's no more than three meters between us, and the rope is thin and meant for hanging game—so thin I doubt it's good for anything more than a little peace of mind between us.

Climbing the glacier is slow work. We're forced to move great distances left and right to navigate around crevasses, and I make the mistake of looking down over the edge into one where the blue jaws of the glacier fall away in an icy prison that must be hundreds of meters deep. Jimmy pries a stone loose from the ice and tosses it in, and we listen to it ricocheting back and forth off the walls as it drops, the sound finally fading away but the stone never hitting bottom.

We climb this way for hours.

The sun beats down and melts the layer of snow covering the glacier, and we climb even slower, using our spears to break footholds in the exposed ice.

Nightfall catches us halfway up. Jimmy stops and loops the rope in as I climb up to where he stands. We carve a thin ledge in the ice and strip off our packs and spear them to the glacier so they won't slide away. Then we sit and drink water and look down and pretend we're not scared.

"We gotta keep movin' up," Jimmy says. "Ain't no way we can make camp here."

"I know it," I say.

"Shouldn't be no differ'nt in the dark, right?"

"Nah," I say. "It's no big deal."

"Jus' one foot in front of the other, right?"

"Yep. One foot in front of the other, and don't slip."

The sunset is blocked, and it seems as though the western ridge has pierced the sky and that the blue is quickly bleeding out of it. The stars that never quite left grow brighter, the sky black, and then the three-quarter moon rises above the eastern ridge and hangs in front of us, seeming close enough to touch.

"Well pluck a duck," Jimmy says, "It's our lucky night."

"Think it's enough to see?"

"It'll jus' have to be, I 'spose."

We stay put and watch for a minute—the stark-white lunar

glow, the marbled surface dotted with shadowed craters.

"Sure is somethin' to look at, ain't it?" Jimmy says.

"Yeah, it sure is something," I say. "Hard to believe there's footprints somewhere up there."

"Footprints? On the moon?"

"Yep. On that moon right there."

"Well, how'd they get there?"

"We were there once. A long, long time ago."

"A human's footprints? No way."

"Yes way."

"How would ya even know?"

"I read all about it."

"Hmm . . .," he says, pondering. "Then I guess it's true."

We wrap our furs tighter and strap on our packs again and climb on in the silver moonlight, choosing our steps carefully. The glacier crust freezes, and I hear Jimmy's feet crunching on the ice ahead of me. I have no idea how high up the summit is or how far down the fall would be.

After a while, Jimmy calls back to me. "Hey, Aubrey."

"Yeah?"

"Even if there was somebody on the moon, what makes ya think their footprints is still up there?"

It's a good question and I'm not sure how to answer it, so I just say: "Because I read it in the book."

Apparently satisfied, Jimmy nods and keeps climbing.

The glacier comes alive at night. Creaking and groaning beneath our feet. We hear a serac cleave off the cliff behind us in the dark and crash down the mountain with a deafening roar that rumbles on forever in the void.

An hour later we come to a wide crevasse and stop at its

edge to search a way around. A cold wind rises from the deadly crack and whistles through the ice, sounding like small children screaming from the deep. The only way around is up and over across a steep patch of solid ice. There's no way we can make it. The crevasse is too wide, the ice leading around it too steep.

I get an idea and tug the rope, pulling Jimmy to me. Then I take out Uncle John's knife and cut the rope between us.

Jimmy looks at me wide-eyed. "What are you doin'?"

"Trust me," I say, "I've got an idea."

I untie the knot at my waist and saw the rope in half again, making two shorter pieces.

"Well, shit," Jimmy says, "there ain't no turnin' back now."

I sit, signaling Jimmy to grip my pack and hold me steady. Then I wrap a length of rope around my homemade shoes and pull it tight and loop it and wrap it again. Five turns, then I double loop and tie it off. Same thing on my other foot. When I finish and stand, five passes of rope run like treads beneath my feet, gripping the ice and giving me traction. Next I hold his pack while Jimmy ties his feet, too.

With no rope between us now, I take the lead and use the moonlight to find a path up and over. The only way to cross is to the right on steep ice, right over the crevasse. One slip and we're gone. Forever. My stomach drops, sweat beads on my brow. One cautious step at a time, we dig our roped feet into the slope, freezing there and breathing out plumes of hot breath as we search the ice before stepping again.

Once, while looking down for a place to set my foot, I see my silhouette in the ice against the reflected moon, and it's as if I have a twin trapped beneath the glacier and I startle with the thought that maybe he's risen to pull me down to join him.

All is silent as we inch our way above the crevasse, neither of us daring to speak. Then I step up and the ice is less steep. Another step and I'm on firmer ground. I turn back and reach a hand to Jimmy and pull him up to join me. He laughs, and it sets me laughing, too. Then his laugh somehow turns to tears, and he grabs me and hugs me. We stand there embracing one another and crying in the moonlight until we both feel silly and pull apart, wiping our eyes and laughing again.

An hour later the storm overtakes us.

We still have a long way to the top and the success of our crevasse crossing quickly fades as dark clouds pass in front of the moon. The moon seems hesitant to leave us alone to our fate, and it makes several attempts to rise above the clouds. But within minutes the moon is swallowed completely, leaving us in utter darkness. The temperature plummets, as if the moon itself had given off some heat, and a wicked wind comes whipping down the glacier in great gusts that threaten to knock us off the mountainside. We lean into the slope and drive our spears into the ice and climb. There's nowhere to go but up. Up into the storm. The wind drives snow into our faces, sends it skating across the ice at our feet, making our steps uncertain and blind.

Jimmy yells something up to me but it's snatched by the wind and carried away and only my name reaches my ears.

We climb on.

The storm intensifies.

My feet go numb with cold. My hands.

Suddenly, the hair on my arms stands up, my scalp tingles, and the cold air smells of metal. Then a blue flash arcs across the sky and lights the snow electric white, the crack of thunder nearly throwing me backwards down the mountain. I look over my shoulder at Jimmy's shadow, shivering behind me, hanging on against the wind. I turn and climb higher into the storm.

Coarse ice crystals grate against my skin, snot runs from my nose and freezes on my face. I stumble, get up again. I have no idea if Jimmy is still behind me, or if he's blown off the glacier, but I reach deep inside myself and summon all of my remaining strength, and I set my teeth and pump my legs and climb. The wind whips wildly, lashing me left and right, and my pack rips free and goes flying off somewhere behind me like a kite. My fingers stiffen, my spear falls from my grasp.

I plunge forward, stepping, stepping, stepping, drop now to my knees, crawling, clawing at the ice, reaching, searching, tilting into empty space, teetering there, pulling back, too late—I free fall into quiet nothingness, the sound of the wind fading above as I flail my arms uselessly in the cold air rushing past.

My back slams into hard ice, forcing the air from my lungs. I lie in the dark, willing myself to breathe again. But either I can't breathe, or I won't, and all is black and still and quiet.

Somewhere high above I can hear the scream of the wind and then even that fades away with my final thought—

Jimmy.

CHAPTER 22
Who Lives Here?

Water dripping.

Echoing and amplified in a cavernous silence.

All around me is blue light.

I turn my head slowly toward the source of the drip, and I know what I see will haunt me forever—

I'm lying on the edge of a sort of subterranean lake, a deep pool melted by the heat rising from some fissure in a dormant volcano. I must be inside the crater. The lake is still and black and it reflects back the thick sheet of blue crater ice hanging as a ceiling above it. And that's not all. It also reflects back what hangs suspended from the retreating grip of that glacial roof. Protruding from the ice, hanging precariously above the lake, is an enormous intercontinental ballistic missile.

There's at least three meters of it exposed, another twenty meters trapped in the ice above. The point of the warhead is red, the green body wide enough that two men couldn't stretch their arms around it, cryptic characters printed there in some violent-looking language, etched yellow triangles arranged in the international nuclear sign. I wonder how long it's been hanging here. I wonder at what rate it's melting free, the ice replaced every season by fresh snowpack above. And I wonder why it didn't detonate, and if it's a dud, or if there's even such a thing when it comes to hydrogen bombs.

I grit my teeth and sit. I can see I've fallen down a crevasse where the crater glacier breaks away from the crater rim, the narrow crack above showing a sliver of blue sky and no trace of the storm that sent me here.

All I can think about is Jimmy. Did he fall into some other crevasse and land in a similar nightmare? Or something worse, maybe? Was he blown off the mountain? I see an image of him sliding down the glacier wall and plunging to his death, and the image makes me cringe.

I force myself to stand, testing for broken bones. Nope, just some bruises and scrapes. I take one last look at the evil thing hanging above that black and bottomless lake, and then I turn away with the image burned forever in my mind.

At first it looks as though I might be trapped down here with civilization's destruction hanging above my head. But then I see a pile of fresh snow on the edge of the lake and when I look up, I see a climbable incline leading out. The ropes are still on my shoes, but the going is slow and tedious. In places where the incline steepens, I have to wedge my feet against one wall and press my back into the other, shimmying up an inch at a time. But as the blue-sky crack above grows, my spirits lift and I climb the last several meters and roll out onto the crater floor.

The sun is up, reflecting white off the fresh snow. I cover my face with my hand, peeping through my fingers and turning to take in my surroundings. I'm on the edge of the crater bowl, snowpack sloping gently down in the center and then rising again to the other side. When I spin nearly all the way around, I see Jimmy sitting on the crater edge, facing away from me with his pack sitting next to him and my pack sitting next to it.

When I tap him on the shoulder, he startles and I have to grab his arm to keep him from falling over the edge.

"Hellfire, man!" he shouts, stepping back from the edge. "You coulda killed me jus' now."

"How long have you been sitting there?"

"Shit. I dunno," he says. "Two, maybe three hours now. Sun jus' come up over there."

"You thought I was dead," I say, "didn't you?"

"Yes'm, I did," he says, picking up his pack. "But dun' go gettin' all sappy 'cause I ain't even finished puzzlin' out whether I's happy or sad about it."

He tries hard to look stoic, but his face breaks into a smile. I shoulder my pack and we start across the crater together.

"Where in hell was ya hidin'?" he asks.

I shudder to think what's suspended beneath our feet.

"Hell is right," is all I say.

The other side looks much friendlier. There's no wind at our elevation, but beneath us billowy clouds float across the sky providing glimpses of the landscape below. A wide glacier, with few visible crevasses, slopes down into a canyon where the ice melt rushes out and becomes a river. The river runs northeast into a pine forest, the trees powdered with fresh snow, and beyond the forest, cupped on three sides by a ring of jagged snowcapped peaks, is an alpine lake so big and blue that it reflects back mountains, trees, and sky, giving it the appearance of another upside down world in itself.

Anxious as I am to get away from the crater and its frozen cargo, we sit on the summit lip, eat handfuls of fresh snow, and look out over the view.

"Ya think she made it?" Jimmy says.

"Huh?" I say, my mouth full of snow.

"The bear," he says. "Do ya think she made it?"

"How do you know it was a she?"

"I dunno," he says, "jus' figured it."

"Yeah, I think she made it."

The sun rises higher and chases the shadows into the folds of the mountains. Far beneath us some enormous predatory bird hovers motionless on a breeze, circling above the river.

"It's so quiet up here," I say.

"I know it," Jimmy says. "And I'd bet my head ya can see three hundred miles right from where we sit."

"We use kilometers where I'm from," I say, "but it doesn't matter because you can't see farther than the cavern walls."

"Ya ever miss it?"

"No, not ever."

"Ya ever think about yer family down there?"

"I miss my dad sometimes."

"Yeah, I figured it so."

"You ever think about yours?"

"I miss my mum mostly," he says.

Jimmy looks away and picks at the snow. After a while, he stands. "Well, we better get on gettin' on," he says. "I'm hungry and this snow ain't helpin' it none."

With the crevasses hidden under fresh snow laid down by last night's storm, it's slower going than I thought it would be, and by the time the roar of the river reaches us, our shadows have disappeared in the pink glow of sunset on the mountain.

We stand on the bottom edge of the glacier and watch the water rush out from beneath our feet and pour into the river, and we watch the river disappear into the twilight forest.

"The river's gotta end up at that lake," Jimmy says.

"That what we're heading for?"

"North's how the train was headin'," he says. "Sides, they's bound to be plenty to eat."

We pick our way down off the glacier and follow the river into the forest. It must run much higher in some other season, because the banks are wide and strewn with boulders and fallen sun-bleached trees, the bone-colored wood water-stripped, the roots still attached and sticking up like gnarled fists. The river runs down the center of this hazard-filled boneyard, reflecting the last light and creating the impression of a silver highway hemmed in on either side by the clean, dark pines.

Jimmy and I both stop at the same time.

Silhouetted against the silver rapids, a fox sits on a boulder staring off downriver with its fluffy tail swooshing back and forth across the surface of the stone. Other than the clock-like swing of its tail, the fox is as still as the stone it sits on, and it looks almost as if it were parked there patiently waiting on some long overdue friend to come up that silvery road.

A rush of wind tickles my ear, and Jimmy's spear flies toward the boulder and disappears, taking the fox with it. One second the fox is sitting there, the next second it's not.

We camp on a high bank beneath the overhanging bows of a tree. I scrounge up wood and build a fire while Jimmy skins out the fox. When the fire burns down, we skewer the meat on pine branches and lay it to roast over the coals. Then we sit in the dark listening to the fat sizzle and smelling the meat cook while we pass the fox's pelt back and forth, admiring it.

Jimmy tosses me the pelt and leans forward and turns the meat, the fox's naked legs flopping from side to side.

"Looked a lot bigger wearin' its fur," he says.

I stroke the pelt, inspecting it in the dim glow of the coals.

Thick brown fur, gray highlights, a black tip at the end of its soft and bushy tail. It's beautiful. Jimmy hands me a skewer of meat; I hand him back the pelt.

"What will you do with it?" I ask.

"The fur?" he says. "Hell, I dunno. Ya want it?"

"No, I don't want it."

"Well, maybe I'll make ya a hat."

The meat is burnt on the outside and half raw yet on the inside, but after almost two days without food we devour it and suck the bones and lick our fingers. Jimmy cracks the bones and eats the marrow, but the idea grosses me out so I toss mine in the fire and watch them blacken. When we finish we're still hungry, and Jimmy gathers pinecones in the dark and sets them in the coals to roast and then we fish them out with sticks and pry them apart and eat the seeds.

If the moon is in the sky, it's trapped somewhere on the other side of the mountain and the night is as black as anything I've ever seen. The coals burn down to just a dim glow beneath the ashes, and we lie on our backs looking up into absolute nothingness and listen to the river rumble down the canyon.

We break camp at dawn, filling our canteens in the river and splashing cold glacier water on our faces before strapping on our packs and heading off downriver. Jimmy ties the fur to the outside of his pack, and as he limps along ahead of me it looks as if the fox has leapt onto his back and is clinging to his shoulders and hitching a ride. We're not gone long when I hear a sort of whimpering behind us. I look back but see nothing among the rocks where we passed.

"Did you hear anything, Jimmy?"

"Jus' the river. Why?"

"No reason."

I pick up a river stick, leaning on it to test its strength, and it feels about the right length so I take it with me for a walking stick and start after Jimmy. Not a minute later, and I hear the whimpering again, this time even closer behind me. I stop, turn. There, following at my heel, is a baby fox. It stops, plops down on its haunches, looks up at me with coal black eyes, and opens its little pink mouth and yawns.

"Jimmy," I call out. "You aren't gonna believe this."

Jimmy backtracks and steps up beside me.

"Shit," he says.

The fox pup trots around behind us, and when we turn, it moves behind us again, as if it were playing some kind of game.

"Take off your pack, Jimmy."

"Why would I?"

"He's following his mama on your back."

Jimmy shrugs off his pack and sets it on the ground. The little fox runs up and buries its face in its mother's fur.

"Should we eat it?" Jimmy says.

"No, we can't eat it," I say, punching him on the arm.

"Well, what'll we do with it then?"

"Let's just bury the fur inside your pack and go on," I say.

Jimmy stuffs the pelt inside his pack, concealing it as best he can with the tattered skins now loosely covering its contents. Then he straps the pack on again and we continue walking.

The fox pup whimpers meekly behind us.

"Don't look back," I say.

We walk for several minutes with nothing but the sound of the river running and then I peek over my shoulder.

"Thought ya said not ta look back," Jimmy says.

"I did say it."

"Then why'd ya look?"

"I don't know."

"Well?"

"Well, what?"

"Is it back there?"

"Yeah, it's back there."

"Shit."

We noon on a sandy shoal where the river splits and pours thick into a deep pool. We sit on our packs and watch the little fox come trotting along the river behind us.

"I'm pretty dang hungry now," Jimmy says.

"Me too," I say, "but we're still not eating it."

The fox lopes up and plops down next to Jimmy's pack. Jimmy stands and snatches his spear, heading off toward the river with it. When I reach to pet the little fox, it shies away, keeping its eyes on Jimmy's pack. I open his pack and pull out the fur and lay it over my lap, patting it as an invitation. The pup takes a half step forward and stops, dropping on his belly.

"Come on, little fox," I say, "it's okay."

I feel funny talking as if it can understand, but I pat the fur again and it shimmies a head closer. We go on like this for the next hour, inch by inch, me talking it toward me, and by the time Jimmy walks back into camp with a half dozen small trout hanging from a string, the fox is sitting on my lap.

"If ya plan on feedin' that whiney little thing," Jimmy says, holding up the fish, "it's comin' outta yer half."

We build a small fire and roast our fish, three for Jimmy, two for me, my third one raw and in the mouth of the pup. He eats it with his little paws holding it down, and it's all he can do to tear small chunks from the fish by biting into its back and thrashing his little head from side to side. After we eat, the pup sits on the riverbank and licks its paws while Jimmy and I swim in the pool. The river water is ice cold, but it feels good to be clean when we finally climb out of it, shivering.

We rinse our tattered clothes in the river and hang them from branches to dry. Then we pull everything out of our packs and spread the packs to air on the sand, and we sit next to them naked with our arms around our knees and skip stones across the pool. I look at Jimmy's thigh, the wound fully healed now, but a nasty red scar there from my crude stitch job.

"Does it still hurt?"

He looks at the scar and shrugs.

"Nah, not really," he says, skipping another stone.

"Never?"

"Only when I think about it."

Jimmy nods to the pup, now running in circles and playing with a pinecone.

"He is kinda cute."

"How do you know it's a he?" I ask.

He shrugs. "I dunno. I jus' figured it."

The pup bats the pinecone and it rolls down the bank into the water. He runs after it and buries his nose in the pool and comes up with the pinecone dripping in his mouth.

"Ya got a name for 'em?" Jimmy asks.

"If we name him, we'll have to keep him."

"Ya already gotta keep 'em," Jimmy says, "ya fed 'em."

"I guess you're right. But I can't think of any name."

Jimmy nods toward the contents of our packs spread out and drying in the sun: furs, broken lengths of rope, canteens, an empty food pouch, my father's pipe, and Uncle John's knife.

"Why dun' ya jus' call 'em Little John, or John, Jr.?"

I remember Uncle John teaching me to clean a fish in two cuts, then giving me his knife. And I remember them bringing his mangled body back and burning it on the bluff. I remember his wife giving birth to his son and naming him John, Jr. And I remember the Park Service slaughtering them, too.

"How about we just call him Junior?" I say.

"Junior it is then," Jimmy says, skipping one last stone. "We better get on if we's gonna reach that lake by dusk."

Junior takes to his name better than he does to keeping up with us. He quickly falls behind, and after waiting for him to catch up a third time, Jimmy threatens to eat him again. I scoop him up and carry him a ways, then I put him in my pack with his mother's fur and we set a fast pace to make up lost time.

All is quiet, with just the sound of the river running and Jimmy's spear and my walking stick knocking against stones as we walk. I feel Junior's hot breath on my ear every few minutes when he pokes his head out and looks around, as if satisfying himself we're heading in the right direction, before retreating into the pack and snuggling into his mother's coat.

Near dusk, with the sky turning cobalt overhead, we come to where the river flows into a deep canyon with no bank on either side, and we're forced to seek higher ground and follow the river by sound as we weave our way through the forest. The forest is bone cold, and the pines stand dark against the deep-blue sky as our breath smokes in the air before us—Jimmy's, mine, and occasionally Junior's tiny breaths over my shoulder. We walk for a long time with the sounds of the river fading to our right and sticks and pine needles crunching under our feet.

Soon, the sky is nearly black, and the trees recede into it so we can only see their faint shadows when we're nearly on top of them. I'm about to suggest we stop and make camp when Jimmy drops to the ground, grabs my arm, and pulls me down with him. He points ahead. We shimmy forward on our bellies and I see why he made us drop out of sight.

The trees end abruptly at the edge of a high bluff, and the bluff looks over the lake now glowing a kind of purple as its still waters reflect the last bit of light. Below us, on a small peninsula that juts out into the lake, is some sort of building shrouded in deep shadows. It looks like a big house, or maybe a lodge. Lighted windows cast yellow rectangles on manicured lawns. Stone steps lead down to an enormous boathouse and a long dock built out into the lake. The dock's edges are lit with gas torches that crisscross one another and cast luminous twin sets of torches on the surface of the water.

"Whataya think it is?" Jimmy whispers.

"Some kind of mansion or something," I whisper back.

"What's a mansion?"

"Just a big fancy house, I guess."

"Oh . . ."

"Like a big tent, but more permanent," I say, realizing he's never seen a house either.

"Who lives here?"

"I'm wondering the same thing."

We lie still and watch while the last bit of light fades, the lake turning from purple to black, the lodge disappearing into shadow save for the lit windows and the torches on the dock. After a while, Junior crawls out of my pack and stands with his front paws on the back of my head and watches with us.

"We better backtrack and make camp," Jimmy says.

I scoop Junior off my back and we shimmy away from the edge. We walk maybe fifty meters into the forest until we find a wind-felled tree. It's too dark to make beds, and we don't dare make a fire, so we lie on the cold ground with the tree between ourselves and the lake. I can hear Jimmy's stomach grumbling next to me, and I wonder if he can hear mine. I fish the pelt from my pack and use it for a pillow. Junior curls up on it also and drops fast asleep beside my head. I feel his tiny ribs rising and falling as he breathes, and I'm sure I even hear his little tummy grumble once, too.

"Hey, Aubrey," Jimmy says.

"Yeah . . ."

"Never mind."

"What is it, Jimmy?"

"I was jus' thinkin'."

"Thinking about what?"

"Well, I was jus' thinkin' that whatever's down there . . . I mean, whatever happens tomorrow . . ."

"Yeah . . ."

"Ah, it's nothin', really," he says, "I jus' was thinkin' stuff. Guess I wanted to say I'm real glad we met."

Junior sneezes in the dark, shifts his position on the fur, and falls right back to sleep. I think Jimmy might say something more, but he doesn't, and all I can hear is the faint rumble of the restless river running down its canyon somewhere.

"Hey, Jimmy?"

"Yeah . . ."

"I'm real glad to have met you, too."

CHAPTER 23
The Lake House at Malthusai

"Knock it off."

Junior licking the salt from my lips.

"All right, all right. What's that sound?"

Swoosh—thwap! Swoosh—thwap! Swoosh—thwap!

Jimmy is fast asleep snoring, his arms wrapped around his pack as if he were cuddling it. I pick Junior up and carry him with me to go investigate. The dawn light beyond the trees is gray and the distant peaks stand black against it, and as I near the edge of the bluff, the pewter lake comes into view. A duck calls, another flapping clumsily across the sky veers to the lake and lands, cutting the smooth surface open like a zipper.

I set Junior on the ground, drop to my belly, and shimmy to the edge. Just as I peek over, the sun rises from between two peaks, blinding me. I narrow my lids against the glare, raise a hand to shield my eyes, and wait for my vision to adjust.

Swoosh—thwap! Swoosh—thwap! Swoosh—thwap!

She fades into my sight like some fiery sex-goddess might in a dream from which I'd never want to wake, and I know in this very moment that I'll never be the same again. Standing on a red clay tennis court, she's hitting balls thrown by a machine. She wears white shoes and a white tennis skirt, her long legs bare, her skin the color of pale honey, and when she hits the ball, her skirt lifts and I can see the hint of her pink underwear. But what attracts me most about her appearance, and why I cannot pull my eyes away, is her thick red hair pulled back from her gorgeous face and tied in a pony tail that sweeps out behind her, splaying open like a burst of flame when she swings, then falling again to rest in the perfect curve of her back.

The balls come fast from the machine, and she delivers them back across the net with expert swings—backhand and forehand and overhand—dancing on the red court, agile and so faery-like I wouldn't be surprised if her red hair spread into wings and she flew away over the treetops. But I hope she never flies away. I want to lie here and watch her forever, and I would if Junior didn't start crying loudly in my ear, the noise threatening to draw her attention to me.

I turn to grab him but he backs away and yips again. I look at his little ribs showing through his fur and think he must be starving. Shimmying away from the edge, I head back toward our camp with Junior yipping at my heel.

Jimmy's awake, propped against the log, digging through his near empty pack.

"What are you looking for?" I ask.

"Anythin' eatable," he says. "Where were ya?"

"Had to take a leak," I say.

I don't know why I lie to him, I just do.

"What was that sound?" he asks.

"What sound?" I say, lying again.

Jimmy just shakes his head and says, "I'm starved."

"Me too. And so is Junior."

He tosses his pack and stands, brushing himself off and looking around.

"Well," he says, "let's leave our stuff here jus' in case and go on and have a look."

When we belly up to the edge, the tennis court is empty. Now that's she's no longer there, holding me spellbound with her beauty, I can see what the place looks like in the light.

The lake is enormous, cupped on all sides by mountains. The lodge below us is built almost entirely of brown stone, its steep roof shingled with red cedar, its gables accented with gray rock. The windows warble in the light like pictures of old leaded glass I've seen in educationals. The face of the lodge angles away from us toward the blue lake, two wings on either side surrounding the red-clay tennis court. The grounds are impeccable, with bursts of little flowers here and hanging baskets of color there. The green lawns are mowed so tight that you can see the lines running in perfect patterns across the grass. At the edge of the property, stone steps lead down to a swath of beach and the enormous boathouse built right up out of the water in stone that matches the lodge. A dock juts out into the lake, hovering just above the water's surface on pylons.

All is quiet and serene, and we sit there for thirty minutes and watch hummingbirds hover at the flowers and the shadows shrink as the sun climbs in the sky.

"Think anyone's home?" Jimmy says.

"I don't know," I say, lying again.

"Think you could boost me over that wall?"

"Maybe."

With Junior whimpering in my arms, we walk through the forest north of the lodge to where we won't be seen, and where the cliffs give way to gentler slopes. We work our way down to the lake and walk the shore back to the wall that separates us from the house. The wall must stand nearly three meters tall, made from impenetrable stone, with a wide arch in its center framing giant wooden doors with iron rings for handles.

"Boost me up," Jimmy says.

"How about you boost me," I say. "I'm lighter."

"Whatever," Jimmy shrugs.

I set Junior down and step into Jimmy's hands. He lifts me up, but I'm still a head short of seeing over.

"It's too high."

I step down. He crouches, tapping his shoulders for me to climb on. I step up, left foot, right, and brace myself against the wall with my palms. He grunts, rises, and the wall slides down past me and disappears until I'm looking in on the garden.

She's standing there on the other side of the wall, looking up at me with her hands hooked on her narrow hips.

"Whataya see?" Jimmy asks, his voice strained beneath me.

She's changed from her tennis skirt into white shorts, her feet bare in the grass, her red hair loose and all around her.

"Who are you?" she asks, her voice calm.

I prop my arms on the edge of the wall.

"I'm Aubrey."

"What?" Jimmy asks.

"Aubrey's a funny name for a boy," she says, smirking.

"I'm not a boy, I'm a man," I say. "What's your name?"

"Hannah."

"Who ya talkin' to?" Jimmy asks, wobbling beneath me.

"Hannah's a funny name for a girl," I say.

"No, it's not," she says. "Besides, what would you know about girls, anyway?"

"I know plenty."

"Well, you can't know that much," she says, "because you don't know enough to use the door right beside you."

"Aubrey," Jimmy says, almost yelling now.

"People don't build walls as an invitation for guests."

She laughs, her face even more beautiful when she does. "So you're telling me you think they build them to invite boys to peek over?"

"Aubrey! Who ya talkin' to?"

"I'm not a boy."

"Well, whatever," she says. "The wall's to keep the flowers in, not to keep anything out. The door isn't locked."

She disappears behind the wall again as Jimmy lowers me. I step down and he crosses his arms and rubs his shoulders and glares at me with his face bright red.

"What the hell, Aubrey," he says, "dun' ya listen? Who was ya talkin' to in there?"

"Come on, I'll show you."

We each grab an iron handle and swing the doors open, soundless on their oiled hinges. Hannah stands just inside the courtyard with the posture of some dignitary doing her duty and receiving guests well beneath her station.

"Welcome to the Lake House at Malthusai," she says.

She turns and walks into the courtyard. Jimmy and I follow without a word. She leads us to a shaded patio overlooking the lake, sweeping her arms toward a large iron table indicating that we should sit, and lowering herself into a chair without waiting.

The heavy chairs are cushioned with thick fabric, and after months of river boulders and fallen trees for furniture, it's the nicest thing I've ever sat in. The table has seats for six, but only Hannah's place is set with plates of fine china, a saucer and cup, a crystal glass, and silver flatware.

She lifts a small golden bell and rings it, and almost before she sets it down again, a woman steps from the house carrying a tray. The woman stops when she sees us, her apron swinging away from her waist and settling again, the ice rattling in its metal pitcher. She turns and disappears back into the house.

I look at Jimmy, Jimmy looks at me, and then we both swivel our heads back to Hannah.

Shortly, the woman reappears carrying a larger tray and she sets place settings to match Hannah's in front of us. She turns our cups over and fills them with steaming tea from an iron pot, and she fills our glasses with ice water from the pitcher. She pauses to look at Junior in my arms. She reaches to pet him, but pulls her hand away and walks back into the house.

When she comes out again, her tray is loaded with food. She sets out a basket of breads. Wood bowls filled with fruit—strawberries, raspberries, oranges, and even mangos. She lifts the steaming lid from a dish of boiled potatoes and asparagus. She sets down pancakes and maple syrup, toast spread with avocado, and a bowl of sliced bananas. On the grass beside the table, she sets a bowl of water and another of fruit and granola. Junior is already squirming in my arms for the food, and when I set him on the grass, he makes for the bowl and buries his little face in it, eating. The woman bows slightly and retreats into the house leaving the three of us alone with our feast.

"Don't be shy," Hannah says.

Jimmy and I look at one another and then we reach for the food and begin to eat without even pausing to put anything on our plates. Our flatware and linens remain untouched as we stuff muffins and bread and fruit into our mouths, chewing and swallowing it before it can be taken away. Hannah sits across from us, sipping her tea and watching with a smile on her face.

The crystal water glass is heavy and cool in my hand and the water tastes deliciously strange after drinking from rivers and streams. I watch Hannah drizzle honey in her tea, stirring it with a tiny spoon. I try to copy her, but I gulp the steaming tea, scald my tongue, and spit it out. She laughs. I eat on.

Fruit, pastries, nuts. Jimmy eats pancakes with his hands, folding them and stuffing them in his mouth. I scoop potatoes and asparagus onto my plate and lift my heavy flatware, but it's been so long since I've used any that I knock the fork against my teeth. We devour nearly everything before us and then the woman comes from the house with even more.

And we eat more.

When I finally push my plate away and rest my hands on my belly and look down, Junior is laid on his side next to his empty dish and breathing heavily with his tongue lolling out. Jimmy finishes eating also, and then the woman reappears and refills our tea, refills our water, and carries everything else away and comes back to sweep the crumbs from the table.

We sit there looking at Hannah as if we've just sat down, no evidence left at all of the feast we just ate except our swollen bellies and our drooping eyes.

"It's nice to have company for breakfast," she says.

"What is this place?" Jimmy asks.

"It's my home," she says. "What's your name?"

"Jimmy."

"Jimmy and Aubrey. And what's the pup's name?"

"Junior," I say. "Do you get many guests?"

"No," she says, "never."

She sips her tea and smiles at us.

Jimmy picks his teeth, I look around.

"Father won't be happy about the pup," she says, after a long silence. "We're not supposed to have pets here."

"You live here with your father?"

"And my mother," she says. "They're off touring, but they should be back tomorrow morning. That was you watching me play tennis this morning, wasn't it?"

I blush and turn away from her. I see Jimmy narrow his eyes at me, realizing I lied.

"Where did you two come from?" she asks.

Jimmy nods toward the forest and the mountain beyond.

"Shut up," she says, setting her teacup down. "You guys crossed the mountains? Have you seen the ocean? I long to see the ocean. I dream about it even. But Daddy says I'm too young to tour yet. Tell me about the ocean."

Jimmy and I start to talk at the same time and stop.

Hannah's eyes dart back and forth between us, and I jump in and keep talking and her eyes settle on me.

"It's amazing," I say. "You have to see it. The water's as blue as you can imagine and it moves with a life of its own."

"Is it big?" she asks, leaning forward, her eyes wide.

"Is it big? I'll tell you, you can see the Earth curve away at the horizon. In the evening, the sun slips into it, and sometimes there's a blast of after light that sets the whole sky on fire."

"Ya can drown in it, too," Jimmy says. "Or get yerself cut to pieces by the Park Service."

"Well, then . . .," she says, picking up her cup and tossing the last of her tea into the grass. "You two look like you could use some rest. Let's see if Gloria's set your rooms, shall we?"

She stands without waiting for an answer.

Jimmy and I slide our heavy chairs out and follow her to

the house. I turn back for Junior, but Hannah waves me along and says she'll have Gloria fix him a comfortable place.

Inside the house is cool. The floors are laid with polished tiles, the walls plastered, the ceilings boxed with timbers. Fresh flowers spring from vases everywhere, and the whole place smells of lavender and pine. She walks us past a study with a fireplace you could stand in, walls of books to the ceiling, and a ladder on wheels with which to reach them. The halls are hung with art, and alcoves display exotic marble statues that watch us pass with dreamy, frozen stares.

Hannah stops in front of an open door.

"Why don't we give you the green room, Aubrey? That's the bath there," she says, pointing across the room to another door left ajar and from which a shaft of white light runs across the floor and climbs the opposite wall. "You'll find everything you need in there. I'll have Gloria see what clothes Daddy can spare. Come with me, Jimmy, we'll give you the blue room."

She pulls the door shut, leaving me standing there alone, taking in the room. Soft light filters in through a high window and lands on an enormous bed turned down with cotton sheets and a green comforter. I walk to the bed and sit—the mattress is soft and springy. The rest of the room is simple. Two lamps. A chest of drawers against one wall, a wood wardrobe against the other. The walls are papered green and inlaid with pictures of yellow birds frozen in flight.

Who made all this stuff, I wonder.

The room is quiet, too quiet. It feels strange to be alone, to be away from Jimmy after all this time. I consider going to find him, but I decide to check out the bathroom instead.

White tile floors, a white clawfoot tub with silver plumbing hanging from it like jewelry. I turn the tap and hot water pours from the waterfall spout. Ah, to have running water again. As the tub fills, I remove my father's pipe from my neck and set it on the counter, strip off my filthy furs, my homemade shoes, and stand in front of the full length mirror.

I don't even recognize myself, and I like it.

Other than glimpses in rivers or streams here and there, I haven't seen my reflection since leaving Holocene II. I'm taller than I was then and my shoulders are wider, my muscles more developed. My skin is tan, my hands calloused and roped with veins. And my shaggy hair hangs almost to my shoulders and it reminds me of Jimmy's.

The steam from the filling tub climbs up the mirror like some fog from the past and my reflection is covered up until just my eyes float there looking back. And then they too recede and leave me looking at nothing but foggy glass.

The water's hot. I grip the tub edges and lower myself in, sitting still to keep from burning. I feel the heat leach away the dirt and grime, the aches and pains. When the water cools, I reach for a bar of soap and scrub. The water turns so dark with dirt that I have to drain it and then fill it again.

Wrapping myself in an enormous soft towel, I step from the tub and search the countertops until I find a toothbrush and some paste. I've done my best with moss and pieces of fur to keep my teeth clean, but the brush takes off layers of grime and leaves them feeling fresh and smooth against my tongue. I find scissors and cut my nails. The clippings are long and dark and they pile on the counter like dead insects.

Back in the room, I find clothes folded neatly at the edge of the bed. On top of the clothes, written in beautiful script on pink stationery is a note that reads:

Take a nap if you'd like one.
Supper will be served on the terrace at dusk.

There's a soft tap on the bedroom door. My heart jumps, thinking maybe it's Hannah. I wrap the towel around my waist, puff out my chest, and open the door. Jimmy's standing there.

"Hey, Jimmy. What's up?"

He hands me a note.

"What's this say?"

"It just says we're having dinner on the terrace."

"Oh," he says, nodding. "Ya look different."

"I took a bath. You should too, it feels great."

"Yeah, okay."

"I'm gonna rest," I say, feeling very drowsy now.

"Sure," he says. "Okay, I'll see ya for dinner then."

As soon as I shut the door, there's another knock.

"What is it, Jimmy?" I ask, opening it again.

"I gotta go."

"You're leaving?"

"No, I gotta go shishi."

"Oh," I say, chuckling. "Just use the toilet."

"Which one's the toilet?"

I invite him in and show him the toilet and how to flush it. He nods, seeming to understand, but looking uncomfortable.

"How do ya know all this stuff?" he asks.

"I grew up with plumbing."

"So ya'll jus' shishi in yer houses?"

"Guess I never thought of it like that," I say, shaking my

head as I walk him to the door and see him out.

The bedding smells of lavender, the pillows smell of pine, and the sheets are warmed from the sun filtering into the quiet room. I'm comfortably full, I'm clean. I feel as if I'm floating in some fantastic fantasy as I close my eyes and picture Hannah's flowing red hair and her perfect angel face.

I fall asleep and I do not dream.

CHAPTER 24
My Sweet, Sweet Hannah

I stir, turn.

The light is gone from the window—

Oh, no, I overslept!

I jump out of bed and flick on the lamp.

The linen slacks are a little too big, but I cinch them with the belt and roll the cuffs to make them fit. I pull on the shirt, slip on the fabric sandals. Then I hang my father's pipe around my neck and comb my fingers through my long hair and pull it away from face. I feel entirely new and civilized as I step from the room and make my way through the house to the terrace.

I find her sitting alone on a wicker chair beside a stone fire pit, holding Junior in her lap, stroking his fur and looking out across the lake. She wears a simple green dress that's striking against her red hair. I've never seen anything so beautiful as she looks sitting there.

She hears me step up and nods to a chair. The fire pit must be fueled with gas because flames rise out of nothing but white sand and seesaw at the air in a light breeze coming off the lake.

"It's not good to take animals from their environment," she says, looking at Junior in her lap. "This little guy should be out there with his mother."

"His mother got eaten," I say.

"Still," she says, frowning slightly, "there's a natural order to things. Whatever ate his mother was fulfilling its role. Who are we to step in and save this one from the same fate?"

"We ate his mother," I say.

"Oh," she says, straightening up and setting Junior on the ground quite suddenly. "You ate meat?"

"Yes. We ate meat."

"What was it like?"

"You've never eaten meat?"

"No," she says, holding her hand to her heart as if her honor has been offended. "We're vegans."

"Well, I was raised vegan, too. I hadn't ever eaten meat until . . . well, until I met Jimmy."

Almost as if I'd called him forth by mentioning his name, Jimmy steps from the house and onto the terrace. His feet are bare, his pants bunched around his waist, the legs rolled up to his knees. His shirt is unbuttoned and flapping in the breeze. He looks very out of place here. He joins us at the fire pit and lowers himself slowly into a seat across from me.

"You both look rested," Hannah says. "Almost human."

Jimmy looks furtively around as if he might be looking for something he lost. Hannah watches him for a while, her eyes curious, her head cocked. Then she turns to me and says:

"Do you play tennis?"

"A little, yeah. I mean, I'm not good or anything, but we had an indoor court where I grew up."

"How about you, Jimmy?" she says. "Do you play tennis?"

Jimmy snaps his head to look at her, his eyes squinted.

"What do yer parents do?"

"Excuse me?"

"All this," Jimmy says, waving his hand across the estate. "What do yer parents do fer it?"

Hannah turns to me. "His manners are quite savage, aren't they? I'll go let Gloria know we're ready for our supper."

She stands, runs her hands along her curves to smooth the wrinkles from her dress, and glides across the terrace to the house, leaving Jimmy and me alone.

"You don't have to be mean. I'll teach you about tennis."

"Ha! Yer gonna teach me?" Jimmy says, leaning forward and planting his hands on his knees. "We dunno nothin' about these people. Nothin'. Who are they? What do they do?"

"I know she's been kind enough to take us in and feed us. She even gave us clothes. The least we can do is be polite."

Jimmy shakes his head.

"You dun' remember nothin', do ya? One look at a pretty face and ya forget ever-thin' we done been through. The cove, the mountains—ever-thin'."

I know he doesn't mean it. He's just being mean because he's jealous, just like with his mother. Hannah's paying more attention to me, and he doesn't like it. But it's not my fault.

"Listen," I say, "I haven't forgotten anything. Let's just go with the flow and see what all this is about."

Hannah steps from the house and waves us over to where a mosquito net drapes the table, suspended from an armature, protecting the gorgeous scene spread there. Bowls of fresh fruit and vases of cut flowers. Candles in glass canisters.

And this time, the table is set for three.

Jimmy ducks through the netting and sits without waiting at the single place setting across from the other two. I wait for Hannah to take her seat, then I sit next to her.

The sun has already dipped behind the mountains and the torch flames on the dock appear and disappear in the shadow of puff-white clouds that pass slowly overhead, pastel-looking in dark skies. The lake seems lit with some energy of its own in the lightness of twilight.

Hannah rings the bell.

The woman appears again and fills our glasses with water and sweet iced tea. Then she delivers a course of toasted bread spread with a rich herb paste that Hannah says is hemp butter.

"Thank you, Gloria. This is Aubrey, and this is Jimmy."

I take Gloria's hand.

"Nice to meet you."

Jimmy ignores her, snatching a piece of bread and eating without waiting, his eyes averted from ours. Junior appears and whines and Jimmy passes him bread beneath the table.

Next, Gloria bring bowls of creamy tomato soup seasoned with an herb that Hannah says is basil.

While we eat, Hannah tells us about the lake.

"It never gets old, looking at this view. You know, this is the deepest lake now in all of America. Well, that's what Daddy says. He would know. I just can't wait for you to see it in the spring. All the minerals wash down from the glaciers and the water is so blue you'd swear it wasn't even real."

"Do you swim in it?" I ask.

"I'm not supposed to," she says, "but I do it sometimes anyway, when my parents are away. Maybe we can all go out for a swim tonight. What do you think?"

"I'd like that," I say.

Jimmy pushes his soup bowl away.

"Is the taste not to your liking?" Hannah asks. "I can have Gloria prepare you something special if you want."

"Ya got any fish?" Jimmy says.

"Oh, no," she says, "we don't eat fish here."

"What, there ain't no fish in yer lake?"

"The lake is swimming with fish. All native species, too. But it's not natural for humans to eat other animals."

"If it ain't natural," Jimmy says, "then why do we got these teeth in our mouths? I'll tell ya what it ain't natural—livin' in a big place like this while others is hidin' out in caves."

Hannah scowls at him.

"I'll forgive your ignorance and just assume you don't understand the human condition."

Jimmy puffs out his cheeks and looks away.

Thankfully, Gloria breaks the tension by bringing out little dishes of mango sorbet and we eat them with tiny spoons that remind me of the one my father fed me with when I was a boy. After clearing away our sorbet dishes, she delivers a cold potato casserole to the table. Hannah watches Jimmy scoop it up and eat it with his hands, letting Junior lick his fingers clean beneath the table. She looks at me and shakes her head. I shrug.

We eat slow, the courses coming one at a time. I notice that Hannah eats only little tastes of things, telling us the names of all the foods. Then she tells us about the flowers around the lodge. She says the lodge is very old and that it once stood on a bluff overlooking the lake. She says that when the dam was built the water rose and brought the lake up and turned the bluff into a peninsula. Jimmy asks her when the dam was built and who built it, but she waves his question away and says it's been there since long before she was born.

"Which was sixteen years ago last month," she adds.

Our final course is a green salad with candied walnuts, and by the time it arrives, the evening alpenglow is sliding down the mountain and spreading across the lake like a luminous pink blanket. The torch reflections rise on the water, twins distorted by gusts of wind running on the lake, rustling across the grass, and softly billowing the netting around the table. The candles, protected in their jars, burn straight and still, and they cast a soft yellow glow over us and the remains of our feast.

As night comes on, Jimmy's face recedes into shadow and his gray eyes slowly disappear until just the reflections of the candle flame hang there in each eye, like two yellow teardrops. He pushes his unfinished salad plate away and stands.

"I'm tired now and need to sleep," he says.

"Of course," Hannah says. "I'm sure Gloria has turned down your bed with fresh sheets."

I don't know what to say, so I don't say anything.

Jimmy reaches beneath the table, scoops up Junior, ducks under the netting, and is gone, his shadow disappearing toward the house. Hannah watches after him, too. I think she might say something when he's gone but she doesn't.

We sit together and stare at the lake, the water darkening as the torch flames brighten on its mirror surface. A thick slice of moon rides above the trees, casting its double on the lake.

Gloria comes out and clears the table. When she returns, she has three stemmed glasses and a crystal bottle filled with red liquid that in the reflection of candlelight looks like blood. She nods toward Jimmy's empty chair, but Hannah shakes her head and she takes the third glass back with her into the house.

Hannah pulls the stopper from the bottle, fills the glasses, and hands one to me. She picks up her glass and swirls the red liquid, smelling it before she takes a sip. I pick up my glass and copy her movements, tasting the sweet bite of bitter at the back of my tongue. It slides warm and heavy down my throat.

"What is this?"

"It's port," she says. "You like it?"

I nod and take another sip.

The night grows dark around us until we're sitting together in a private world enclosed by the mosquito net. We drink and watch the candle flames reflect through the crystal decanter of port. The red glow highlights Hannah's hair and her green eyes burn with an emerald sparkle as she sips her wine and looks at me. The port sits like an ember in my gut, slowly radiating heat outward until even my fingertips tingle with warm excitement. Hannah lifts the stopper again and refills our glasses.

"You must have been very brave to cross the mountains," she says, breaking a long silence.

"Nah, it was nothing really," I say, feeling myself blush.

"How long did it take you?"

"Two days total on the upper mountain, maybe another three on the approach, I think."

"It must be lovely to be so close to the stars. I'll bet you felt you could reach up and pluck them from the sky like fruit."

"Have you never been to the mountains?"

"No," she says, with a look of disappointment. "I've never been anywhere but here. But that will all change soon enough now. Now I'll get to tour. How long have you known Jimmy?"

"Since early summer, I guess."

"And how did you two meet?"

I'm not sure how much to tell, or if she'd even understand. I remember Jimmy's warning that we don't know anything about her yet, and part of me knows he's right. But her green eyes smile at me with patient understanding, and her freckled face is so open, her look so soft, that I can't imagine her being anything but sweet and pure and kind.

Nervous, I sip my port and set it down. Then I pick it up and sip it again. The warmth oozes into my chest and rises to my head, and I feel my cheeks flush, my heart quicken.

"Okay," I say, "I have to tell you something, but I'll warn you first—you might find it hard to believe."

"You might be surprised what I'd believe," she says, lifting an eyebrow and sipping her port. "Please, do tell."

I look at her face, feel the wine wash away my inhibitions, and without thinking, everything pours from my mouth:

"The thing is this—I'm not from up here. I mean, I'm not from the surface. I grew up many kilometers underground and we didn't think any of this existed anymore up here. The lake, the trees, the ocean—anything. Then a terrible accident happened on a train—well, a kind of train that travels underground—and I climbed out of the wreck and onto the surface and nearly died. I met Jimmy and he really helped me a lot. He did. His family helped me too. But then they got slaughtered and we set out to find out what's going on, who's behind things. Then I saw you. Anyway, this probably isn't making any sense, is it?"

"It makes perfect sense," she says.

"You mean you believe me?"

"Believe you?" she says, a sexy, mischievous smile curling on her lips. "Of course I believe you."

"Are you joking with me, or you really do?"

"I knew it all already," she says. "And what I didn't know I pieced together when you showed up."

"What?" I close my eyes and shake my head, trying to clear

the fog because the port is making me feel funny and I can't be hearing her right. "You knew? How did you know?"

She drains her port, the smile still on her face.

"Because we had been expecting you, silly."

"What do you mean you were expecting me?"

"We've been worried sick with wondering what happened to you. But let's not think about that now. Daddy will explain everything to you tomorrow. Right now, let's enjoy the night and go for a swim, shall we? Come on."

She stands and passes through the mosquito net and with her silhouette cast on the sheer netting by the torchlight, she slides her dress free from her shoulders and slips it off.

She steps out of it and runs down to the dock.

I stand and the world spins for several seconds, then rights itself and sits glimmering before me, magical and incandescent, the night filled with mystery. Our conversation slips away into some dark faraway place, and I duck beneath the netting and step over Hannah's green dress where it lies piled on the grass.

I run after her.

She walks along the dock ahead of me, her perfect body appearing and then disappearing in the light of the torches as she passes. When she reaches the dock's end, she stands for one moment with her arms upstretched, as if to embrace the crescent moon that hangs pale above the lake, then she dives headfirst into the water with a splash.

I stand at the edge of the dock and watch her swim away, floating on her back and kicking the water playfully.

"Dive in," she calls. "You'll love it. I promise. The water feels like cool silk against your skin."

I strip off my shirt and hop free of my new pants, almost

pulling off my undershorts, too, remembering how Jimmy and I swam naked, but I blush thinking about it and leave them on. Piling my clothes in a heap on the dock, I dive in after her.

The cold water shocks me sober.

There's something I should be thinking about now, I know there is, but before it floats to the surface of my mind, Hannah appears from underwater in front of me, her hair slicked away from porcelain features, her red lips parted, her teeth glinting white in the moonlight as she spits water in my face.

"Try to catch me if you can," she says, giggling.

She takes off. I swim after her, the moon shattering into a million miniatures of itself as I stroke across the black water. All I can think about is Hannah, Hannah wanting me to chase, Hannah ahead of me nearly naked in the lake.

I overtake her and wrap my arms around her from behind. She turns, wraps hers around me, her body warm and inviting in the cool lake. In each other's arms, we float in a shimmering sea of moonlight and our breath blows hot against the cold air rising from the lake, mixing together like smoke between us.

I lean forward and close the distance and touch my lips to hers. She takes me in and we kiss, long and deep, our tongues searching one another. She tastes sweet and oh so much more intoxicating than any port could ever be.

Hannah—my sweet, sweet, Hannah.

CHAPTER 25
Dr. Radcliffe

Jimmy isn't in his room.

A shaft of morning sun landing on the untouched bed and his borrowed clothes sitting folded on its end.

I search the house but it's empty. I search the yard but see no sign of either Jimmy or Junior. I hike the bluff to our camp. Jimmy's pack is gone. My empty pack sits propped beside the wind-felled log, right where I left it the other morning when I lied to Jimmy about seeing Hannah play tennis. I feel absolutely terrible about letting him walk away from the table last night without a word.

When I get back to the lake house, Hannah is standing at the edge of the dock, her white dress flapping in the wind and hugging her curves. I come to stand beside her.

"I can't find Jimmy," I say.

Hannah stands with perfect posture, her chin raised to the wind and her red hair waving behind her on the breeze.

"Did you hear me? Jimmy's gone."

She turns to me.

"Gloria said he made camp in the woods not far from her cottage. Just down the beach there a ways. She brought him food and supplies this morning. He'll be fine."

I touch her arm.

"Hannah, what did you mean last night when you said you'd been waiting for me?"

"Daddy will explain everything," she says.

"When can I talk to him then?"

With one graceful motion, she lifts her arm out over the water and points. I follow her finger and skylight a boat in the distance growing ever so slow and steady as it approaches. Hannah stands close beside me and I wonder if she can tell that I'm nervous, if she can smell my sweat. I can smell the soap on her skin and a light perfume in her hair and the wind presses her dress against her just enough to expose the curve of her breasts. I want to kiss her again and feel her in my arms. I'm nervous to meet her father, and I don't know if it's because of the questions I have for him, or because I can't stop thinking about kissing his daughter.

The boat comes closer into view—

It's an antique wooden motorboat like some I've seen in educationals from the twentieth century. The bow is polished wood with brass fixtures reflecting the sun. It must be powered by electric motors for the boat moves across the water without sound. Two figures sit in the boat with perfect posture, like dignitaries on some parade float.

I see right away they're Hannah's mother and father.

Her mother has Hannah's red hair, and she gracefully lifts a hand to wave. She might be Hannah's own future reflection cast years from now across the lake. Her father, piloting the boat, has silver hair that looks almost metallic in the glint of the sun. Something about his face seems familiar to me, even from such a distance. I lift my hand to shade my eyes and focus on his features. As the boat moves closer, the outline of his face evolves and his nose comes into view. Then the arch of his brow. Lastly, I see the blue sparkle of his irises shining like two

Benitoite lanterns in his shaded sockets. He turns and says something to his wife and when he looks back, his blue eyes flicker three times as he blinks.

I know who he reminds me of—Dr. Radcliffe.

"Is your father related to Dr. Radcliffe?"

Hannah turns to me. "My father is Dr. Radcliffe."

"I knew it. He is related then. He must be a descendant of Dr. Robert Radcliffe, the founder of Holocene II?"

"No," she says, a smile curling around her lips, "he is the same Dr. Robert Radcliffe who founded Holocene II."

Before I can ask her what she means, the bow of the boat sinks into the water as it slows and glides past us and comes to rest with perfect precision beside the dock. A step plate folds out on silent mechanical hinges and secures the boat to the dock with some kind of magnetic connection. Dr. Radcliffe steps down onto the dock and turns to take his wife's hand and she steps down beside him.

Then they turn and stand before us. He's not much older than the Dr. Radcliffe I saw in the founder's video they showed us on testing day, and when he smiles and blinks at me, I know it's him, even though it's impossible because that video was recorded nine hundred years ago.

"Dr. Radcliffe?"

"You must have many questions," he says, nodding his head and blinking. "Trust that they will all be answered in time. But first let me welcome you. We had given you up for gone. This is my wife, Catherine."

She stretches out her delicate hand and I take it in mine. She looks so much like an older version of Hannah that I can't stop looking back and forth between the two and comparing.

Dr. Radcliffe wraps his arm around me and leads me from the dock. Hannah and her mother stay behind chatting.

"I hope Hannah has made you comfortable here," he says, smiling down at me. "Your journey looks quite good on you, young man. Let's retire to my study; I'll clear up a few things."

He shows me to his study and asks me if I'm thirsty and I say that I am even though I'm not. He leaves to fetch us iced tea. My mind is running with questions, my pulse races. I need to steady my nerves. I walk around the study and inspect the walls of books. From floor to ceiling they're stacked in no certain order from Socrates to Charles Darwin and everything in between, including the plays of Tennessee Williams and the works of William Shakespeare. I've dreamed of reading books like this. Real books bound in leather, crisp pages yellowed with time. Not the sterile graphite letters displayed on my lesson slate down in Holocene II. Spotting an ancient leather-bound collection entitled *The Complete Works of Leo Tolstoy*, I slide out the first book of four comprising *War and Peace*. I open the cover and look at the title page. The English translation I'm holding was printed in 1910. I can't imagine it—something that old resting in my hand. I want to sit and read it, maybe lock myself inside the study and read them all.

Dr. Radcliffe steps through the door and closes it again.

I snap the book closed and slide it back into its slot.

He hands me an iced tea.

"Good choice," he says, indicating the book with a nod. "Have you read it?"

"It wasn't in the Foundation library," I say, nervous.

"Oh, yes, that's right," he says, as if just remembering who I am. "Well, you'll have plenty of time to read them now. Let's take a seat and have a chat, shall we?"

He leads me to a brocaded chair beside the fire. I sit; he sits next to me. I watch the gas flames dance in the fireplace shadows. He sips his tea, I sip mine. He slides a polished-agate coaster free from a stack of coasters on the table and places his glass down on it. I slide a coaster free and place mine next to his, and our glasses sit there side by side, catching the light filtering through the study windows, the ice cubes swirling slow and then finally coming to rest in the amber tea. The room is silent except for a clock ticking loudly somewhere on a shelf.

Dr. Radcliffe clears his throat.

"Well then, let's start at the very beginning and I'll do my best to explain how we've arrived where we're sitting here today. Sound good?"

"Okay," I say, because I can't think of anything else.

"Many years ago," he says, his voice grave, his tone that of one beginning a speech, "before we were locked underground, I was trusted to lead a very important venture between private enterprise and our government."

"Holocene II, right?"

"That's right," he says.

"That's nothing new," I say.

"Hear me out, lad. There'll be plenty that's new."

"Sorry. Okay. Go on."

"Good. So, many of us, mostly men who had become very wealthy in biotechnology and energy science, believed that we were on the verge of making great leaps in human longevity."

"Lifespan?"

"Boy, let me talk."

"Sorry . . ."

"These advancements in longevity, or lifespan as you say, appealed to many people in positions of power for the obvious reasons. Men have always sought ways to defy their mortality, always. Even I. But my interest was for other reasons. You see, the planet had fallen victim to an emerging catastrophe that was centuries in the making. Our populations had swollen to record levels—levels not even imagined possible just decades before. Small groups of people in the world controlled nearly all the world's resources. Billions of others lived in complete poverty, working almost as slaves to provide the luxuries my peers took for granted. And beyond the human suffering, there was an even greater cost. We were quickly destroying the planet."

"You mean global warming."

"Yes. That and worse."

"But I've read all this in lesson slates."

"You're not a very patient fellow, are you?"

"I just want to know what's going on."

"Listen and you'll find out."

"Okay. Go on—go on."

"One of my companies had been making great progress with senescence and liquid computers."

"Senescence?"

"Aging. Biology. Biotech, my boy. It was the new frontier. We had created computers that could be injected into the body, becoming part of the human immune system. Tiny computers that reproduce themselves. Computers smaller than a white blood cell. Computers powered by the very glucose that powers our own cells. And we believed that these computers would make man immortal, or as immortal as anyone should ever want to be. We learned to rewire human DNA, allowing cells to reproduce without the telomeres shortening, totally eliminating the Hayflick limit that causes us to age. But cancer, you might ask, what of cancer?"

He pauses, leans forward, gulps his tea.

"We discovered that the aging process is partly a defense against cancer, and when we removed the limits on cell division, test subjects were overrun with cancers. But with this new liquid-computer tech, we solved the cancer problem. Once injected, these computers search out diseased cells, including cancerous cells, and they attach to the cell wall and release a protein that causes the bad cell to destroy itself. And we did it. We made it work, I tell you. First on rats, then on monkeys. Then we made it work on ourselves. We extended our lives a hundred years. Then five hundred. Now, we've refined the serum and we can extend a human life to almost a millennium. I was the first human to undergo the treatment and that was over nine hundred years ago."

"Wait just a minute," I say, not believing what I'm hearing. "You're telling me that you're nine hundred years old?"

My question hangs in the room. There's a long silence and all I can hear is the ticking of the clock. Tick-tick-tick . . .

"Nine hundred and seventy-three last May," he says.

"I don't believe you."

"That doesn't make it any less true," he says.

"Well, if it is true, then I don't understand. We're all taught in Holocene II that we work until we're thirty-five and then retire to Eden. We don't grow old so we don't burden society, so we don't overuse limited resources. But here you are almost a thousand years old now? No sickness, you say? No burden? Please, just tell me what's happened. I don't understand."

"Here, maybe some slides will help . . ."

Reaching to the table, he slides open a drawer and removes a small remote. He presses a button and the fire dies. Then blackout shades lower in front of the windows and the light disappears from the study in a retreating line that runs like a wave of shadow over me and the glasses of tea between us, and over Dr. Radcliffe until the last crack of light is sucked through the bottom of the shades and all is dim. A screen drops from the ceiling and lowers in front of us.

He clicks a button and an image flicks onto the screen—

An aerial photo of the ocean showing an island of garbage of all kinds floating off to the horizon.

"Increased ocean carbon killed the coral reefs, killed the sea life. A billion people were short of protein."

He clicks another image on the screen—

An image of mass exodus, refugees lined up as far as the dusty horizon to receive bags of biscuit powder being handed out from air-dropped pallets being guarded by U.S. soldiers.

"Even genetically engineered agriculture had no chance of holding off mass starvation with rapidly increasing populations. And birth rates actually rose, if you can believe it. Seems the hungrier people got, the more children they had."

Click—

Forklifts and dozers methodically pushing a wall of bodies, wooden and swollen, tumbling and piling into pits.

"Overuse of antibiotics created resistant staph and these bacteria borrowed our own DNA to become hyper-infectious. Epidemics spread through cities in waves of putrid death not imagined since the Black Plague."

Click—

Bodies in burning tenement doorways, tanks, and armored trucks passing through deserted streets.

"Here we had known centuries of peace like none before, and we rewarded this good fortune by reproducing at record levels, consuming the planet. And soon, scarcity of resources led us back to our barbaric roots. But this time with better weapons. And this is why I agreed to oversee Holocene II."

I look at the screen, the bodies, the desolation.

"But I thought we were a biological research center?"

"We were," he says. "We are."

"So how are we connected to the War? And how are you here after all these years? And why is there no ice up here?"

"That's what I'm getting at, young man," he says, his voice irritated in the dark beside me. "Try to show some patience."

"Of course. Go on, please."

"First, I'm a pacifist, Aubrey. You must know this. I'm a scientist, a lover of nature, and my entire life has always been about working to improve the planet and our life on it. And that is why I agreed to do the research I did in Holocene II. We believed the overpopulation problem was really a health and education problem. We believed that an educated and healthy society would lead to lower birth rates and manageable resource practices. And in my innocence, I imagined a perfect world where humans lived to be a thousand, where populations were stable and small—a utopia where a man's wisdom could grow for a millennium before passing the torch to a new generation. I believed in a world of peace. But while we were doing our work in Holocene II, the world was anything but peaceful. We sucked the Earth dry of its oil reserves and built nuclear power plants at record levels in spite of the risks."

"But we solved the energy problem," I say. "At least that's what I learned. Don't our wave generators produce unlimited power from electromagnetic fields?"

"Yes, they do," he says, his shadow nodding. "But when corporate scientists discovered that technology, the rich few who controlled it withheld the energy supply to create demand, to keep prices up, to keep profits up. The entire world could have enjoyed free energy were it not for greed. Always greed. And so nothing was solved."

Click—

A coastline covered in black oil.

Click—

An abandoned nuclear plant, its reactors cracked open and sinking into the barren and polluted ground.

Click—

Crowds of protestors encircling Washington D.C., their faces masked, their fists raised.

"Then the real trouble began," he says. "The governments of other countries, nuclear countries, began to be overthrown by their people. Pakistan, then India. Russia, and even China, too. There was no way to keep up relations. No agreements remaining, no understanding that nuclear arms were off the table, no concern for mutually assured destruction. These young rebel governments began flexing their power. They used the threat of nuclear strikes to demand money and resources from countries that had them. They extorted us. Every day our government and its remaining allies were gambling with destruction, and the planet was being raped in the process."

"So what did you do?"

"Well, it became clear to me that I could never share our

longevity breakthroughs with anyone. We knew the rich would hoard it and sell it. And even worse, we knew this one percent that pulled the puppet strings of government would have a thousand years to grow more powerful, more connected. And they would never allow an educated and healthy population to exist. They wouldn't allow it because they maintained their power with instability and inequality."

"Didn't people check on what you were doing?"

"No. Our government partners were occupied elsewhere. They were occupied with the War."

He clicks the remote again and a slideshow of horrific images flashes across the screen—

War and destruction.

Whole cities rendered into twisted craters of rubble.

Skyscrapers collapsed, ships blown out of the ocean.

And then the mushroom cloud of nuclear destruction.

A satellite image of the Hawaiian Islands. The next image and an entire island is gone beneath a haze of nuclear smoke. Pictures of both devastated U.S. coastlines—Washington, D.C. a charred nuclear wasteland, New York City one big pile of crushed concrete and twisted steel, Los Angeles ripped to shreds and flooded with polluted ocean waters.

And then I remember the missile I saw hanging from that ice-ceiling over that subterranean crater lake I fell into, and I know what Dr. Radcliffe is showing me is real.

He clicks the slideshow off, and the screen retracts into the ceiling. Then the shades lift and the light comes back into the room, cutting across Dr. Radcliffe where he sits solemn in his chair, cutting across our iced teas sitting on their coasters with melted ice and sweating glasses, cutting across where I sit and cutting up my body. Then the light comes on into my eyes.

"What happened next?" I ask.

He stands and walks to the window and looks out.

"Everything was destroyed," he says. "Bases, cities, towns. There were many more missiles than anyone had imagined. Even our own government was bombed out of its bunkers. Seems nearly the only thing untouched was Holocene II."

"Why weren't we bombed?"

He turns to face me again.

"We were too new, too secret. Plus, our mission wasn't strictly military so we never made it onto any target maps. We sat there forgotten, living in our self-contained city five kilometers under New Mexico's bedrock."

He sits again, crossing his legs and sighing.

"We tried, Aubrey. You have to know we tried. Everything we sent up to sample the surface told us it was uninhabitable. Radiation, disease, pollution. A nuclear winter dropped like a deadly curtain and the few remaining peoples suffered a terrible demise. Our resources were limited, our space confined. We didn't know what to do. But it was clear that we would soon outgrow our own underground home. Then I had an idea. I had been working on virtual reality environments for the brain, and it occurred to me that rather than suffering a lifetime underground, people need only work their productive years and then we could deliver them into a virtual heaven and keep their consciousness alive for ever, even longer than if I kept their bodies alive with the medical discoveries we had made."

"Eden?" I ask.

"Eden," he nods. "The few of us on Level 1 created Eden. And so Holocene II as you know it was born. One level cut off from the next and everyone supporting the cause."

"But I thought you were the first to go to Eden? You even said it yourself in the video they show us."

He lowers his head.

"It's the one thing I'm really ashamed of. But I had to disappear or the others would have questioned my never aging and all would have been lost. Sometimes the ends do justify the means, Aubrey. This was just one of those times."

"But I still don't understand," I say. "I get all of this, but here we are on the surface, in the world. There is no ice. There is no radiation. Why can't we live up here now?"

And then I remember the moral dilemma question on my test. The very last question that I blindly answered with a stab of my finger. And it hits me why I'm here. Why I was chosen. Not just for my test score, but because I must have answered that I would keep the infected level locked to their fate to prevent the spread of a virus that could wipe out our species.

"Do we have a virus in Holocene II?" I say. "Something that will infect the planet? Oh, no! Did I bring something up with me when that train crashed? Please tell me I didn't."

"You're half right there," he says, blinking and leaning forward to rest his hands on his knees. "What I'm about to tell you may be a shock at first."

I lean forward to listen. "Tell me."

"Eventually, we discovered the ice retreating, the radiation fading, and it was safe for us to investigate the surface. What we found surprised us. With no humans on the planet—or almost no humans, anyway—the Earth had begun to heal itself. Species we thought to be extinct had returned. Endangered species were flourishing. We discovered paradise in the making.

A real Eden right here on the planet. Then we found humans. Small nomadic groups of them. Primitive. Violent. Descendants of survivors on the surface. And they were beginning it all again. Starting everything over. Rummaging through the rubble of cities, discovering their grandparents' technology, developing weapons. Fighting one another. Slaughtering species wholesale for food and for fun. Breeding. Multiplying again unchecked."

"But did they have a virus or something?" I cut him off. "Some infectious disease that put life on the planet at risk?"

"I thought you'd have figured it out by now," he says, blinking and shaking his head.

"Figured out what?"

"We don't just carry an infection, Aubrey—we are the infection. Humans are the virus. We're parasites."

"What? Parasites?"

"Yes, the worst parasites. We reproduce with no internal limitations. We consume and destroy and make war. We have no predator except ourselves, and left unchecked we destroy ourselves every time. And we destroy the planet along with us. Humankind is the thing that must be contained. Man must be checked. We were nature's mistake—the only species worth extinction is our very own."

"You're the Park Service?" I ask, my voice cracking, my legs shaking in the chair. "You're the ones who slaughtered my friend's family in that cove?"

"I know nothing about that," he says, blinking three times before his face falls into an almost believable look of sadness. "We made a choice long ago."

"What choice?"

"The only choice."

"What choice?" I shout.

"We dedicated all of North America as National Park and we swore to protect it. And we must protect it, Aubrey."

"Your plan is to exterminate all humankind?" I say, my voice sounding suddenly small and far away.

"Our plan is to prevent another apocalypse. To let the Earth exist as it was meant to exist. To let some better species evolve. And the plan is working. But not fast enough."

I shake my head, confused.

"What about Holocene II?"

"We kept it for its production capacity, of course."

"You mean those drones we make?"

"And food, and supplies. And now you."

"Why me? Why am I here?"

"I'm dying, Aubrey. My wife is dying. We're all dying. There is a limit to our longevity, and we're all reaching it fast. We had hoped to accomplish our mission in one lifetime. To wipe out the human race and then, at last, ourselves with it. But we've failed. It's taken longer than we thought it would—the human disease has proved a resilient one. Luckily, we had frozen Catherine's eggs and my sperm and we were able to use a surrogate to have Hannah. Our lovely daughter Hannah. And now Hannah is ready for a mate, a partner to continue the mission after we're gone. And that mate is you, Aubrey. You're the chosen one. Your DNA is a perfect match. Our models say it will combine with Hannah's in all the best ways."

"You want me to have kids with Hannah?"

"Yes. Don't you see—you and Hannah and your children will finish the work we've started here."

"Why are you telling me all this?"

"Because I need to know if you're on board. There's not much time, Aubrey. We thought you were lost for good, dead in the park, and we've already begun harvesting donor sperm from lesser candidates down in Holocene II. Of course, having you here is so much better than that."

I sit reeling in the chair—sweating, sick. The study spins, my head throbs. The clock ticks the loud seconds by. The ice tea glasses stand before me in agate pools of sweat dripping from their sides, the golden liquid catching the light like some foreign elixir of a world too contrary even to fully imagine.

A tap on the door, it opens. Mrs. Radcliffe looks in.

"Lunch is ready, you two."

"We'll be taking it to go," Dr. Radcliffe says.

"To go where?"

"I plan to show Aubrey here the Park."

"Oh, sweet Cosmos," she says, as if cursing or calling on some higher power. "Hasn't he had enough of your lecturing by now? I'm sure he's just exhausted."

I sit and watch their banter volley across the room as if I'm not really here. Perhaps I'm still in a theatre watching the drama unfold onscreen, or maybe reading it in some lesson slate play.

"Aubrey . . ."

"Huh? What?"

"Are you allergic to anything?

"Allergic?"

"Food?" she says. "Allergic to any foods?"

"He's fine," Dr. Radcliffe says. "He's a healthy boy."

"Growing fast as a weed, too, I'll bet," she says. "I'll have Gloria pack him double sandwiches then and bring them out."

She retreats from the room and closes the door.

Dr. Radcliffe reaches forward, picks up his tea, and drains it in one gulp. Then he stands and holds out his hand.

"Come with me, Aubrey," he says, his blue eyes blinking. "I'd like to show you the world you will inherit."

CHAPTER 26
The Foundation

I push his hand away.

Rush from the study.

Burst from the house.

A windstorm has risen on the lake, whitecaps chopping its surface, pounding the shore. The world seems different. Alien. Violent in its apathy. I want to scream. I want to run. I want to hide away somewhere and die. I feel sicker than sick, my guts twisted up in some evil fist of knowledge that won't release me from its guilty grip. Jimmy was right—we didn't know who these people were.

I feel a hand on my shoulder and turn—

Hannah stands beside me.

"What's wrong?"

"What's wrong?" I ask, mocking her. "Your father. You. This place. It's all wrong.

"Why would you say that?"

"You're the Park Service. You butchered Jimmy's family."

"I don't know what you're talking about," she exclaims.

"Ships. Drones. The Park Service. They came in while they were hunting whales and murdered everyone. Even the kids in the cove. They almost killed Jimmy, too. Don't you get it?

Hannah reaches for my hand. I pull it away.

"I'm sorry," she says. "I really am."

"I had to collect the bodies, Hannah. I had to burn them.

Have you ever smelled a burning body?"

"Please, just hear me out," she pleads. "I promise you that I knew nothing about this. But I do know my father, and he's a gentle man. He wouldn't have anything to do with murdering people. Besides, you can't do any good without knowing what the situation is, right? Let's just go along and see for ourselves."

I look at her emerald eyes sparkling in the stormy light, her red hair tossing in the breeze, a hint of freckles on her cheeks.

"Go along where?"

"To tour the park," she says. "Daddy's taking us on tour."

"Oh, that's just cute. A tour."

"Come on. I've never left the lake house, and today we get to go and see the world. Don't spoil it for me, Aubrey. Please. Don't you want to see it, too?"

I look toward the dock where the waiting boat rolls in the waves, the metal step plate screeching as it loses its magnetic connection and grates across the wood. Dr. Radcliffe stands looking at us from the wheel, his coat flapping wildly, a streak of white appearing on his shadowed face when he smiles.

I cross my arms and plant my feet.

"I want nothing to do with the Park Service."

"But how will we ever know?" she asks. "Let's just go and see. This will all be ours someday soon anyway. We can change it then if we want to. Besides, what good can you do out there in the woods on your own? You can starve. You can die."

She's right. There's nothing I can do out there. Jimmy and I were beat and starving when we stumbled on the lake house. Maybe I should just pretend to go along until I've heard them out, seen what there is to see.

"Fine," I say. "I'll go. But just to see."

Hannah smiles. Without giving me a second to change my mind, she grasps my hand and leads me to the boat.

Her mother runs from the house, holding a hat on her head and carrying lunches wrapped in cloth with her free hand.

"Are you coming, Mom?" Hannah asks.

"Not this time, sweetie," she says, handing us the lunches. "I'm tired and need to rest. I'll see you when you get back."

The boat pulls away before the step plate can even fully retract, and I look back and see Hannah's mother standing on the dock looking after us, holding her blowing hat, a strange look of resolved sadness giving her the appearance of Hannah's forlorn reflection cast in shadows and retreating into the past.

Dr. Radcliffe adjusts the throttles and steers our course. Hannah and I sit on the bench behind him. She takes my hand in hers and puts it in her lap, and I let her even though I find small comfort in the gesture. The wind intensifies and the boat drives against it, my breath pushed into my lungs, my eyes watering. Dark clouds fly in with the wind and suck the color from the world, turning the water a lifeless gray. Even Hannah's hair whipping about in the wind seems less red and more rust. As the boat battles the wind in its endless crossing, the lake house disappears behind us, the snowcapped peaks lining the far shore grow closer, and I feel like I'm on some underworld ferry delivering me to my punishment for some unforgivable sin I've committed, or perhaps for just the sin of being born.

The wind stops at once, and Hannah releases my hand.

I look back and see a strange visible line we crossed, where one side is gray and rippled with whitecaps and the other is as smooth as blue glass, like some border crossing with invisible guards blowing hell from their lungs.

"This is so exciting," Hannah says.

"What?" I say. "You've never been on the boat?"

"Of course," she says, "but only on cruises around the lake. We're going down. I've never been down."

Dr. Radcliffe looks back at us and grins like a tour guide, steering the boat toward a towering concrete dam stretching between two mountain peaks in front of us. On one side of the dam, the steel doors of a giant mitre gate stand open like jaws, and we cruise through them into an enclosed chamber. The gates grind against the pressure of the water behind us and the daylight fades to just a sliver. Then the doors snap shut, leaving us floating in total darkness.

Hannah takes my hand again.

LED lights blink on and the chamber is lit with an eerie glow that reflects off the oil-black water and shimmers against the gray concrete walls. The water level begins to lower, being sucked away somewhere deep beneath us. The boat sinks into the chamber locks, and the LED lights shrink above in the receding ceiling. We drop twenty, fifty, a hundred meters. Then we drop more, descending until all around us is murky black. I can just see the outline of Dr. Radcliffe's shadow sitting in the captain's chair ahead of us, as if he's piloting some boat-sized casket down into a watery concrete tomb.

A great sucking sound rises from the far concrete wall and the water begins to turn in a boil there. Then the crescent of an arch appears and grows as we drop until a tall set of steel doors are exposed. The water levels off, the doors swing open, and a cryptic underground channel of water stretches away in the dim glow of more LED lights. The boat's silent engines engage with a slight jerk beneath my feet, and we glide into the channel.

I watch the tunnel walls slide by for what seems like hours because there's nothing here in the gray underworld to mark the passage of time. The LED ceiling lights pass over us in a hypnotic pulsing of light and shadow, light and shadow, and I watch Dr. Radcliffe's image fade in and out ahead of us as if he were being passed over again and again by some searchlight.

Now a red light appears in the distance, as if some sleeping cyclops crustacean burrowed here beneath the mountain lake has sensed our approach and opened its evil eye. The red light grows closer; the end of the tunnel comes into view. The boat cruises into a cavernous underground shipyard bay. Ceilings draped in shadow, inky water eerily still. Silhouettes of waiting cranes hovering over deserted docks. The cold glint of steel. A submarine moored in a maintenance berth, the Foundation Valknut crest etched on its exposed side.

"Ouch," Hannah says, "you're hurting me."

I realize I'm squeezing Hannah's hand without meaning to. She winces with pain and pulls it away.

Dr. Radcliffe guides the boat to a berth, the magnetic step plate folds out. Then he steps onto the dock and turns to help us from the boat. Hannah takes his hand. I refuse it.

"Welcome to the Foundation," he says.

The red light casts the cavern bay in an eerie illumination, playing shadows on Dr. Radcliffe's face, as if some hellish fire were burning deep beneath the ink-black surface of the water

"This is gloomy," Hannah says. "You and Mom spend all that time away down here?"

"No, no," Dr. Radcliffe answers with a chuckle and his trademark blink. "This is our office, so to speak. We work here, but much of the time we're out touring the park."

"What is this place?" I ask.

"You know it as Level 1," he says.

"But this is nowhere near Holocene II."

"You're quite correct, of course. This was an underground military installation we discovered after coming to the surface. For some reason it was left intact."

"So we're beneath the lake right now?" I ask.

He nods. "The lake is three hundred meters above us. The dam allows us to flood the locks and pass small boats between here and the surface of the lake."

"How did that submarine get in here?"

He points to a taller archway on the other side of the bay.

"That tunnel leads in a series of step locks all the way to the Pacific. Most of our vessels are out working, of course, but they cycle home for maintenance."

"Yeah, right," I huff. "*Working*."

"What about the other coast, Daddy?"

"Great question, Hannah. We have plans for an Atlantic tunnel, but the distance has proven difficult, even for nuclear borers. Right now, we go around using a deep-water channel where the Panama Canal once was. It does leave us weaker in the eastern seas, though."

"Where does the train come up?" I ask.

"Follow me," he says. "I'll give you the nickel tour."

"The what tour?" Hannah asks.

"Oh, just a silly saying from when people used money."

He leads us from the docks onto the shore where several metal buildings stand, their alloy walls reflecting back the red light that seems to come from everywhere and nowhere in this dungeon place. Stopping at a door, he punches a code into a keypad and the door slides open.

"This is our sintering plant."

"What's sintering, Daddy?" Hannah asks.

"Well, the long name is atomic diffusion manufacturing. It's how we produce what we need without having complex assembly lines or scaled economies. You would have seen these on Level 4, Aubrey, if you'd gone down instead of up."

We pass through the door into a wide hall of bright-white light. Dr. Radcliffe leads us to a glass window and stops. Inside, a series of robotic arms move in precise and mindless jerks, guiding laser beams down to nozzles spraying bursts of metal powder. As they work, gleaming titanium cylinders grow like tall mushrooms on platforms.

"What are they making?"

He points to an LCD display.

Revolving there against a black-grid background is a virtual three-dimensional rendering of a small silver missile.

I look back through the glass as the missiles take shape on their platforms. When they're complete, the machines pause to cool them with bursts of nitrogen, and then the platforms open and the missiles drop onto a conveyor belt to be carried away. The lasers begin again and more missiles sprout from the alloy.

"Can't they make other things?" Hannah asks.

"Oh, yes," he says. "Anything you can dream up and draft into the computer. And not just alloys either, but plastics too. We have much larger machines down on Level 4, of course."

"I've seen enough of this," I say.

"Let's carry on then, shall we?"

He leads us away from the window and down the hall and

through a door into another room. This room is dim and cool with fans whirring in the ceiling and black tables illuminated by hanging spotlights. Stacked on the tables, garish and gleaming, an array of newly minted munitions casings wait to be loaded. Behind the tables, against the wall, I spot canisters marked with chemical names, some of which I recognize from lessons:

POTASSIUM PERMANGANATE

AMMONIUM PERCHLORATE COMPOSITE

MAGNESIUM POWDER

MERCURY NITRIDE

TETRAZINE

Against the farthest wall stands an indestructible black box riddled with rivets and hinges and small windows glowing blue. Red lettering on its side reads—ANTIMATTER.

We cross the room in silence, our footsteps echoing loudly on the concrete floor. I don't realize I'm holding my breath until we exit outside into the cavern again, back in the low red glow, standing in an open-air courtyard looking at a hologram starscape hanging above a bubbling fountain. The courtyard is surrounded by upper floors of doors covered in scaffolding.

"These are our living quarters," Dr. Radcliffe says. "As you can see, we're doing a little maintenance."

We cross the courtyard and exit beneath an archway onto a pathway leading to a footbridge over a sunken channel of train tracks. The tracks arrive from a tunnel with a closed iron door and pass beneath the bridge to a terminal. And there, next to the terminal, beneath me on the bridge, is the source of the red glow: a circular building sunken into the carven floor, its dome ceiling opaque and throbbing with deep-red light. An LCD sign above the door reads WELCOME TO EDEN.

"That's Eden?" I ask. "Under that dome?"

"Yes," Dr. Radcliffe says. "This is where we would have received you had the train not been crushed in that rockslide. And had you made it here, we could have prepared you more slowly for your new role and the shock of seeing the surface."

"Why was the train on the surface anyway?"

"Well, even though we're below the lake here, this is still quite an elevation, and there's a nasty fault line to skirt in the pass. I'm hoping to find a workaround. Maybe you can help."

I look down at the train dock at Eden, an offshoot channel obviously designed to receive a car of retirees in a narrow corral with a small platform leading only to the metal door.

"Can we see it?"

"See what? The fault line?"

"No. Eden."

"Let's save Eden for another time," he says, turning away. "Right now I want to show you both the world."

Hannah steals a look at me and smiles. Her face is the only thing that seems alive in the red pulsing light rising up from the dome of Eden. I wish I were as excited as she is. I follow along, reminding myself I'm just going to gather information.

We move from the bridge onto a tarmac surface, walk past another row of metal buildings, and pass through one of several open hangar doors carved into the cavern's far wall.

The tall, curved ceiling is lit with the familiar LED floods, and lined up on the polished hangar floor is a fleet of gleaming PZ-51 Ranger drones. At the far hangar wall, a steel door sits open, revealing an upward sloping runway disappearing into the cavern wall. A drone taxis toward it and stops. An old man with an electronic clipboard steps up and inspects the drone, circling it slowly, touching the missile batteries hanging from its wings, and checking them against his clipboard. He's the first person we've seen down here. When he's finished counting the warheads, he steps back and gives a thumbs up toward the mirrored glass of an elevated office overlooking the hangar. The drone noses silently forward, its front wheel sinking into the runway channel and locking into an electromagnetic shuttle. I recognize the catapult launch system from an engineering lesson plan. There's a moment of silence followed by a steadily building whine and then a loud click as the drone disappears in a flash of gray up the runway shaft, a sucking sound filling the vacuum of its exit. It's there and then it isn't.

The man with the clipboard turns to us. He looks old and tired, wrinkles around his mouth, bags beneath his eyes. But I guess everyone down here would be old. Really old.

"This the kid?" he says, waving his clipboard at me.

"The very one," Dr. Radcliffe says.

"Nice to meet you," he says. "I'm Dr. Taft."

I shake his hand but say nothing.

"Chatty fellow, aren't you? Just call me Taft. And aren't you a lucky lad being called up into the arms of this beauty? This must be your lovely Hannah, Robert." He takes Hannah's hand, raises it to his whiskery lips, and kisses it. "I can't believe you've kept her from us all these years. You look exactly like your mother, young lady. And that's a fine compliment."

Hannah pulls her hand back and rubs it, blushing.

"Your sightseer's all set and ready to go," he says, turning to Dr. Radcliffe. "Flight plan's programmed just as you asked."

He waves his clipboard at the mirrored glass and another drone moves forward from the fleet and taxis to the runway opening. This drone is smaller, carries less munitions, and has a glass observation bubble hanging suspended from its belly with several seats for passengers. A door opens, steps fold out.

I cross my arms.

"You expect me to get in that thing?"

Dr. Taft looks at Dr. Radcliffe, Dr. Radcliffe shrugs.

"It looks exciting," Hannah says.

"It looks unsafe."

"Nothing to be afraid of," Dr. Radcliffe says, stepping up into the drone.

"Who said I was afraid? I'm not afraid."

We climb the steps, duck into the body, and descend again into the glass observation bubble. I buckle into my seat and look out at Dr. Taft. He laughs and says something but there's no sound audible through the thick glass. Then he waves his clipboard toward the mirrored window again and the drone moves forward. I feel the front drop as the wheel locks into the launch shuttle.

Dr. Radcliffe crosses his arms in front of his chest, leans back in the seat, and says, "Hold on, kids."

Without warning, the drone rockets forward and slams me into the seat and we race up through a blur of black tunnel—

Up, up, up, and then we shoot free from the side of the mountain and launch weightless into the big blue sky.

CHAPTER 27
Touring the Park

At first, I panic.

Hanging in open space, the glass observation bubble our only protection, my muscles tense, anticipating a fatal fall. Then, deciding to trust the seat, I relax and watch the world spread out beneath us, seeing how truly large the lake is. It sits cupped between the mountains like an upheld sea, twisting around into hidden fjords not visible from the shore.

"Look," Hannah says, pointing.

The lake house is a tiny speck beneath us, the peninsula fading to a sliver as we climb. The drone turns east and blazes across the mountains, passing over snowy peaks until they give way to arid mountain ranges that roll down into desert plains. The drone dives, plunging toward ground, and I instinctively pull my feet off the floor as if to brace for a crash that would vaporize all of us anyway, but the drone levels out and jets across the desert only a few hundred meters above the sand.

The desert goes on for minutes, and kilometers cruise pass fast as I watch the bright sun directly overhead cast our shadow like a giant bird racing beneath us on the surface of the sand, the winged shadow growing and shrinking as we pass over high dunes and the low valleys between them. The sands eventually thin, revealing tufts of dry grass and lone trees standing like lunar sentinels in the moonscape land. Then the desert floor falls away and we dive into a wide red-rock canyon flying over domes and hoodoos and ruddy reefs of rock connected by long spans of weather-carved bridges high above deep river narrows zigzagging on the canyon floor.

Hannah takes my hand in hers and squeezes it.

"Wow," she says. "It's so amazing."

Dr. Radcliffe inspects our faces, seemingly more interested in seeing our reaction to the landscape than he is in seeing the landscape itself. But then if he really is nine hundred years old, he's seen it all plenty of times before I'm sure.

The canyon rises to a tableland plateau, the plateau drops to prairie, and we race so close to the surface that we drive out herds of grazing buffalo and set them thundering off across the plains in front of us, kicking up great clouds of dust as we pass. Amazed, I look back and see thousands of them charging after us, tossing their shaggy-horned heads, wrestling invisible reins.

"Majestic, aren't they?" Dr. Radcliffe says, watching me look. "Hard to believe they used to slaughter them for pelts and leave the naked carcasses to bloat and rot in the sun."

"I don't believe it," Hannah says. "Who could kill them like that? And who would waste the whole animal?"

"We did, dear," he whispers. "We did."

The drone flies smooth and silent, propelled by its electric engines, and from my quiet seat inside the protected bubble it almost seems as though I'm watching some 3D theme park ride of a wild and long lost America. But it's real, and I'm seeing it with my own eyes.

The drone accelerates now, and the vistas pass by so fast that only snapshots of things appear and then disappear kilometers behind us in a flash. Shallow lakes littered with white cranes frozen on one foot, all head-cocked as if listening to us pass overhead. Golden fields stretching in every direction with invisible winds seething across the headed grass. Trees appear and grow thicker. As we blaze by a swath of yellow-leaf forest, a million starlings rise before our drone and swell in a massive murmuration blacking the sun. Several soft thuds knock against the viewing-bubble glass, and we bust through them, leaving a blue hole bored through the flock. I turn and watch as the sky-lit tunnel swells slowly closed behind us.

Now we climb from the valleys, nose up, ascending a mountain where patches of snow shine like frosty jewels in the shadowed crags. Then we cut through a ceiling of cloud and when it clears, the world is winter white before us all around, and we follow the line of a snow-covered ridge.

Hannah grasps my arm. "Look!" she says, pointing.

Puffs of pure powder rise from the steep slope, stirred by the prancing hooves of mountain goats thrusting in a single-file line through deep drifts of snow and cresting the ridge to walk in a long row on its back. Their shaggy white coats and long bearded faces give them the appearance of ancient men bent to the ridgeline, climbing to some high house of worship.

As the drone climbs above the mountains, Hannah opens her cloth-wrapped lunch, and I realize that I haven't eaten all day. By the look of the sun, it must be early afternoon already. Without taking our eyes off the passing terrain, we sip fruit juice and eat cute veggie sandwiches with their crusts cut off. I even find a package of algaecrisps from Holocene II.

The drone clears the mountain range and turns northeast and cruises to lower altitudes where the sun drops behind us and lights the northern Midwest wetlands in a golden glow. We drop lower and parkland forests of spruce and alder rise into view. I notice patches of small brown hills moving on the wetland plains. I lean forward and look closer. I see brown fur, high haunches, head-bent and moving slow, grazing. When one swings its massive head to track us as we pass, I see the giant curved tusks and the lolling trunk.

"Are those mastodons?" I say, pointing.

"Holy moly," Hannah says.

"Woolly mammoths," Dr. Radcliffe says, a level of pride in his voice. "They're one of my proudest achievements. Brought them back from complete extinction with a five-thousand-year-old tooth. I'd bring back mastodons too, but so far a suitable DNA sample has eluded us. Maybe you two will do it."

It's hard for me to believe we just passed a heard of wooly mammoth. I remember reading about them in my lesson plans, about how modern man hunted them to extinction when the glaciers of North America retreated. But here they are—real wooly mammoths, walking the Earth and grazing on American grass as if they'd never left, as if we'd never arrived.

"See there?" Dr. Radcliffe says, indicating massive rivers of ice twisting through northern valleys. "The great lakes."

"They look like glaciers, Dad."

"So they are, sweetie. So they are. Now that humankind isn't pumping all that carbon into the atmosphere, the long overdue glacial period can return to do its work."

We bank southeast, flying over hills set afire with turning leaves, and Hannah points out a row of glassy alpine lakes. I point out a green river valley and ridges of rock that rise from the treeline like humps of landlocked whales. After a while, Dr. Radcliffe points our attention to a wide, white-water falls dropping in stages and narrowing into a river that snakes away and widens into a tideland estuary of a distant bay.

"That's the Potomac," he says.

"The Potomac?"

"Washington, D.C.—that was our country's capital."

Hannah and I lean forward and search the river banks, but no sign of any monument or building remains.

"Was it all destroyed in the War?"

"Much of it," Dr. Radcliffe says. "But we've been hard at work razing the ruins and returning things to their natural state. New York was the most difficult, as you might imagine, but you'd be surprised how much help we had from rising seas and earthquakes. It was as if we'd held some great force of nature at bay. Something patient. Some force deep inside the Earth that rose to sweep away our history the minute we were gone and no longer carving up her surface. Or almost gone, anyway."

We recline in our seats and look over the passing world, each of us silent with our own thoughts.

The drone climbs.

Turns south.

Accelerates.

We move so fast, I watch the coastline slide by beneath us, cutting the blue water into jagged inlets, bays and saltwater lagoons that glimmer for kilometers beneath the waving heads of palm trees quickly disappearing behind us. Rocky bluffs, sandy beaches. Great reefs reaching out like pink fingers disappearing at the dark line of some deep ocean shelf. I spot a line of black dashes following the coast south, and I know they're whales. I'm reminded of the horror in that cove and the Park Service slaughtering Jimmy's family, but from this distance I can also see the slaughter of that whale and hear its muffled cries as the harpoons pierced its flesh and its blood leaked into the sea.

The drone rises above some turbulence, and I see the horn of land we're following, another sea bordering its other side. I know from my lessons that we're traveling over what used to be the state of Florida. From this height, the white-sand beaches glow in the afternoon sun like bright electrified borders between the green vegetated land and the blue Atlantic Ocean.

The drone drives the land out and then descends over a stretch of island keys dotting south from the Continent like the humps of giant turtles walking out to sea.

The landing gear drops; the drone drops.

A runway appears before us, distorted heat waves rising from its surface. The drone eases in and touches down. Brakes and slows. Taxis now to the end of the runway where it turns in a roundabout and comes to rest facing the way we came.

CHAPTER 28
Stories and Storms

We step out into the humid, tropical air.

The steps retract, the door seals shut, and the drone lowers on its hydraulic landing gear. Dr. Radcliffe places his hands in the small of his back and stretches, and it occurs to me for the first time how very tired he looks. He leads us off the runway down weathered steps toward a white-sand beach where small waves drift in and slide up the shore and hiss as they sift the sand and drain back again.

At the bottom of the steps, just above the beach, a path leads us to a manufactured cabin sunken into the hillside, its covered porch providing unobstructed ocean views. It looks like some time has passed since it's been used. The windows are streaked with salt; a drift of windblown sand is piled in front of the metal door. Dr. Radcliffe lifts a weatherproof cover from a keypad and types in a code. The door locks retract with a click. He opens the door and ducks inside, and we follow.

The cabin is small but comfortably furnished with a main room overlooking the ocean, a small kitchen, a solar bathroom, and two windowless bedrooms in the back.

"What is this place?" I ask.

"It's one of our outposts," Dr. Radcliffe says.

"Is this where you and Mom stay when you tour?"

"One of many," he says. "This is the southernmost border of the Park. The Continent too, for that matter."

"What's out there beyond?"

"It's a big world," he says, looking out the window and sighing. "We'll need to have that talk another time. Right now, I'm tired. Why don't you two go out and explore."

"But, Daddy," Hannah says, "the Park Service?"

"This island is a safe zone," he assures her. "The drones overlook it. Other than maybe being bitten by mosquitos, you two have nothing to fear here."

He retreats into a back bedroom and pulls the door closed. Hannah and I kick off our shoes and head outside.

We walk barefoot along the beach, beneath the soft light filtering through shoreline palms and dappling the quiet waves. I take her hand in mine. A hermit crab scuttles along the beach. Bits of pink coral. A white shell.

"Isn't it great?" she says. "It's everything I ever imagined and more. The world, I mean. I read about it, and I dreamt about it, but I never knew it could be so beautiful. Did you ever think it could?"

I smell the salt breeze, feel my toes sink in the warm sand.

"No. I couldn't have imagined it being so . . . real. I read about the world, too. That's all I did was read. But we were five kilometers underground and taught that all this was gone for good."

Hannah stops and turns to face me. Her long lashes catch the light like threads of fire gold that flicker when she blinks, and she looks at me with the most intensity I've ever known.

"You do want to protect it, don't you, Aubrey?"

"Yes. I do," I say. "It's too beautiful not to."

"Oh, good," she sighs. "I knew you would."

"But we'll have to figure out a better way. Some way that

works without killing people."

"Do you like people, Aubrey?"

"I like you."

Her lips curl in a smile. She lifts onto her toes and kisses me. Her mouth is soft, her tongue warm. I reach to pull her closer, but she breaks away and jogs down the beach laughing, her red hair bouncing in the breeze, her feet kicking up white sand. I chase after her. She's fast. The sand slows me down, but I've grown strong since I've been above ground and I pump my legs and take long strides and just as I'm about to overtake her, my toe catches a buried stone and I trip and fall on my face and eat a mouthful of sand. I sit, rubbing my toe and spitting sand. Hannah stands over me laughing. I grab her wrist and pull her down and we wrestle on the beach. We roll into a wave and she screams from the sudden chill of the water. I laugh, she punches my shoulder. We crawl higher on the beach together, away from the waves, and we lie there side by side looking up at the blue sky and listening to the surf.

I remember the electric beach down in Holocene II and all my Sundays there dreaming of the real ocean, wishing I lived in another time, in another life. And here I am living another life. And not just any other life, either—a life beyond any life I dared to ever dream . . .

We walk back to the cabin in the magic glow of twilight, the tall palms leaning shadowed against a purple sky, the white luminescent sand warm beneath my feet, the ocean breeze cool on my cheek. I look over my shoulder at the impressions our feet leave in the sand, side by side footprints like invisible lovers forever walking on the deserted beaches of time. A high wave rolls dark up the shore and slides back again, wiping the sand clean and sweeping the invisible lovers out to sea.

When we reach the cabin, Dr. Radcliffe is sitting on the porch in a folding lounge chair with two empty chairs beside him. A candle flickers in a star-stamped lantern, casting a tiny constellation on the deck at our feet.

"Nice night for a walk,' he says, almost to himself.

Hannah bends down and kisses her father on the forehead and then she drapes herself into the seat next to him. I sit too.

"Rain's coming," he says.

"Rain?" Hannah says.

"Probably some thunder with it."

"How can you tell?" I ask.

"I can smell it," he says. "That, and it comes almost every night this time of year."

"You come here a lot?"

He nods, gazing out to sea. We sit listening to the waves until the light fades and only the candle stars and the white sand and the broken tumble of the surf are visible in the night.

"I met your mother here," he says, out of nowhere.

"You always told me you met at work," Hannah says.

"We were here working," he says. "Well, sort of working. Officially, we were here for a company retreat—celebrating our first patent for an injectable liquid computer. Unofficially, those of us on the board were celebrating our partnership with the government to take over the labs at Holocene II. We were a big company. I hadn't met your mother, but I'd seen her. Hard to miss that red hair. She was gorgeous. Well, she still is . . ."

His story trails off, his mind apparently drifting elsewhere, and he stretches his feet and rubs them together as he stares at the black ocean as though he were expecting a ship to return.

Hannah tugs his sleeve. "Tell us how you met, Dad."

"It was a Sunday afternoon. Everyone was getting liquored up with the tourists on margaritas in the pub."

"Margaritas?"

"It's a nasty tequila drink. I excused myself and went for a walk to see a very famous writer's house they had turned into a museum. The museum was closed, and all I got to see through the gates were fifty cats lying on the porch. As soon as I hit the main street again, a crack of thunder lit the sky and the rain came down as if the whole ocean had been carried into the air and dropped. I ducked into a creamery to stay dry."

"A creamery?"

"An ice cream shop, dear. Thirty seconds later, your mom stepped in, dripping. We looked at one another standing there soaked as two seals, but neither of us said a word. We just watched the rain. And boy, did it rain. Water rose in the streets, flooded the sidewalks. It poured halfway into the creamery, forcing us both together at the far wall. A stray dog came in and joined us. Shook us both wet, I remember. A rooster, too."

"Are there still roosters here, Daddy?"

"No, they were domestic animals mostly. Twenty-some billion had to be exterminated. There are red junglefowl here, though, and if you see one you'll swear it's a rooster like you've read about. That's where they came from anyway."

"Okay, back to you and Mom . . ."

"We stood in the creamery marooned on a little dry patch in the back. The rooster watching the dog, the dog watching me, and me watching your mom. I was starstruck, lost in her stormy red hair as she stared out into the rain. I asked the kid behind the counter how long it usually kept up like it was. He just shrugged and said it was hurricane season in Florida, as if that were all the answer my question deserved. The rain kept coming and I kept staring at your mom. Finally, she looked at me with those green eyes. I was struck dumb and said the stupidest thing I could have said."

"Oh, no," Hannah cuts in. "What'd you say, Dad?"

"Can I buy you an ice cream?"

"That's not bad. It's kinda cute."

"You think so?"

"Yeah. What'd she say?"

"She smiled at me and said: 'I thought you'd never ask.'"

"Why haven't you told me that story before, Dad? It's so absolutely romantic."

"Romance makes me shy," he says, shrugging. "Or maybe because I don't like to think about the way things were before. About all those poor people who used to live here. There was much worse than rain coming and they had no idea."

"What do you mean by much worse?" I ask.

"The War," he says. "The dark years of the War."

I wait, hoping he'll say more, but he doesn't. He just sits there rubbing his feet together and staring out into the dark.

Soon, a drop of rain slaps against the metal roof above the porch. Another drop. Then, as if those lone two raindrops had given us fair warning, the rain dumps down. It slams against the roof and rushes off the edges in a shower onto the beach. It falls in massive drops, dimpling the sand. Waves wash up and smooth the sand clear, and the rain pounds the dimples back again. The candle flickers wildly in its stamped lantern and the stars dance on the slats of the porch.

Dr. Radcliffe stands and lifts the lantern and blows out the candle. He opens the door and holds it for us and then follows us in and closes it, sealing the storm outside in the night.

After we eat a sad supper of dried fruits and algaecrisps, Dr. Radcliffe folds the sofa out for himself, telling Hannah and me to take the beds. We share a longing glance behind his back and then Hannah shrugs and disappears into her bedroom.

My room is small, and when I crawl beneath the covers and click off the LED light, it's completely dark and completely silent. Sealed inside the pod, wedged inside the hill, you'd never know there was a tempest raging just outside.

I open my eyes, close them, open them again. I can see no difference in the total black of the room and the total black of my mind. I drift off into a dream—

I dream that I'm back underground, that I wake in my old bed and look out the window over a deserted Level 3. Dark and empty, the blue benitoite glowing in the cavern roof. I rush from our living quarters and race through the empty square to the elevators just as the door is closing on my father inside. Dropping to my knees, I scream, but my voice is swallowed by five kilometers of rock overhead.

Sometime in the night, she crawls into bed with me.

Her body presses into mine, her mouth searches out my mouth, her hands search out my hands, moving them to her, and we lie tangled beneath the sheets—excited, electric, alive.

Then suddenly she's gone.

I hear the door click shut and I'm alone again.

I smell her on my pillow and taste her on my tongue and I drift off into a sweet sleep with no dreams.

In the morning the world is shades of gray. Gray sky, gray surf. The wet sand stretches away like a glistening gray highway littered with the green-ribbed carcasses of palm fronds torn from the trees and blown out to sea and washed ashore.

Dr. Radcliffe seals the pod door and leads us up the steps to the waiting drone. We lift off the gray runway into gray skies, and the drone climbs high and cruises fast on a direct course northwest toward home. When we're above the clouds, he flips a switch and the observation bubble glass tints against the sun.

We say very little to each other.

Midway across the Continent, we enter a thunderstorm. Outside the glass, giant clouds float across angry skies like an army of electric jellies—their ominous interiors pulsing, veins of flashing blue bouncing off one another like blind sky-bound behemoths charged with blue-beating hearts, streaks of rocket lightning striking between them in some strange transfusion of energy tethering them together in the foreboding sky.

As we leave the dark thunderheads sparking in the distance behind us, I see the shadows of two other drones go jetting by below. I wonder where they're off to and why.

Part Four

CHAPTER 29
Days of Rain

The next day it rains.

Hannah and I sit in front of the fire and watch the clouds settle over the lake. We sip tea and tell each other about our lives. We have a lot in common. We both grew up isolated. We both dreamed of finding adventure. And she likes to read as much as I do. After talking with her, it's clear that I wasn't called up here to run things, but rather to help Hannah run things. Well, that and for my sperm, I guess. With the scientists slowly dying off, we'll need to have children if we plan to keep the Foundation staffed.

I ask Hannah why none of the other scientists have kids, and she says they made a pact not to have any. She says they voted and her mom and dad were chosen to freeze samples of his sperm and her eggs, just in case they needed to continue the human race. And she says she's glad because it would suck to never have been born.

"How would you know?" I ask.

"How would I know what?"

"If it would suck to never be born."

"I just know," she says.

"Yeah, but you wouldn't know if you hadn't been born."

"So?"

"So, that's the point. If you wouldn't even know what you were missing, how would it suck?

She shakes her head and says: "Boys."

We sit and sip our tea. After a time, I ask Hannah how she feels about our arranged relationship, about me being selected because of my DNA and a test score, about her having no choice. She tells me she hated the idea, fought with her parents about it. Says she threatened to run away even. Then she tells me she felt relieved when she heard about the train accident and that they thought I was dead.

"Oh, really?" I say, setting my tea cup down loudly on its saucer. "You were happy that I was dead?"

"I didn't say happy," she answers. "I said relieved."

"Same difference."

"No it isn't," she says. "Besides, I didn't even know you."

"Well, what's changed now?"

"It's all changed."

"Why? When?"

"When you stuck your head over that fence."

"Really?"

"Yes, really. The moment that I saw you . . . well, I guess I liked you right away."

"You like me?"

"Yes," she says, giggling. "I guess I do."

"You like me a lot?

She looks down and bites her lip. "Maybe I always have."

"What do you mean?"

"I felt like I'd known you before. In dreams, perhaps."

"You knew me?"

"I knew your face already, I knew your voice."

"Well, I felt the same way about you."

"I know," she says. "I know."

"Well, don't you want me to say it?"

"Say what?"

"Say that I like you a lot, too."

"You don't have to say it."

"What if I want to say it?"

"I won't stop you."

"Fine, I won't say it."

"That's okay, too," she says, sipping her tea.

"I like you a lot," I say.

She smiles. "I know."

The rain falls for days.

Dr. Radcliffe leaves for the Foundation to deal with some pressing issue, and Hannah's mother spends most of her time sleeping in her room. It's clear she's not well. I ask Hannah about her mother's health, but she only says that the fatigue comes and goes and that she'll snap out of it soon.

The house has a basement laboratory and Hannah spends afternoons down there working. White walls, white floor, white lab coat—the only color in the whole place is her red hair.

At first, I hang out and watch over her shoulder as she isolates damaged brain cells on viewing slides and peers at them through microscopes. But I get bored. I get bored and a little bit embarrassed because I don't understand what she's doing.

"What are you doing now?" I ask, watching as she places a slide in the centrifuge and spins it.

"Neuron regeneration," she says.

"I thought neurons didn't regenerate."

"That's the problem," she says. "They regenerate some in the hippocampus, and a few other places, but for some strange reason most neurogenesis stops after we're born."

"Is that a problem?"

"It's a big problem."

"Why?"

"Well, when you've tricked your other cells into dividing perfectly forever, you end up with neurons much older than they're meant to be. It's the one thing we haven't solved."

"Is that why your parents are dying?"

A tear runs down her cheek. She wipes it with the back of her hand and leans over the microscope again.

"Maybe you'd rather go read something?" she mumbles, without looking up. "I'll take a break when this rain stops."

I nod, even though she can't see me, already looking back into her scope, her body still and taut, her hair pulled back and tied. I back from the lab and head upstairs.

As I pass the main room I see Mrs. Radcliffe reclining in a rocker, staring out the window at the lake. I stop in the hall and look at her for a moment. Her hands are folded over a knitted blanket in her lap and her hair spills red around the dark-wood chair. She's watching the rain tease the gray surface of the lake and her gaze is so far away she doesn't even notice me standing just three meters from her. She looks sad. Regretful, maybe. I can't help but see their similarity—her here dying and Hannah down below so desperately trying to stop it.

She looks too thoughtful to disturb, so I continue on.

I walk in the study and the lights fade on, the fire springs to life in the hearth. The wind drives rain against the windows, and through the water-streaked panes I see the trees lashing on the bluff above, like some distant world seen in a blurry dream.

I walk the shelves of books, running my fingers along their aged spines. This must be all that remains. Out of millions of books, these alone survived the War and its aftermath. I can see the writers spread through time, thousands of years, thousands of writers, hunched over keyboards, tapping away at a tapestry of words, and I wonder if any of these writers knew that their thoughts would survive long after they were gone. These are the true immortals. I don't see books. I see doors into other worlds. Windows into minds. The life of man spinning beyond time. This can't all be wrong. It can't be bad.

My fingers stop on an ancient book, the author's name inscribed in gold upon its spine. Melville. Now that's a name. I slide the book out, the spine stiff, the glue cracking as I open the cover. Well, hello. *Moby Dick.*

I carry the book to the chair beside the fire.

Something outside catches my eye. I look up, focusing past the rain to the trees on the bluff. For a moment, I'd swear I see Jimmy standing up there in the wind. But when I look closer, it's just a stump with one dead branch held up in a permanent wave, saying hello, or perhaps saying goodbye.

I open the book and read.

CHAPTER 30
Gloria

A knock on the door.

Must be Hannah.

"Come in."

The door opens, and Gloria steps in with several outfits of clothes, probably from Dr. Radcliffe's closet. She lays them on the foot of the bed and looks me over.

"It's awfully early to be in bed," she says. "Are you sick?"

It's the first time she's spoken to me. Her voice is tenor soft and she reminds me a little of Jimmy's mother.

"I'm taking a nap."

"Long nap," she says. "I haven't seen you out once."

"Is it still raining?" I ask.

"Coming down in sheets," she says.

"I'd be feeling fine if this rain would stop."

She sighs, picks up a shirt from the pile of clothes, unfolds it, and then refolds it again.

"You know," she says, lifting an eyebrow, "sometimes the weather is a reflection of what's going on inside of us."

"You mean I'm making it rain?"

"No," she says, refolding a pair of slacks. "It just means that sometimes the way you feel about the weather has more to do with how you feel than it does with the weather."

I prop myself up on my elbows.

"Can I ask you a question?"

"Sure," she says.

"Have you seen Jimmy?"

She smiles.

"Yes, I see him almost every day. He's been helping out over at our place."

"So he's okay then?"

"He's okay."

Silence now, the clock ticking loudly on the dresser. When she finishes refolding the clothes, I think she might leave, but she picks a shirt off the freshly folded stack, snaps it open, inspects it, and begins to fold it a third time.

"Can I ask you something else?"

"You can ask me anything," she says.

I look away from her and study the covers at my waist.

"Well, what is it?"

"I forgot already. It wasn't anything, really."

"The answer is yes," she says.

"Yes what?"

She sets the shirt on the stack, steps closer, and sits on the edge of the bed. She looks down at me and smiles.

"Yes, he asks about you, too."

"He does?"

"Of course he does," she says. "He misses you."

"What about Junior?"

"You mean that little pup? Ha! Other than eating us out of our bungalow, he's doing just fine. You can't hardly tell the two of them apart. Wherever Jimmy is, there's that little fox on his heel mewling away about something."

I sit up, looking at her closer now. Her dark hair is bobbed short, the roots streaked with gray. She has deep sun wrinkles around her eyes and little brown spots on her cheek.

"How old are you?" I ask.

"That's a funny question to ask a woman, you know."

"I mean, are you as old as everybody else?"

"Do you mean to ask me if I'm as old as Mrs. Radcliffe and her husband are?"

"Yes," I say, nodding.

"No," she says, shaking her head. "I don't understand how they are the way they are, or what they do. But they've been very good to us. They found us alone after our family had been killed. They took us in. Raised us like their own. That was a long time ago. Maybe forty years now. I was very young."

"You said us."

"Me and my brother Tom. You haven't met him yet, but he does all the maintenance and landscaping around here. He's a hell of a gardener too, even if he isn't much of a talker."

"Who killed your family?"

"The machines," she says, looking away.

"Sorry."

There's a long silence. I'm worried she might leave and I don't want her to, so I change the subject.

"Tell me about Hannah."

The mention of Hannah's name makes her smile.

"Well, she's a special girl. But you know that. She's full of life, that girl is. She couldn't wait to be born. Came a full two weeks early, and even then I was in labor less than two hours."

"In labor?" I say. "You're Hannah's mother?"

"I carried her," she says, patting her belly. "I wish I were her mother. Sometimes I feel like I am. Other times not; mostly when she's being a brat like only she can be. I claim nothing to do with spoiling her the way they have. But she's a good girl with a big heart. And smart as they come, too."

"Maybe you could tell Jimmy that?" I say.

"Hey now," she says. "I'm sure Jimmy has his own reasons for feeling how he does. Just the same as you do."

"Yeah, I guess so."

She reaches out and musses my hair with her hand.

"How about we shake these rainy day blues together, eh? Let me make you some dinner, and then I'll give you a haircut. See if there isn't a young man hiding beneath this shaggy head."

"Okay," I say, laughing. "But I don't want too much cut off. I like to keep it longer. Like Jimmy's."

CHAPTER 31
Mrs. Radcliffe

"Good morning."

Mrs. Radcliffe walks in the kitchen and catches me with my fist frozen in the jar of breakfast bars.

"Uh, good morning to you, too," I stammer. "I was just looking for something to eat."

"Oh, you don't want those old things," she says, "they're as stale as one of my husband's speeches. Come sit down here. I'll make you a proper breakfast."

I take a seat at the table.

She clicks on the stove and sets a kettle of water to boil. Then she opens the wood-paneled refrigerator and lays out ingredients. She chops potatoes and mushrooms and tofu. She dices an onion, turning her head away and wiping her eyes with the sleeve of her robe. She pours the water into a teapot, sets the kettle on a warmer. She takes down a pan from where they hang and sets it on the flame. She drizzles oil in the pan and slides the ingredients from the cutting board in. A wonderful smell of caramelized onion and roasted potato fills the small kitchen. When the skillet is sizzling, she opens a seasoning tin and sprinkles on a pinch of herbs and then tips the pan and slides the stir fry onto a plate and sets the steaming plate in front of me. She hands me linen and a fork. Then she pulls down two mugs and fills them with hot tea. She sets one mug in front of me, and she sits across from me cradling the other in her hands, sipping her tea, watching me eat.

"Your haircut looks nice," she says.

"Thanks," I say, between bites. "Gloria cut it yesterday."

"She told me."

"Where is Gloria?"

"Sunday's her day off. She's a better cook than I am."

"No, I didn't mean that at all," I say, worried I've offended her. "This is great. Really great. I was just curious is all."

She smiles and sips her tea. A minute later, she says:

"Can you believe we used to eat everything precooked, like they do below? But when you have as much time as we've had, you need to find some way to fill it."

"Who built all of this?" I ask, looking up from my plate and rotating my head in a circle to indicate the house.

"Well, the old stone foundation for the lake house was already here. We restored it. Brought up a generator. Tapped a natural gas reservoir. It was an outpost at first and we shared it with the other scientists—a place to relax and take time away from work. But it seems most of us don't know what to do with ourselves if we're not working. Eventually nobody else came, so we moved in."

"Does anybody come up now?"

"Nobody's been out here since Hannah was born."

"Was the wooden boat here, too?"

"No," she chuckles. "That's Robert's little obsession."

"Robert?"

"My husband," she says. "Dr. Radcliffe. He comes from boating people. He built that boat as a kind of tribute. It's a replica of his family's old cruiser. He was happier then, I think. When he had something to do with his hands."

She stares out the water-streaked window where the rain falls down steadily against the gray. I finish eating and rise to rinse the plate, but she waves me back down in my seat and takes my plate to the sink. She returns with the kettle and refills our teas and then sits again.

"How about you?" I ask her.

"Me?"

"Do you have any hobbies?"

"Oh, I've tried lots of things. Centuries ago, I found an old piano out touring and managed to bring it here and restore it. I'd always wanted to learn. But with nobody to teach me and nobody to play for, the damn thing just sat in the front room until I couldn't stand the sight of it anymore." She stares off through the archway into the front room, as if the piano might reappear there now that she's mentioned it. Her attention turns back to me. "I noticed you like to read."

"Yes, I love books."

"I did also," she says.

"You did?"

She sips her tea and nods. "I did. At first, it was nice to have all the time in the world. Time to just relax and read. And read I did. I read every book in that study. Every book in our Foundation's digital library. Then I read them all again."

"You've read all those books in there twice?"

"Some three or four times."

"That's amazing."

"What do you do with a thousand years?"

"Oh, I can think of endless things," I say. "I'd do anything I wanted to. Everything I ever dreamed."

She looks at me and sighs. "Oh, to be young again."

"I would," I say. "I'd do everything."

"Well, why have you been lying in bed for two days then?"

"The stupid rain," I say.

"Well, so much for doing everything you ever dreamed. Here you are already wasting days because of a little rain."

"But it hasn't let up . . ."

"I know. Can you imagine a rain that settles inside of you and never lets up? A rain that soaks your soul in sadness? A rain like that has the power to drown all those dreams."

I raise my cup, realize it's empty, and set it down again.

"What about your husband?" I ask. "Don't you two love spending time together? Touring the park, or whatever you do? He told us how you met. In that rainstorm."

"Oh, he did, did he?" she says, looking at the window again, as if seeing the creamery scene play out there on the gray pane of glass. "Aubrey, do you love my daughter?" she asks, without looking away from the window.

Her question catches me off guard. I pick up my cup to buy time with a drink. Still empty. I set it down and spin it slowly on the table in front of me.

"It's okay if you're shy," she says.

"I'm not shy."

"It's endearing."

"I'm not."

She smiles. "I knew I loved Robert the minute I saw him," she says. "I loved him so much."

"But you don't anymore?"

She breaks her gaze away from the window and looks at me, considering my question for a long time.

"I think I loved him enough for two lifetimes," she says.

"But not enough for nine."

"I never thought about that."

"We've been together a very long time, Aubrey. Too long. Maybe we've just been alive too long."

"You didn't want to live so long?"

"I thought I did once. But now I think people were meant to have a certain amount of time and that's it. We got greedy. Things need to turn over. Renew. Recycle. Refresh."

"But couldn't a person end their life anytime they wanted? I mean, I'm not suggesting—"

"Some of us have turned to suicide. Dr. Freeland ventured into the park and let the drones get him. Old Wesley jumped from the dam. Others have died in curious accidents. You'd be surprised just how many mishaps happen in nine hundred years. But deciding to end your life is a special kind of horror, a horror I find worse than waiting forever for life to end."

"Well, why did you go along with it then? Extending your life so long, I mean."

"It was my discovery that made it possible."

"It was?"

"Yes, it was."

"But Dr. Rad—"

"Oh, he takes credit for everything. I would have won the Nobel Prize if he'd made my discovery public."

She gazes down into her empty mug, a look of regret on her furrowed brow. Then she looks up and continues:

"I was passionate about longevity when I was young. I had this silly idea that the progress of science was halted because of the human life span. I felt that just as we reached our true potential, we died, taking all that knowledge with us. Most scientists are lucky to make one breakthrough discovery in their lifetime. Do you know why? Because they spend their early career learning what the scientists before them knew. And just as they become experts, they're lucky to add some small new discovery to the community of knowledge, and then they die. I thought if only we lived for hundreds of years working on a problem, we could advance our knowledge in enormous leaps. Science. Science. Science. Everything I did was for science."

She sits still, staring at the table in front of her.

A gust of wind drives rain against the window.

My cup is cool in my hand.

"What changed?"

"I don't know," she says. "I think things just accumulate in our brains over so many years. Too much judgment, maybe. Even too much knowledge. They collect in our consciousness like so much empty clutter. It destroys our spirit. Youth has its advantages, you know."

"I don't see any advantages," I say.

"Well, that's one of them," she says. "Ignorance."

"Ignorance is an advantage?"

"Of course. It allows you to hope, doesn't it? It lets you take action without all the facts. Less thinking, more action—that's what youth gives you. That and lots of mistakes."

"What's so good about mistakes?"

"Mistakes can be very beautiful. Mistakes lead to surprises. Even joy. And joy makes life worth living. I missed life because I was working. I missed my youth, my fertile years. And then Hannah came and changed everything. I watched her grow in Gloria's womb and I was so very jealous. I'm ashamed I was so jealous. And then to watch her be born. Oh, to see it. To see her breast feed. So thirsty for that nourishment that I couldn't give her. It filled me with regret. But I love her so incredibly much, Aubrey. And now I see things differently. I see we were wrong about living this long. And maybe we were wrong about other things too. Maybe we were wrong about—"

"Morning."

I turn to see Hannah standing in the kitchen entry.

"Good morning," I say.

She walks over and pulls herself down a mug.

"Looks like somebody's having a tea party and I wasn't invited," she says. "Mind if I join you?"

"I was just talking about you," her mother says.

Hannah refills the kettle and sets it to boil.

"Should I be embarrassed?" she asks.

"Oh yes," I say. "She was telling me all of your secrets."

"Is that true, Mom?"

Mrs. Radcliffe laughs. "Of course not, honey. You know I don't know any of your secrets to tell. Pull up a chair and let's all plan a picnic. I think this rain is going to clear."

CHAPTER 32
One, Two, It's All Through

Hannah serves.

I pop the ball back, close to the net.

She springs forward and returns to my off side. I race across the court, sending it back deep. She catches the ball just before a second bounce and drives it between her legs. I dive for it but miss and lie on the ground panting.

She stands over me smiling.

"Good game."

"Yeah right," I laugh. "You said the same thing after the last three games you whipped me on."

She extends a hand, laughing, and helps me to my feet. We walk to the table and sit in the shade. Hannah pours us iced tea.

"Is it hot out here?" I ask, shaking my shirt for some air. "Or is it just me chasing your returns all over the court?"

"No, it's hot," she says, "because I'm hot, too, and you barely had me moving at all."

"Very funny."

"Well, enjoy it anyway," she says. "It's September already and we won't get many more nice days like this."

She picks up a fallen leaf from the table, nodding to a small maple nearby, a ring of bright-red leaves around its base.

"Is that a Japanese Maple? I read about them."

"No," she says. "It's called a Fullmoon Maple. See how the leaves are rounder. Mother loves trees and flowers. She brings all kinds of things back from the park. That's why Daddy built the wall. He said we have to keep things from spreading where they don't belong."

I look over the rest of the yard. Gardens of late blooming flowers. A fruit tree. Perfect green grass. Then I see a man on the lawn and he startles me up in my chair until I notice he's pushing a mechanical mower.

"Who's that?"

"That's Tom. Gloria's brother. And there's Jimmy, too."

I follow her gaze and see Jimmy on the edge of the lawn, raking the grass clippings onto a fabric tarp. Jimmy looks good. His weight is back up to normal, his limp nearly gone. Junior is twice the size he was when I saw him last, just a week ago now, and he's chasing the rake and swatting at it as Jimmy works.

"I'm going to bring them some tea," I say, taking two clean glasses off the tray and filling them from the pitcher.

Tom sees me coming and stops, wiping his brow with his sleeve and leaning on the mower handle. When I offer the tea, he takes it and drains the glass. He clucks his tongue and hands the glass back.

"Thank you." Then he leans into the mower and pushes on, leaving me with both glasses, one empty, one full.

I walk across the lawn to Jimmy.

He drops the rake and bends over and gathers up the tarp. Heaving it over his shoulder, he walks right past me without making eye contact and the tarp hits my arm, knocking the glass from my hand. Junior stops to sniff at the tea and lick the wet grass. He looks up at me, his dark eyes showing no recognition, and then he lopes off and follows Jimmy out the open gate without looking back.

"Hey!"

The shout comes from behind me—

"Come give an old man a hand, will you?"

I turn and see Dr. Radcliffe standing at the boat, holding an armload of supplies. Snatching up the fallen glass, I jog to the table and return it. Hannah stands and hugs me.

"Sorry," she says.

Then we hurry to the dock to help her father unload.

Hannah and I take an armload each and carry them into the kitchen where Gloria inventories the supplies. Dr. Radcliffe brings in the last load as Mrs. Radcliffe appears in the doorway.

"Did you get my medicine?"

"There wasn't any," he answers.

"You know I need it, Robert," she says, her voice irritated. "This headache is making me mad."

"I said there wasn't any, dear. The train comes tomorrow."

"Fine," she sighs. "I'll be in bed. Don't disturb me unless the house catches fire. No, don't disturb me even then."

"Oh, Mommy," Hannah says, frowning. "Let me run you a nice bath and we'll get you hydrated and tucked in for a nap."

Hannah takes her mother's arm and leads her away toward the back of the house.

Gloria opens cupboards, making space for the supplies.

"Come with me, Aubrey," Dr. Radcliffe says. "I brought a little something back for you."

I follow him down the hall to my room and into my bathroom. He sets a plastic case on the counter, and stands me in front of the mirror. He's maybe six inches taller than I am, and a shaft of light streams in the high window and illuminates his white hair, creating the impression of some haloed saint I might have seen in an educational, standing behind me with his hands resting on my shoulders as if in a manner of blessing.

He reaches around and twists the hot water tap on.

"Wet your face well," he says. "Open up those pores."

I cup my hands and fill them with hot water and lean forward and splash it on my face. When I look up again, he's whipping soap with a brush in a small stone pestle. He puts two fingers beneath my chin, lifts my dripping face, and applies the lather to my cheeks, my lip, my jaw. When he releases my chin, I look at my white-soap beard in the mirror. Then he snaps the case open and plucks out a razor and turns my hand over and slaps the razor in my palm.

"Draw it down slow, not too much pressure."

"But I don't have any whiskers yet," I say.

"If you don't, you will soon," he says, waving his finger in an indication for me to continue. "My father taught me when I was your age. Besides, we can't have you running around here looking like a savage."

I bring the razor to my lathered cheek and draw it down slow, cutting a clean path in the cream.

"Be careful around the chin," he warns.

Steam rises on the mirror as I shave, never quite blocking my face, but obscuring Dr. Radcliffe's reflection and creating the appearance of another me, alone, shaving in another world, on the other side of the foggy glass.

When I finish, Dr. Radcliffe wets a towel in the hot water, rings it out, and hands it to me. I hold the towel to my face, breathing in the hot damp air. Then I pull the towel away and look at myself in the mirror. I look the same as when we started, other than a spot of blood where I nicked my chin.

Dr. Radcliffe pats me on the back.

"Well done, well done. Now you're a man. The kit's yours to keep. Come with me. I want to show you something."

The basement is quiet, the laboratory dark.

I follow Dr. Radcliffe across the tile floor to the far wall where he stops and lifts the lid on a keypad, its electric glow washing his face an eerie blue in the shadows of the lab. He looks at me, hesitating. I look away. I hear him punch in four numbers. Then, with a series of clicks, a panel in the wall pops out and slides open, revealing a large room lit with LED lights.

I follow him inside and watch as he slaps a red button with his palm and the door slides shut and seals.

The room is five meters across and five meters deep, with walls made of polished steel, a toilet shielded by a partition, and several wall-mounted cots. But what interests me is the farthest wall and a built-in command center. A desktop, a chair. A panel of controls and switches, a joystick of sorts. Mounted above the desk, a dozen screens show various live video feeds from around the park. Aerial images from cameras mounted on high-flying drones. Shoreline images from ships patrolling the coasts. Snowy regions, arid regions, tropical regions—all trapped like spooky movie sets in the silent monitors there.

"Pretty neat, isn't it?" Dr. Radcliffe says.

My eyes dart from screen to screen.

Screen one: a drone drills down its camera on a herd of elk, their velvet heads lifted toward two males facing off, their antlers raised, their lips curled as if bugling.

Screen two: a ship's camera pans fast, focusing a telephoto lens on sea lions hauling out of the surf onto a rocky shore.

Screen three: a drone glides over a forest fire, glimpses of flames between plumes of black smoke.

"Do you put out the fires?"

"Not when they're started by lightning," he says.

"What is this place?"

"Well, it's half control room, half safe room."

"Safe room?"

"For protection," he says. "Drones patrol the mountains and the perimeter of the lake pretty close, but the lake and its shores are a safe zone. I'm actually surprised you and your friend made it through. We retreat down here in case hostiles show up. Steel walls over reinforced concrete, two-inch solid Kevlar door, thousand P.S.I. electromagnetic locks—nothing gets in here. Food and water for a month over there. Batteries, too. You can hide in here and guide in the drones and take out whatever threat is above."

"Have you ever had to use it?"

He shakes his head. "Not really. We did have a bear once."

"A bear?"

"Yeah, before the wall. Marched right into the house and joined us for supper. You should have seen Catherine's face."

"Did you kill it?"

"Of course not," he says, obviously offended. "We waited down here for it to leave, then waited some more just to be safe. I'd already planned to build the wall with all these invasive plants my wife brings home. But that's not really why we're down here today." He slides the chair out. "Have a seat?"

"You want me to sit?"

"Well, who else would I be talking to?" he asks, chuckling. "One of my other personalities?"

I slide into the chair and sit at the controls.

"This is a miniature command center," he says. "We have bigger ones at the Foundation. The drones are all programmed with flight plans and auto-targeting features, so there's really nothing to do. But you can override the programs and pilot a drone or a ship remote from here. Sometimes just to look around, sometimes to neutralize an abnormal threat."

"What's an abnormal threat?"

"Oh, things the drones don't look for. In the early years packs of wild dogs, or livestock. Things like that. Not so much anymore. Most species that remain are native. Except humans, of course. But the drones target them without prompting."

"How do they target humans?"

He reaches over my shoulder and taps a key, then another. One of the screens switches to a nighttime scene where two infrared silhouettes walk across a dark field, one bulky, one small and bent, walking with a strange padding gate.

"This was just the other week," he says. "It's all automatic. Watch. Thermal imaging, mainly. Humans have unique infrared signatures. Sometimes mutations or strange clothing cause us problems, but the drones can map movement and compare it to a database. Not much is hot like a human, but nothing walks like one. Not even this funny specimen."

I watch the screen. The man seems to sense something, stops and turns. The smaller man keeps going until he hits the end of his leash and jerks back around. I recognize them now. Then two blasts of bright light fill the dark screen, and when they fade, the two men lie in heaps with the red draining out of them. My legs twitch; I want to stand and leave

Dr. Radcliffe taps another key and the horrific scene is replaced by a graph.

"As you can see," he says, "we've had both successes and setbacks over the years."

With bold red characters, the graph shows the current estimated above ground world populations at 25,754. It graphs the history, too, showing decades as high as 350,000, and others much lower, one as low as 2,900. As we watch, the count drops by three to 25,751.

"These are only estimates, of course," Dr. Radcliffe says, pointing to the bottom of the graph where the margin of error is displayed. "But we track land covered, drone sightings, kill data. And the algorithms are usually pretty damn close."

He taps another key, another graph—

This one says at the current pace, total extermination will be achieved in 357 years.

"But don't be fooled," he says. "these numbers can change fast. The Americas are largely under control. But other places remain problematic."

"What places?"

"Well, strange things are happening in China, for example. We lost a drone there, and when we sent another to retrieve its weapons, we lost that one, too. What we need is a new strategy, my boy. We need fresh blood, fresh ideas. We need you."

"Me? What am I supposed to do?"

He spins the chair so I'm facing him and he reaches down and taps his finger against my breastplate.

"First, when I know you're really ready, we get you off this terrible clock that's ticking inside of you."

"And how do we do that?"

"I'm glad you asked."

He steps over to a locked refrigerator, punches in another

code, and the door pops loose. He opens it and pulls out a clear case of preloaded syringes. Opening the case, he removes a syringe, and holds it up to the LED light. The red fluid inside shimmers with a life of its own.

"This makes you a god, Aubrey," he says, holding it out to me. "At least as close to one as there ever will be."

I reach for the syringe, but he pulls it back.

"Not yet, young man," he says, giving me a subtle head shake and a grin. "Not until I'm convinced that you're ready."

"That's all it takes?" I ask. "One shot?"

"That's it," he says, tucking the syringe back in its case and putting the case back in the refrigerator. "Your body does the rest. Everything you need, you already have. This unlocks it."

He shuts the refrigerator door. The lock clicks closed.

"Once I take that, then what?"

"Then we need to get you and Hannah working on some kids. She'll be mature in another year or two."

"You said I'm not ready?"

"I said: I'm not convinced you're ready."

"How do I get ready?"

"Now there's the bright young man I've been looking for. I like the way you think, Aubrey. I knew we chose right when we chose you." He points to the screen. "We need to come up with an actionable plan to get that number to absolute zero."

"And once it's at zero, what will you do?" I ask.

"No, you mean what will *you* do?" he corrects. "I'll be long gone, unfortunately."

"Well, what will I do then?"

He slides the chair out, with me in it, lifts me to my feet and lays his arm over my shoulder.

"What I'm about to show you," he says, "no one else has seen, not even my wife."

Then he sits down and slides up to the desk. He hits a yellow button on the panel, a hatch pops open revealing a keyhole. He reaches under his shirt collar and slips a chain over his head, a small silver key dangles at its end. He slides the key into the hole and turns it. The lid opens, revealing two red toggles protected with reverse finger guards labeled PHASE 1 and PHASE 2. Next to the toggles a yellow button reads: LIVE FEED. He reaches in and presses the button. The screens all go dark, then three click back on. One screen shows a view of the lake from the house, another screen shows the Foundation cavern. But the third screen looks foreign, until I look closer and recognize the Transfer Station of Holocene II where I boarded the train that set me on this journey. The elevators stand closed, the loaders parked and still, the silent train waiting at its platform. It must be rest hours.

"I can't tell you how I dreamed of this," Dr. Radcliffe says, holding his hands suspended over the toggles and wiggling his fingers like some pianist about to perform. "To be the last man, to draw the last breath, to think the last human thought. What would it be like? Now it's slipped away. Gone, gone, gone. But you can be the one, Aubrey. You can be the last man."

"You want to be the last man alive?"

"No," he says, shaking his head slowly. "I want to be the last man to die. You see, I used to be afraid of dying, Aubrey. That fear helped motivate my work. It had a place. But I've come to see it differently now. The fear of death is the fear of being forgotten. Of being irrelevant. Overlooked. It's not death that scares men, it's life going on without them. But to sit right here and welcome the end of all humankind, to have the honor, no, the privilege, of handing the planet back to nature . . ."

"You look forward to it?"

"It's a glorious gift, young man. A glorious fine gift. And it's a gift I'm giving to you."

"What about Hannah?" I say, not wanting to sit and listen to this madness alone. "Shouldn't you be telling this to her?"

"Hannah's my only daughter, I love her. She's probably smarter than you are. No offense meant, but it's true. But she also has a soft heart, you see. A nurturing instinct. And when the time comes, you'll have children, don't forget. You can't trust a mother to make a rational choice."

"But what is this rational choice?"

"To pull these switches."

"And what do these switches do?"

"When the above ground population reaches absolute zero, and after a grace period to be sure, of course, you'll come down here and toggle these switches—Phase 1, Phase 2."

He snaps his fingers, the pop echoing in the closed room.

"And just like that it all ends. One, two, it's all through. You can watch in the monitors if you'd like. I always thought I'd walk outside and meet it with open arms."

"Meet what?"

"The wave," he says, as if I should know.

"What wave?"

He points to the lake view screen.

"You see that monolith of stone there? Just right of the dam, hanging over the lake?"

"Yes, I see it."

"It might not look like much from here, but that stone is

larger than ten thousand of these houses. Look at it compared to the dam. It's bigger than the dam. This second switch labeled Phase 2 closes the locks, seals the launch tunnels, and floods the Foundation with lake water. Then it detonates small nuclear charges bored deep into that stone, and that stone there slides into the lake."

"I don't get it," I say, shaking my head.

"The wave, boy, the wave. I got the idea from Lituya Bay up in Alaska, mid-twentieth century. One of my fellows was studying it to help map potential asteroid tsunami patterns."

"Tsunami?"

"An earthquake sent a massive slide into the enclosed bay, and a wave rose seventeen-hundred feet up the other shore, snapping every tree in its path and washing everything back with it, even the topsoil. Don't you see the beauty of it? This wave won't be near as high by the time it reaches the house here, not with the size of this lake, but it'll be a hundred meters for sure. Maybe two. It'll wipe out the lake house, the bungalow down the beach, everything. And when it retreats, it will take every last trace to the bottom of the lake. It even cleans up the mess, you see. It'll be like we were never even here."

"Well, what about the people down in Holocene II?"

He waves his hand, as if batting away an invisible fly.

"By the time you hit the second switch, they'll be flooded."

"Flooded?" I ask, a sick feeling rising in my gut.

"What do you think the Phase 1 switch does?"

"You mean it drowns them?"

"That's exactly what I mean. Phase 1 opens an ocean gate in the train tubes and floods Holocene II. When it's time, you can watch it all on the monitors there," he says, pointing.

"You mean they're all living down there every day with the threat of being drowned while they sleep? And they don't even know it? I was living like that?"

He stares up at me, a look of genuine confusion.

"We live every day with the threat of disaster. People used to believe in God's wrath, not knowing when he would strike us down again. He even flooded the Earth himself once, they say. Don't believe in God? Asteroids then. Comets. Or how about the nuclear bombs that rained down? We all live at the whimsy of chance. We're pathetic, powerless little people."

"So you plan to murder everyone alive."

"Such ugly words," he says. "This is the only moral choice, Aubrey. It's the right thing for this planet and all the peaceful life left on it. We had our chance. We failed."

He clicks the lid shut, removes the key and hangs it around his neck. Then he rises and pushes the chair in. He walks to the safe room door and slaps a green button with his palm and the door slides open. I stand looking at the blank screens.

"Don't worry," he says. "It's a lot to digest in one meal. That's why I'm not convinced you're ready. But when you are ready, you'll know. You'll know, and I'll know. Now come on, let's go see about some dinner."

CHAPTER 33
I Love You, Dad

I wake thrashing with my legs tangled in wet sheets.

A dream, a nightmare—what was it?

I kick the covers off, and roll onto my side.

The sun has yet to rise, and the window above my bed glows faint silver in the dawn, casting the room in shadow. The wallpaper picks up the low light and the yellow birds shimmer, as if flapping to free themselves from their paper prison.

My hand reaches up instinctively, grabbing my father's pipe where it hangs from the bedpost.

Then I remember—

I remember the safe room and Dr. Radcliffe's crazy video feeds, the train sitting idle on the Transfer Station platform in Holocene II. I remember him telling Mrs. Radcliffe yesterday that the train arrives today. Then I remember Hannah handing me that leaf and saying that it was September already.

My father retires in September.

My father—he'll be on that train to Eden.

I jump out of bed. Everyone is still sleeping when I creep into the hall, stopping in the kitchen to drink a glass of water and fill my pockets with breakfast bars. Then I step from the house out into the cool, gray morning.

The lake is still as poured lead, and the predawn sky hangs heavy above it. My breath smokes, silver frost covers the grass, crunching beneath my feet as I walk down to the dock.

I twist the boathouse knob. The door opens. The wooden boat floats there waiting, its lacquered steering wheel catching the low light from the high windows. Above the wooden boat, suspended from the ceiling by an electric lift, hangs another boat crafted from carbon fiber, its cockpit enclosed in glass, the Foundation crest on its hull. Must be a backup for bad weather.

The boat rocks slightly when I step into it and sit behind the wheel, the cushioned seat soft, the polished-wood throttle knob cold as steel. I search the gauges in the dim light, but see no instructions and no key. Next to the wheel is a circular pushbutton cut from a deep-red jewel, and I wonder if it isn't some precious ruby recovered from the ruins they razed to reclaim the park. I press the button—the electric engines whir to life; a small churn of water echoes softly off the stone walls.

I see no way to open the boathouse doors, and I assume they must be automatic.

"Here goes everything," I mutter to myself as I push the throttle forward, just a little. Nothing. A little more throttle—still nothing. I press the throttle all the way open and the water churns violently behind the boat, but still it doesn't move. Then I see a drive switch and when I press it, the boat launches forward, rams into the closed boathouse doors and fishtails in the water, fighting to get out. I panic, leaving the throttle wide open. The doors part and the boat blasts through them, scraping against the wood as it shoots out into the glassy lake, the automatic doors drawing themselves closed behind us.

I get a grip on myself, pull the throttle back to midpoint, and steer toward the dam. I look back once more to see the lake house disappearing into the shadows of the bluff.

The boat cuts through the clean water and throws a wake

behind it that fans out and rolls away, leaving the water smooth and unmarked, the only evidence of a crossing arriving as small waves on either shore, hopefully long after I'm gone.

The wind is cool on my face. The air smells of wet leaves. It feels nice to be out in the boat, moving across the water. The sun rises from behind the jagged mountains, its golden light forcing the gray down to the surface of the lake. I can see why Dr. Radcliffe prefers this open-air antique to the covered thing he has hanging in the boathouse. I fish a breakfast bar from my pocket and eat it. Mrs. Radcliffe was right. They are stale.

I notice the stone monolith hanging from the mountain, perched above the lake—a granite slab so immense it wouldn't fit in Level 3 of Holocene II. I try to guess where the nuclear charges are hidden, how it might shear off. Would the wave come right away? I feel the threat of that enormous stone, and my stomach twists up with anxiety. I toss the breakfast bar into the water, drop the throttle, and speed toward the dam.

I don't see the mitre gates open, and it dawns on me that I have no idea how to work the locks. I pull the throttle back, the boat sinks into the water, and I cruise slowly toward the gates, hoping that they're automatic also. They are. As I approach, the gates grind open and I steer the boat in, ease the throttle back, and coast the last few meters. Then the automatic doors shut behind me and darkness swallows the boat.

I sit in absolute black, the boat rocking on its own ebbing wake. Smells of wet concrete, gear grease. The lonely drip of water. Just when I think the locks might not be automatic after all, that I might be trapped here in the dark, the LED lights snap on, and the water begins to drain away, lowering the boat.

It takes a long time to drop, longer than I remember.

Without Hannah by my side, and without Dr. Radcliffe at the wheel, I feel anxious being three hundred meters down in a concrete chamber, the weight of an entire lake pressing above my head. I bring my hand to my chest, grip my father's pipe there, and remember why I'm here.

The archway appears, the water level equalizes, and the gates open, the LED lights reflecting off the wet concrete walls. I engage the drive switch, nudge the throttle forward, and idle into the underground channel.

When I cruise from the channel into the red glow of the cavern bay, the Foundation docks are deserted, the submarine gone. It's quiet. The only sound is a soft tumble of water draining away somewhere on the far side of the cavern.

I guide the boat to the same dock Dr. Radcliffe brought us to and look for a tie off, but before I can find one, the step plate folds out automatically and clamps itself onto the dock.

I press the ruby button and kill the engines.

Onshore, I walk past the galvanized door of the sintering plant and skirt the edges of the living quarters, grateful for the scaffolding that blocks the windows. I make my way to the pathway bridge that overlooks the sunken train channel.

I see right away that I was right . . .

The tunnel gates stand open, the train hovers motionless at the loading platform, the cargo cars loaded with supplies from Holocene II. The passenger car is corralled into the receiving dock of Eden, steep walls on either side blocking any exit, the train car open onto a narrow platform leading up to the door and the LCD sign that reads: WELCOME TO EDEN.

There's no sign of life anywhere.

I hop over the bridge rail and drop down onto the roof of

the train, working my way up to the passenger car docked at Eden. I creep to the front of the car, and edge toward the side. The roof slopes away and there's nothing to hold onto, so I drop onto my butt, slide off the roof, kick free of the car, and land on the platform.

Well, that was simpler than I thought. I have absolutely no idea how I'll get back up, but getting down sure was easy.

The LCD sign blinks, and the door slides open.

The platform must be pressure sensitive.

I walk to the open door and peek in on a yellow hallway. I'm nervous. Remembering my father's words, I breathe good energy in, and breathe bad energy out. Then I step over the threshold and into the hall. The door slides shut behind me.

The hall leads to a large circular room. Across the room, another steel door, a blank LCD display and a speaker mounted above it. Other than one ordinary door marked BATHROOM, the walls are entirely covered with digital screens showing video loops of nature scenes—waterfalls, beaches, the forest.

On the largest screen, an animated woman smiles while she talks about Eden: "Soon, your every dream will come true. Just think—anything you want will be yours. You can visit the Sahara, dive with sharks, even walk on the moon. And the best part is you can do it with everyone you love, every day."

Several rows of padded seats face the screen, and a woman sits in the front watching, her posture rigid, her hands folded in her lap. She wears the familiar gray jumpsuit of Holocene II.

"Hello," my voice echoes off the walls. "I'm Aubrey."

She turns to look at me, then looks back at the screen.

"Are you up from Holocene II?"

She looks back again and nods, but says nothing.

"What level are you from?"

"Now serving Doris Tiegs," a robotic voice says.

I look toward the speaker—

DORIS TIEGS is displayed on the LCD screen.

The steel door slides open.

The woman stands and tugs at her sleeves, adjusting her jumpsuit. She casts a nervous glance my way as she walks past me to the open door. It slides closed behind her, and I'm alone in the room. The animated woman starts her loop again:

"Soon, your every dream will come true . . ."

I missed him. I missed my dad. Maybe if I'd been a little less selfish, less wrapped up with Hannah, maybe I would have remembered in time to catch him. It's too late now. I'll never forgive myself for missing him. For not being able to tell him—

What's that smell? Is that tobacco? Pipe tobacco?

I reach in my shirt and lift my father's pipe to my nose—nothing. Any odor has been long washed away. I look down the yellow hall but it's empty. My eyes search the room, landing on the bathroom door. I step to the door, twist the handle, and pull it open. A cloud of smoke billows out, and when it clears, my father stands there with a guilty smile.

"Dad?"

"Son?"

He steps from the bathroom and I throw my arms around him. At first he's stiff, his arms at his side. Then he softens, reaching his free hand around me and patting my back. I realize I'm as tall as he is now, and nearly as big, too. I bury my nose in his neck and smell his familiar scent of tobacco and soap. It suddenly feels awkward to be hugging him, so I let go and step back and look at his face. He looks younger than I remember, almost innocent somehow.

"What are you doing, Dad?"

He holds up a makeshift pipe, teeth marks already on its stem, smoke still curling from its bowl.

"Guess the darn habit's harder to kick than I thought. I wanted one last smoke. Your mother doesn't like the smell, you know. Never did. Hey, you still got the pipe I gave you?"

"Of course I have it."

I lift the pipe from my shirt so he can see it.

"Good," he says. "Keep passing it on. How are you, Son? You look different. They don't have barbers up here?"

"It's nothing like we've been told up here."

"No, I'm sure it's not. But I always knew you'd be the one they called up. I knew it. I'm proud of you."

"Dad, I need to talk to you."

"I mean it, Son. I'm proud of you. Really proud. All of Holocene II is. And your mother will be, too. I'm so excited to see her, I'm jumping outta my skin like a seven-year cicada before the War." He looks down at the pipe in his hand. "Ah, heck, I'm so darn nervous I'm puffing away in a bathroom like some learning annex kid getting high on busybee algae."

"There's no ice, Dad."

"What's that you say?"

"It was all a lie."

"What was a lie, Son?"

"Everything was. The ice, the radiation, the disappeared atmosphere. All a bunch of damn lies."

"When did you start talking like this? I don't like it."

"Dad! Aren't you listening to me? We've been kept locked up like prisoners, Dad. Locked up with lies."

The virtual woman begins her loop again:

"Soon, your every dream will come true . . ."

My father frowns, lifts a hand, lets it drop.

"I don't know what you're saying, Aubrey."

"Dr. Radcliffe is alive."

"Dr. Radcliffe?"

"Yes. After all this time. He's nearly a thousand years old, and he never went to Eden."

"Are you okay, Son?"

"Are you hearing me? They lied."

"I'm sure they have a good reason," he says.

"Yeah, they think humans are a virus."

"We have a virus?"

"No!" I shout, "We are the virus."

He reaches out and rests a hand on my shoulder.

"Hey, hey, calm down now, kiddo. I'm sure you've got things mixed up. You're all worked up here. This is my big day, Son. Let's not spoil it, okay? Everything'll be fine. And if they need a smart fellow to straighten things out up here, they've picked the right one with you."

"Now serving Jonathon Van Houten," the speaker says.

The steel door slides open.

I look up at my father's name on the LCD screen:

JONATHON VAN HOUTEN.

I knew his name was Jon, but I never knew it was short for Jonathon. I wonder what else I don't know about him, what else I'll never have the chance to know now.

"That's me, Son. Lucky they go alphabetical or we might have missed saying goodbye."

He leans down and sets his pipe on one of the seats.

When he straightens, I grab his hand in both of mine and bring it to my chest.

"You don't have to go, Dad. We can walk out of here right now. I've got a boat. We can take it up to the surface. The sun is up there shining sure as we're standing here. You don't have to retire. There's no reason to retire. No reason to walk through that door."

His eyes are wet when I finish. He reaches his free hand up, clenches it around my hands, and steps toward me. We stand like that, chest to chest, hands locked at our hearts.

"I love you, Son, but you're wrong. There's every reason in the world for me to walk through that door."

I feel a tear roll down my cheek, because I know he's right. He's waited a long time for this moment. More than fifteen years raising me by himself, my name reminding him every day of the woman he loves waiting for him here in Eden.

"Will you tell her I love her?"

"Of course I will," he says. "Of course I will."

I wipe away another tear.

"Don't cry, Son. We'll see you soon enough."

I wish it were true. I wish I were going into Eden with him right now. But I can't bring myself to tell him that it may well be another thousand years before I do.

"Now serving Jonathon Van Houten."

He turns away and steps toward the door. Then he stops and turns back. He reaches in his pocket and pulls out a sealed plastic case and presses it into my palm.

"Won't be needing my tobacco in there," he says.

I don't know what to say, so I fight back the tears and say nothing. He wraps his hands behind my neck, pulls me forward and kisses the top of my head, just like he used to do when I was a young boy. Then he turns and walks across the room and through the door without looking back.

As the door seals closed, I say:

"I love you, Dad."

CHAPTER 34
But What About Eden?

Just Great.

The door's locked.

Turning back, I enter the round room again.

I look at the closed door to Eden, the blank LCD screen that had displayed my father's name just moments ago. I see his makeshift pipe abandoned on the seat where he left it, and I'm overcome with longing already to see him again. Then I notice a sort of phone hanging on the wall. A sign above it reads:

RETIREMENT ANXIETY HELP LINE

I pluck the receiver off its cradle and hold it up to my ear. After a few seconds, it beeps and a voice comes on:

"How may I help you?"

"I'm stuck down here."

"Anxiety is a common response to change," the scripted voice drones out. "You'll feel much better once you're invited inside for a tour of the retirement process. And if you'd like, we can—hey, wait a minute," the voice changes from scripted to sincere, "we don't show any other retirees. What's your name? Where did you come from?"

"My name is Aubrey. I came from the lake house."

There's a muffled pause on the other end, someone talking in the background. Then another voice comes on:

"Aubrey, is that you?"

"Who's this?"

"This is Dr. Taft. We met the other day, remember? How did you get in there? Never mind, I'll be right down."

Less than a minute later, a hidden panel in the wall opens and Dr. Taft waves me into a vestibule leading to a staircase.

"My goodness, boy," he says, shaking his head. "You're lucky you didn't walk through the wrong door and get rendered into Eden. We need you around here, you know."

"Sorry," I say, "I was just looking around."

"Well, I'm glad you're here anyway," he says. "Radcliffe is much too slow about things, and it's high time we got you up to speed. Come on up. Today's the perfect day to visit Eden."

He hits a button and the panel seals shut.

I follow him up the long flight of stairs and through a door into a control room where several scientists look up from their workstations, their backs hunched, their fingers frozen at their keyboards. They take me in with red-rimmed eyes, then return to their work without a word. They sit in front of a wall-length window overlooking an enormous circular pool surrounded by a metal catwalk and covered with a domed ceiling. The pool is pulsing with red bursts of electricity that light the scientists' faces, giving them the appearance of old men staring into some giant flickering fireplace.

"Is that Eden?" I ask.

"Yes. And you're just in time to see how it works," he says, pointing to an LCD display on one of the workstations.

The display shows another circular room, smaller, more sterile, with a strange chair mounted in its center. The chair faces a wall flashing with more relaxing nature scenes. A door slides open, and a naked woman steps into the room with her arms crossed over her breasts. I recognize her as the woman I just met from Holocene II, although her head has been shaved and she looks thinner stripped of her jumpsuit.

She steps up into the chair and sits, her eyes darting around the room before settling on the screen, the waterfall scene there making her smile. The lights dim slightly. The chair reclines on automatic hinges. She takes a deep breath and leans back, her body relaxing into the contours of the seat. When her head hits the headrest, a syringe darts out and pushes a needle into her neck. She winces. Then she smiles, and her eyes slowly close. She looks young and peaceful sleeping naked in the chair.

Then the chair transforms, locking her ankles and wrists in place. A strap unfolds around her chest, cinching her into the seat. Braces flip out and trap her head. A panel in the ceiling opens and robotic arms descend, a steel disc encapsulating her head. A whining sound rises on the display speaker, and then the arm pulls away, taking the top of her skull with it. Her mouth opens in a sort of sleeping sigh. I gape at the exposed folds of her brain, vomit rising in my throat. Another arm lowers, covering her head. It lifts with a soft vacuum sound, pulling her brain free. A smaller arm slips a blade underneath, severing the brainstem. Her jaw drops completely open, her bottom teeth showing, her tongue lolling out. The arm lifts her brain toward the ceiling, slides away on its track, and disappears into an opening in the far wall. Her body sits strapped in the chair, her jaw resting on her chest, her open skull empty and red. The straps free from her ankles, her wrists, her chest. The head braces retract. A trapdoor opens in the floor, and the chair tilts forward until the dead weight of her brainless body slides off, disappearing in a tangle of limp limbs into the hole.

"Watch here now," Dr. Taft says, pointing at the window.

The mechanical arm slides through the wall carrying her steaming brain out over the circular pool.

"Why is there smoke coming off her brain?" I ask, choking back my sudden need to vomit again.

"It's cold in there," he says. "Twenty below in the pool."

"Why isn't it frozen?"

"Glycerin," he says, drawling the word as if it were some key ingredient in a favorite recipe. "Electrical currents move better in a cold brine, plus it helps to preserve tissue. We mix glycerin in to keep it from freezing."

One of the scientists taps his keyboard and a rope of wires rises from the red pool, a plastic coupling on its end. Another scientist guides the brain down with a joystick, lining up the brainstem with the coupling. The coupling senses the stem and constricts, connecting the brain to the wires. Then the arm releases its suction and the brain plunks softly into the pool and disappears. The red light pulses a little brighter, as if greeting the newest member of Eden.

"Can you locate individual people?" I ask, thinking maybe I can see my mother. "I mean, can you see what they're dreaming up? What they're remembering?"

He shakes his head. "Dreaming up? Remembering? What has Radcliffe told you? Besides, we don't bother tracking who's who. And it really wouldn't matter much anyhow, seeing as they all get tethered together in test groups."

"What do you mean test groups?"

"Test groups for peaceful habitation."

"Peaceful habitation?"

"I know," he says, tossing up his hands. "Sounds crazy to me, too. We all know there's no way in eternity humans could ever live in harmony with themselves, let alone the rest of the planet. But some of us needed proof."

His voice seems far away—his words foreign, his message delayed. I look directly at him, confused.

"You mean to tell me you run tests on them?"

"Oh, it's quite harmless," he says.

"Harmless how?"

"They have no idea who they are, really, or who they were. No memory, no willful participation. They're all good as dead when we loop them in. Of course, we make sure to erase any traumatic events every time we begin a new test."

"I'm confused here," I say, truly baffled by what he's said. "What kinds of tests did you say you run?"

"Oh, all kinds. You name it. We feed hypothetical worlds into the system and see how they respond. We accelerate their time, expedite the results. We've tried every government, every form of economy. We've tried too few resources, too many, just enough. We've tried different social structures. We've even toyed with neuroanatomical differences in the sexes. Increasing sexual dimorphism, decreasing it, and eliminating it all together. And with every test, we get the same result. Humans reproduce unchecked. They over consume, and destroy their environment. Then they destroy one another. Every test. Every time."

"But what about Eden?" I ask, trembling. "What about living in a virtual paradise forever with the people you love?

"Nursery rhymes," he says. "Nothing but nursery rhymes."

"It's all a lie?"

"We needed to tell the poor people something to make life bearable down there. The truth would be inhumane"

The horror of what he's saying hits me hard.

"So you're telling me this is one big test incubator?" I say, gesturing wildly toward the window. "That all these brains are nothing but test subjects?"

"What you're looking at," he answers, "is a giant petri-dish culture of the worst parasites to ever be created. And we have nearly nine-hundred years of test results to prove it. But, who knows—maybe you'll find something different."

The red pulsing makes me dizzy.

My flesh breaks out in sweat, my knees buckle.

I turn back to the LCD display just in time to see the chair tilting forward and my father's lifeless body sloughing away into the open trapdoor in the killing room floor.

I lurch backward, reeling, falling, reaching. I grab Dr. Taft and turn and puke on his coat.

He grips my shoulders. "What's wrong with you, boy?"

I place my hands on his chest and thrust him away from me. He loses his balance and falls flailing on top of the desk, knocking keyboards and monitors onto the floor. The scientists scramble to their feet and stand motionless, staring at me, not quite knowing what to do.

I race for the exit and plunge into the dim red light of the underground cavern.

I pause to bend over and puke again.

Then I rush to the boat.

CHAPTER 35
My Last Mistake

"You use them for social experiments?"

Dr. Radcliffe looks up from his book.

"Ah," he sighs, nodding, "looks like someone's been on a little field trip."

I step farther into the study.

"You murdered my father!"

"I wouldn't call it that," he says.

"Of course, you wouldn't!" I shout. "You'd use some fancy term to rationalize it, just like you do with everything."

He waves to the empty chair.

"Have a seat. Let's talk."

"I'm tired of talking," I say, standing my ground.

He closes his book and sets it aside.

"I wanted Eden to work. I really did. But the brain just doesn't go on the same without the body. It doesn't dream, it doesn't remember. It reverts to some primal state. Responding to stimuli—sure. But with no volition of its own. None, I tell you. And no connection to the prior life of its donor."

"So you enslave them as test subjects?"

"I did it for the greater good," he replies, throwing up his hands and letting them fall in his lap again. "I thought maybe we'd find some way humans could live peaceably. Some system of government, some environment of equality. I didn't do it to harm anyone, Aubrey. I did it in hopes of freeing Holocene II one day. Can't you see that?"

"I see that you're a sick, sick man," I say, spitting on the carpet to show my contempt. "A sick and evil man."

He leans forward and looks at my spit stain

"Well, you might be right there, kid. We're all evil men. And that's the problem. That's why we need to be destroyed. The whole stinking human race."

I stand there staring at him, wishing I could pick up a fire poker and bash in his skull. But my anger dissipates into self-loathing. I'm just as guilty as he is. Guilty of going along with him, guilty of buying into his crazy dogma. I should have been firmer with my father, more insistent. I should have made him leave with me. He'd have known what to do. The thought of his body sliding off that chair makes my stomach turn again.

"You need to pull it together," I hear Dr. Radcliffe say.

"What's that?"

"You need to focus on what's important here. We've got a job to do, and not much time to prepare. You'll have the whole planet. You'll have Hannah. You'll have as long as it takes to accomplish what needs to be done, and then you'll have the honor of being the last man."

"The last man? Really? That again? What's the point of such a perfect planet if nobody's here to enjoy it anyway?"

"To let some greater thing come to be, of course."

"I don't believe you even know what you're saying."

"You've got a lot to learn yet, young man. Why don't you come with me in the morning? I'm leaving at first light to inspect what murderous things some of your precious humans have been doing up north. I'd like for you to see it yourself."

I shake my head.

"You'll come around," he says, picking up his book again. "You're a smart boy, and there's no other choice."

"I do have one question for you."

"Sure," he says. "Anything."

"If you needed me so bad, why weren't you looking for me after the train crashed?"

"We did search for you," he says. "We looked everywhere. We mobilized most of our fleet to the west coast trying to find you. We never thought you'd already look like one of them."

"One of who?"

"Those savages."

"What savages?"

"In that cove," he says. "I'm just glad you survived."

Just when I thought things couldn't get any worse, a new and darker horror grips my heart and rips it from my chest—

It was me they were looking for. I brought all those drones to the cove. The first fly-by that killed Uncle John. The warship that mowed down the men. The drones that slaughtered the woman and the kids. Me! They were looking for me.

"Where are you going?" Dr. Radcliffe asks.

"I need some fresh air."

"Good thing there's a whole world full of it out there," he says, chuckling. "And put my boat back in the boathouse, will you? Smells like rain tonight."

The wooden door closes in the rock wall behind me with a solid and final thud. I pause and consider going back and saying goodbye to Hannah, but decide against it.

I walk the shore and climb the bluff to where Jimmy and I first saw the lake house. I remember how magical it looked that night with the windows lit and the torches burning. I remember being mesmerized the next morning by Hannah hitting balls. Stopping, I look down at the lawns, the tennis courts, the dock. It doesn't seem like much of anything to me now.

Heading into the forest, I find the fallen tree where Jimmy and I spent that night. My old pack is still there, empty and blackened with mildew. I reach down and pick it up, something heavy in its bottom. I reach inside and find Uncle John's knife. I turn it in my hand, as cold and hard and real as the fact that I drew those drones that murdered him.

I walk into the forest, down toward the river, retracing the way Jimmy and I came up. My mind wanders and I walk in a trance, navigating by some faded memory of our having come this way before, without actually recognizing anything I pass.

I think about the horror of that day, the cannons, the men vaporizing into bloody mist. I think about the women, the kids, the bodies stacked on the funeral pyre burning in the night. I think about my father's lifeless body sliding into that trap, his brain suspended in the mindless grip of that robotic arm. And I think about my mother lost forever in that rancid red soup.

It's dusk when I reach the river. The trees are dark, the water black. The only light comes from the sun-bleached stones littering the riverbank where they seem to glow in the shadows of coming night. I bend down and pick one up, cold and heavy in my hand. I hear a branch break and turn toward the sound, listening for a minute, a minute more. But all I hear is the deep river flowing quietly past. Calm comes over me. A kind of peace I haven't known for a long time. I slip the stone in my pack. Then I choose another and slip it in, too. I bend and pick up stone after stone, adding each to the pack, and when the pack is full, I cinch it closed, and lift it to check the weight.

Heavy enough. I swing the pack, hoist it onto my back, slip my arms beneath the straps, and knot the ends tight at my chest.

I pick Uncle John's knife from my pocket and pitch it into the river. Then I wade in after it. My legs shiver uncontrollably in the cold, the current tugging my waist, and my breath steams in front of me like some ghost escaping already from my chest. I look up at the dark sky. Not a single star in sight. I guess no one is looking down after all. There's just me here all alone, looking up, looking around, looking anywhere to avoid looking at this new loneliness I've found.

My legs stop trembling and I feel my thoughts numb.

I step farther into the river and give myself to the current, my feet dragging on the bottom for a moment before slipping into the depths. Then I lean back and let the heavy pack take me down.

It's peaceful—the silence, the cold.

I feel the pack knock against the rocky riverbed, drag along the bottom, catch a snag and then stop.

I'm weightless. I open my eyes and watch the shadows of my life rippling away on the dark surface above. I exhale my last breath and empty my lungs, the bubbles carried away in the swift current. I close my eyes and imagine my father cupping my head in his hands, kissing my hair, telling me he loves me.

Then I open my mouth to fill my lungs—

I can't do it. My body won't respond to my command, my lungs won't inhale. Panic overtakes me—survival instinct, maybe even regret. I twist and turn in the straps, kicking my legs, flailing my arms. Then I hear my father's words, "Breathe good energy in, breath bad energy out," and I relax and settle into my fate, my arms going limp and dangling in the current at my side. I laugh inside to think that this is where everything led. Somehow it all seems unimportant to me now, even silly. But here it is for real, the final moment, my last mistake.

My lungs give up their fight. I gasp the cold river in.

CHAPTER 36
You Don't Look Like an Angel

Mouth on my mouth.

Fists pounding on my chest.

Coughing, spitting, breathe.

Hands rubbing my arms, my legs. Wet sandpaper on my cheek. A fire fades into view. When I sit up, Jimmy and Junior are both looking at me. Jimmy's stripped to just his underwear, his dry clothes wrapped around me. I see my wet clothes spread on rocks near the fire, drying.

"What happened?" I ask.

"You's know what happened," Jimmy says.

"But you don't look like an angel."

"You's dun' look like much yerself."

"Did you follow me?"

"No," he says, "I followed Junior. Junior followed ya."

Junior sneezes, licks my face again. It doesn't matter who followed who, I'm just happy that they're both here. Then I see my father's pipe resting on a rock beside my clothes, the plastic case of tobacco he gave me just this morning sitting next to it. Seeing them there reminds me of what happened, and tears well up in my eyes. The fire blurs. I shake.

"It's okay," Jimmy says. "It's okay. Jus' relax."

He rubs my arms again and I feel the circulation returning in waves of tingling pain. I look down at my hands, white and wrinkled and lifeless in the light of the fire.

"I'm sorry," I say.

"Dun' be sorry. There's nothing to be sorry for."

"Oh, yes, there is," I insist, tears coming fast now, my voice cracking in my swollen throat. "I'm sorry for letting you down. I'm sorry for betraying you, for taking sides with Radcliffe. I'm sorry for your family, for leading the Park Service to them. I'm sorry for everything, Jimmy."

"So they are the Park Service?"

"That and worse," I say. "They killed my dad, Jimmy. And I watched it. They cut out his brain. Now they've got it kept in some sort of sick torture test. My mother's, too."

Jimmy moves down to my legs, kneading them with warm hands. They too begin to ache as the circulation returns.

"I've got to do something," I say. "I've got to free them from that terrible place."

Jimmy looks confused. "Thought you said they's dead?"

"They are and they aren't."

"How can ya be both?"

"That's the horror of it. They're not alive, at least not as themselves. But they're not completely dead, either." I pause to look into the fire, the flames crackling in the cold air. "Jimmy, why'd you want me to burn the bodies in the cove?"

"To release their souls," he says.

"You believe in souls?"

"I really dunno," he says, his eyes wet now, too. "There's somethin' leaves us when we die. There jus' has to be."

"Will you help me?"

He moves down to my feet, rubbing warmth back into my toes. "Help you with what?"

"Help me set my family free."

"I'll never forget what ya did for me," he says. "You's jus' tell me what ya need, buddy, and I'm with ya all the way."

Junior hops into my lap and looks up at me. I reach to pet him, my arms stiff and slow. He licks my hand.

"Looks like Junior's with ya, too," Jimmy says, laughing. "Now let's get ya back into yer own damn clothes 'fore I freeze my nuts off here and die myself."

Hannah comes to me in the night.

I wake to find her sitting on the edge of my bed, the silver moon framed in the window, her wavy red hair gray in its light.

When I sit, she startles, as if she was the one sleeping, not me. She turns and smiles. Then she leans down and kisses me on the lips, lingering for a moment before pulling away and touching my cheek.

"Are you all right?" she whispers.

"I don't know," I say, shaking my head. "I think so."

"Daddy told me what happened. I'm so sorry. I can't even imagine what seeing that must have been like."

I shrug and look away, not wanting to cry again.

"Why don't we wait and talk about Eden later when you're ready," she says, stroking my hair. "We'll find a better way."

I nod and pull her into my arms, never wanting to let her go, but knowing that I might have to. I smell her hair and kiss her head and tell her everything will be okay.

I don't tell her there'll be no Eden left to talk about.

CHAPTER 37
How Many Miles Down to Babylon?

"Pisscrap!"

Jimmy punches the locked doorknob.

"Pisscrap?"

"It's somethin' my pa said. Ya sure there's even another'n in there anyhow?"

"Yeah, I'm sure," I say, trying the boathouse knob myself. "It's hanging from a lift in the cross beams. I saw it myself."

Jimmy turns and looks out across the lake.

"Maybe we can make a raft or somethin'?"

"We'd never make it in a raft," I say. "And how would we work the locks?"

"How do ya work 'em anyway?"

"I don't know, they just open. Probably a cryptographic signature from the boat."

"Crypto-what?"

"An electronic signal."

"Like lightning?"

"Boy, we've got a lot to catch you up on."

"Whatever. We jus' better do somethin' 'fore the rest of the house wakes up. When did the creepy old man leave?"

I look back at the sleeping house, a single light burning in the kitchen window. "I'm not sure. He said yesterday he was heading out at first light. His bed was empty when I checked."

"What about his wife?"

"She has her own room."

"They sleep separate?"

"She's sick a lot."

"Hannah?"

"Sleeping like a princess."

Jimmy steps away from the locked door, and walks farther down the dock, peering around at the front of the boathouse.

"I've got an idea," he says. Then he jumps in the water.

I see right away what his plan is. My breath catches as I lower myself into the cold lake, joining Jimmy where he treads water in front of the boathouse.

"Ready?" he says, "One, two, three."

We gulp in breaths, dive underwater and swim beneath the doors. When we surface inside the shadowed boathouse, Jimmy climbs up on the dock, and reaches a hand to help me up after him. He looks funny in his dripping clothes, and I must too.

"Double pisscrap," he says. "He ain't even gone yet."

The wooden boat floats beside the dock, the carbon fiber boat suspended above it. I stand there, looking at the boats, wondering what to do. Water drips down my face, tickling my nose. I smell the varnish, the wet stone. Then I hear the jingle of approaching keys. Jimmy grabs my arm, his eyes wide with panic. Frantic, I look for a place to hide. Stepping into the boat, I scurry beneath the cockpit and open a panel, hoping that the storage bay is big enough to fit us. We scramble inside the bow, and I close the panel just as the boathouse door opens.

We lie perfectly still amidst the life vests and coils of rope. My heart hammers. I breathe slow, trying to not make a sound. I can feel Jimmy's chest rise and fall beside me in the dark.

The boat rocks when Dr. Radcliffe steps aboard, and I just

hope he didn't see our wet footprints on the dock, or hear us crawling in here to hide. I breathe a little easier when I feel the electric engines spin on. Then the boat moves gently forward, and I know we've exited the boathouse because a crack of light shows around the edges of the closed panel. Jimmy pats my back as a silent good job. I smile even though he can't see it.

The boat accelerates across the lake, rising and falling over waves, the hull slapping the surface of the water, jostling Jimmy and me woodenly in the dark. It takes a long time crossing, or at least it seems like it does, confined in a crawlspace just on the other side of Dr. Radcliffe's feet.

At last, the boat slows, and I know we've cruised inside the locks because the crack of light around the panel disappears again. Jimmy grips my arm when he feels the boat dropping. I pat his hand to let him know everything is okay. As the boat lowers into the deep locks, Dr. Radcliffe begins to sing, his words echoing off the walls of the concrete shaft—

How many miles down to Babylon? / Three score miles more and ten. / Can I find my way by candle-light? / Yes, there and maybe back again. / For if your hull is nimble and your oars light, / You may just get there by candle-light.

It must be some childhood nursery rhyme he remembers, and I'm embarrassed listening to him sing it—feels as if we're eavesdropping on a private moment.

We reach the bottom of the locks. I hear the lower gates open on their gears, and I feel the boat glide forward into the underground channel. Dr. Radcliffe doesn't sing again, and I'm glad for the silence, even though we nearly have to hold our breath it's so quiet. A few minutes later, we slow to a stop, and I hear the step plate fold out and clamp onto the dock. Then the motors shut off, and the boat rocks as Dr. Radcliffe steps out of it, his footsteps retreating up the dock.

Jimmy and I lie there for five minutes, maybe ten. Finally deciding there's nothing to be gained by waiting any longer, I pop the panel free and climb out into the dim red glow of the underground cavern. Jimmy climbs out behind me and looks around, his head turning slowly, his eyes fast and furtive.

"What is this place?"

"It's the Foundation headquarters."

"Foundation?"

I drop my eyes from his, the full connection hitting me for the first time. "The Park Service," I say.

Keeping low and out of sight, we tiptoe up the docks onto the shore. When we arrive at the locked metal door of the sintering plant, I stop and look at the keypad.

"What's the plan?" Jimmy asks, scanning the buildings.

"We're going to blow up Eden," I say.

"I figured that," he says, looking at me like I'm stupid.

"You got your strike-a-light?"

"Yer gonna blow up Eden with a pyrite and flint?"

"Just give it to me."

Jimmy stuffs his hand in his pocket and pulls out a small leather case, still damp from our swim. He opens it and empties the round flint and flat pyrite stone into my palm. I strip my father's pipe off my neck, pull out the plastic tobacco canister he gave me, thankful that it's water tight, and load the stringy tobacco in the bowl.

"Fine time for a smoke," Jimmy says, shaking his head.

I stuff the canister back in my pocket, put the loaded pipe in my mouth, and strike the flint on the pyrite over the bowl, sucking air through to coax the spark to take. Three, four, five loud strikes in the quiet cavern. and then a curl of smoke rises from the bed of tobacco. Several short puffs get it going, and I turn away and cover my cough, handing the pipe to Jimmy.

"Smoke it."

"What?"

"Puff it fast," I say. "We need to burn the tobacco down."

We pass the pipe back and forth, puffing until we're both green. When the tobacco is burned down and blackened, I use the round flint stone to grind the ash to a fine powder inside the bowl. Then I lean down with the pipe in my mouth, tilt the bowl to the keypad and blow. Black charcoal powder plumes out and settles on the keypad in an almost unnoticeable film.

"Come on," I say, grabbing Jimmy and pulling him away from the door. "Let's hide."

We retreat toward the docks and duck behind the base of a gantry crane used for pulling big boats out of the water. I hang the pipe around my neck, peek around the crane, and watch our cloud of tobacco smoke dissipate into the red shadows.

"You think anyone will come?" Jimmy asks.

"Someone has to go in there eventually," I say.

"Who all's down in this creepy place?"

"Just a bunch of old scientists, mostly."

"What's inside the door?"

"You ask a lot of questions."

"Wouldn't you?" he says, huffing.

A half hour later, we get lucky. An old man in a white lab coat shuffles up to the door and punches in his code without even looking down at the keypad. I'm sure he's done it ten thousand times by now. We wait ten minutes until he comes out again, and then we wait another ten just to be sure he isn't coming back before we sneak up to the door. I bend down and look at the keypad. Of the nine possible numbers, 3, 4, 5, and 7 have been wiped free of their tobacco-dust coating. It doesn't tell the code, but now I have it narrowed down to 24 possible combinations of these four numbers. I try the easy one first: 3457. Nothing. I reverse it: 7543. This could take a while. On my fifteenth try, I get it: 5734—the door slides open.

Jimmy and I step inside and walk past the window looking in on the atomic diffusion machines, their lasers building silicon computer chips now and dropping them on the conveyor belt. The door at the end of the hall is unlocked, and we enter the dark munitions room. I head to the far wall and look over the canisters of chemicals.

"This is what we need," I say, turning around. I stop when I see Jimmy standing at a table with a silver missile in his hand. "Jimmy?" He doesn't answer. I step over and lay my hand on his shoulder. "I know," I say, "I feel it, too. I'm sorry."

He sets the missile down, his trance broken.

"What?"

"I said I'm sorry."

"No," he says, "ya said you's found what we need."

"Yeah, over here." I lead him to the stack of canisters and point to the white lettering—

POTASSIUM PERMANGANATE.

"Ya know I cain't read," he says.

"My dad called them Condy's Crystals," I say. "We used them underground for treating our water."

"Treatin' water? What good's that do us?"

"That's not all they do," I say, righting one of the canisters and screwing off the lid. "You mix this stuff with glycerin and you got yourself a rocket to the moon."

"Is that glycerin over there?" Jimmy points to the glowing vault marked ANTIMATTER.

"No, that's not glycerin."

Jimmy eyes the blue pulsing window.

"Well, what is it?"

"You don't wanna know."

"Well, is there glycerin somewhere else here?"

"Not here, no. But the pool at Eden is filled with it. And probably glucose, too. I figure if we dump enough of these potassium crystals in there, we'll start a chemical reaction that will light the whole thing up and free the brains."

"Like the funeral fire?"

"Just like the funeral fire."

We exit the munitions room carrying two canisters each, one on either shoulder. We pass through the courtyard with its hologram starscape hovering over the fountain, and creep past the scaffolding on the scientists' living quarters. Everything is eerily quiet. We pass under the archway onto the main path, and I lead Jimmy to the door that I burst out of just yesterday after watching them kill my father. We step over my dry puke, still visible on the ground.

I lower one of my canisters, freeing my hand, and look for the keypad but there isn't one.

"Great," I say, frustrated. "Just great. What's that word your dad used to say? Pisscrap?"

Jimmy sets down one of his canisters, reaches out, and pulls the door open. He smirks at me as we shoulder our loads again and walk through the door into Eden.

CHAPTER 38
You're Free Now

The lights are dim, the hallway empty.

When we reach the control room, I crack the door and peek in. The room is dark, the workstations deserted. The LCD display is still on and the killing chair sits eerily empty.

We step inside and close the door quietly behind us.

Jimmy walks to the window and looks out over the pool.

"What the hell is it?" he asks, almost to himself.

"Hell is exactly what it is," I say, carrying my canisters to the door that leads onto the catwalk around the pool, setting them down, and examining the latch.

Jimmy joins me.

"What's the plan?"

"When we step through this door, it's gonna be way cold. We won't have much time."

"How cold?"

"Twenty below."

"How cold's that?"

"Remember the mountain?"

"How could I forget?"

"Much colder than that."

Jimmy straightens, cradling his canisters.

"Whataya waitin' for?" he says. "Load me up and lead the way. Let's do this."

I stack my canisters on top of his, only his eyes showing

above the load. Grabbing the lever, I unseal the door. A blast of cold air hits my face, my breath smokes in the red light from the pool. I push the door open and step out onto the catwalk.

Jimmy steps past me, and I close the door and seal it with the lever on the inside. We shimmy left, away from the door, away from the window. I take the canisters one at a time from Jimmy's arms and set them upright on the catwalk.

"This is some kind of cold," Jimmy says, shivering.

"I know it," I say, my teeth chattering already.

Together, we screw the lids off the canisters. I look over the rail at the red, pulsing water below. I see shadows of hoses and wires that look like sea kelp with brains floating at their ends, and I'm reminded of Jimmy's family on that bloody day in that bloody cove.

"Okay, we have to dump it fast—"

Jimmy taps me on the shoulder. I turn and see why . . .

The lights are on in the control room. We press ourselves against the wall and watch. Nobody comes to the window, but I see shadows playing on the glass. Minutes go by. My body shivers violently; I clench my teeth to stop the chatter clacking in my skull. My hands shake, my legs too. I know from biology lessons that my hypothalamus is taking over now, pulling blood from my extremities and regulating my core temperature. I look at Jimmy and see his nose is turning blue, his lips, too. His eyes are wide with fear. I feel dizzy, like I'm suffocating, and when I take a deep breath, the subzero air bites my lungs.

Still the shadows move in the control room . . .

Jimmy's legs buckle, straighten again. I grab him and hold him upright, sharing our body heat, watching the window over his shoulder. Finally, the light snaps off and the window is dark again. I shake Jimmy from his stupor. He looks confused, then he pulls his shirt off over his head.

"I'm hot," he says.

"You're not hot," I say, pulling his shirt back down before he can get it off. "You're hypothermic. I need you to focus. Do what I do. Okay? Come on, pal, I can't do this without you."

Jimmy's eyes refocus, his mind coming back. He nods. We grab a canister each and balance them against the catwalk rail.

"Do it fast," I say, my voice feeble and shaking. "Then the other canister, then we hit the door."

We tip the canisters, but nothing comes out.

I tip mine back and look inside. The potassium crystals are clumped together in the cold, forming a kind of lid. I reach in and break the crystals free with my frozen hand. Quick now, all four canisters. We tip them again and the potassium pours out, mixing into a black cloud and landing in the pool.

We set the empty canisters down, grab the others, tip them into the pool too, smoke already rising from red bubbles there.

I love you, Mom, I love you, Dad. You're free now.

We run to the door, but the door won't budge. I check the lever, push again—nothing. I slam my shoulder against it, but it holds solid. I turn to Jimmy in a panic.

"The door's locked!"

Jimmy tries it—no luck.

"Whoever was in there must have bolted it from inside."

I look into the pool for one moment and see a bright-blue flame dancing on the water's red surface. I rush back and grab two empty canisters, handing one to Jimmy. I bash the canister against the control room glass. Jimmy steps up and joins me. My hands are freezing, but adrenalin pushes away the pain. One two, one two—we smash at the glass in unison. I see a flash of white, a giant ball of flame reflected on the glass. Jimmy panics, hammers wildly against the glass, his canister bouncing free from his hand and falling into the pool with a splash. He runs back for another. I hammer on. A small crack appears. Another whack and it spiders larger. Jimmy beside me now, hitting the weak spot with me. Heat on my neck, the fireball growing, the cracking glass, sizzling chemical flames, potassium smoke, the water bubbling already in a boil. I pull back for one last mighty whack. The explosion shockwave rips the canister from my hand and shatters the glass and throws me through it.

I come to on the floor, flames licking against the broken window. Jimmy is slumped over the workstation desk, half in, half out. I jump to my feet and pull him into the control room, away from the fire. His ear is bleeding, his cheek cut.

I shake him conscious.

"We gotta go now, buddy."

His head lolls, lifts, lolls again.

"Can you walk?"

Arm in arm, we exit the control room and limp down the hall, shaking from adrenaline, shaking from the cold.

Outside, in the red cavern glow again, we jog toward the dock, hoping we won't be seen. I hear doors banging, voices shouting. A siren begins to wail. We scamper down the dock, step aboard the boat, and crawl down into the dark hull. I pull the panel closed and snuggle into the far corner with Jimmy.

"We did it," he says, his voice loud, his breathing labored.

"Keep it down," I say, "I think you blew out your ear."

"You's flew out of here?"

"You blew out your ear."

"Oh," he says, lowering his voice a little. "But we did it. Sure as that siren out there, we did it."

It sounds like he's laughing, but then I realize he's actually crying. I take him in my arms, and rock him in the dark.

"We sure did, buddy. We sure did."

CHAPTER 39
You Got a Better Plan?

"Fire," Jimmy moans. "Hellfire run."

I clamp my hand on his mouth. "Shh . . . you're okay."

The boat is moving fast, the bow tilted high. Other than the rhythmic sound of the hull slapping the water, we ride the rest of the way in silence. The boat slows, the bow drops, and I hear Hannah calling out from the dock:

"Daddy! Oh, hurry, Daddy! Mom's not well."

The boat stops, the step plate folds out.

"What is it, honey?" Dr. Radcliffe asks, panic in his voice.

"She won't wake up, Daddy. Come quick."

The boat rocks violently as he jumps out. I crack the panel and watch him stride up the dock toward the house, Hannah running ahead of him waving for him to come faster. When they're both inside, I slide the panel free.

"Come on, Jimmy. Let's hustle."

Jimmy crawls out after me, squinting in the light. He looks terrible. Dried blood in his hair, a garish gash on his cheek, one eye swollen shut. I appear to be unscathed, other than both my hands stained brown from digging the potassium crystals free.

"What'll we do now?" Jimmy asks, peeking over the side of the boat at the house.

"Let's get out of here," I say.

"Ya mean out of the boat, or out of here here?"

"I mean out of here here," I say. "The whole place."

"What about Hannah?"

My heart hurts, my head drops.

"Maybe we'll come back for her later," I say, not really believing I'll ever get the chance. "When things settle down, maybe. See if she wants to leave."

"Well, ya wanna go in for any supplies?"

"Nah . . . it's too risky."

I cross my arms and look longingly at the house, knowing we need to leave, but not really wanting to. Jimmy eyes me.

"Sure ya wanna leave?"

"We have to."

"Okay," he says, "I know this must be hard for ya, so I'll make the plan. Let's beat feet for the gate and get out of here. We'll stop at Gloria's, grab grub and my gear, pick up Junior. Then we can follow the river out until we're safe away."

"Then what?"

"We'll make camp for the night."

"And what will we do after that?"

"I dunno," he says, irritated. "You got a better plan?"

"I'm sorry," I say, realizing I'm being a jerk. "It's a good plan. Anything's better than sitting here waiting for Doctor Evil to come back. Can you run? On three. One, two, three."

We scramble off the boat and run for it. Jimmy's limping pretty well, so I slow down to keep his pace. When we get to the gate, it's unlocked, as always. We step out, close the wooden door, and hustle along shore toward Gloria's. The afternoon is quiet, the lake calm, and it feels funny to be running. Almost as if we're playing some game and there isn't really anything to be frightened of. And what are we frightened of? An old man and his sick wife? Then it hits me, what we've done. Or what we haven't done. We haven't solved anything by destroying Eden.

"What is it?" Jimmy asks, stopping and turning around.

I realize I'm standing still, my feet planted on the ground.

"It's her, ain't it?"

"It isn't her."

"Yes, it is."

"I've gotta go back, Jimmy."

He kicks a rock into the lake.

"I knew it was her."

"It's not her."

"Well, what is it then?"

"We destroyed Eden, but now what? Next month another train of retirees comes up. And what will they do with them? Slaughter them is what they'll do." Then I remember the safe room and the switches. "They'll slaughter them if Dr. Radcliffe hasn't drowned them all first."

Jimmy bends over and picks up a stick. He flexes it in his hands, looking back over my shoulder toward the lake house.

"What are ya sayin'?"

"I'm saying think about the Park Service."

"What about 'em?"

"They'll just keep on killing people, won't they? I mean, they'll even be hunting us once we leave this lake."

Jimmy snaps the stick in two and looks at it in his hands, weighing the halves.

"Whataya wanna do?"

"I don't know," I say, pulling at my hair as if an idea might be hiding there. "We go back and buy some time, I guess. Try to get that doomsday key away from Radcliffe."

"Ya dun' think he'll suspect us blowin' up Eden?"

"He might suspect something if I don't show up soon. But he didn't seem to know we were his hidden cargo, and there's no other way down there, so how could it be us?"

"So yer jus' gonna go back like nothin' happened?"

"That's the plan."

"What am I supposed to do?"

"Go clean up and lay low," I say. "Wait."

"Lay low and wait for what?"

"I'll need your help taking over when the time comes."

"Yer crazy, man," he says, "straight crazy."

"Maybe so," I say. "You in or out?"

"I like ya crazy."

"Does that mean you're in?"

"I'm in," he says, tossing both sticks in the lake. "But jus' for the record, yer plan ain't no better'n mine was."

CHAPTER 40

Why is Courage Wasted on the Young?

The door is cracked.

I stop in the dim blade of light dividing the dark hall and check my appearance, smoothing my rumpled shirt, running my fingers through my hair. My hands are stained a deep shade of potassium brown, clearly visible in the low light. I stuff them in my pockets, nudge the door open, and step into the room.

The bedroom is large, soft carpet, thick curtains drawn tight, an incandescent lamp burning low beside a massive bed, and it smells of mothballs and iodine. I see them gathered there around her bed, already in some sad vigil. Mrs. Radcliffe lies propped up on pillows, her eyes closed, her arms resting at her sides. Dr. Radcliffe sits on the edge of the bed, Hannah sits next to him with her head buried in her hands, the soft light on her red hair giving her the appearance of Mrs. Radcliffe's ghost mourning her own passing. And for a moment, I think she might be dead. But then I see Gloria, standing beside the bed inspecting a silver thermometer in the lamplight.

"Still running a fever," she says.

She dips a towel in a bucket of ice water, rings it out, and lays it across Mrs. Radcliffe's brow, slapping Dr. Radcliffe's hand away from his wife's cheek.

"Give the poor woman a little breathing room."

Dr. Radcliffe opens his mouth to say something to her, but stops short when he sees me. His face hardens. He says:

"Where have you been, young man?"

I stand in the doorway with my hands in my pockets.

"Where have I been?"

"It's not a difficult question," he says.

"Daddy," Hannah says, pushing his knee. "Not now."

"Eden was destroyed in a fire this morning. Sabotaged. I'd like to know just where Aubrey was when it was set."

Hannah turns to me, drilling into me with those green eyes through the slits of narrowed lids. She appears to be thinking, deciding something. Then, without looking away, she says:

"Well, Aubrey couldn't have had anything to do with it because he was here with me all day."

Gloria glances at Hannah, a confused look on her face.

I decide to act surprised.

"Did you say destroyed by fire?"

Dr. Radcliffe looks from me to Hannah and back again.

"It's served its purpose anyway," he says. "We don't need Eden anymore. Let's talk about this another time."

"Served its purpose?" I say. "You mean you plan to let the retirees live when they come up?"

"I said let's talk about this another time."

"I want to talk about it now," I say, stepping closer.

"This is hardly the place," he says, nodding to his sick wife.

My hands clench in my pockets, the left one gripping my father's tobacco case.

"You didn't seem to have any problem talking about things right after you slaughtered my father."

"Enough!" he shouts, leaping to his feet and pointing to the open door behind me. "Get out of here."

Hannah tugs his shirt tail. "You don't need to yell, Daddy.

Aubrey's right, we do need to talk about things."

"Your mother is ill," he says. "This is not the time."

Hannah looks at her mother. "She's dying, Daddy."

"You don't know that."

"Yes I do. She's dying just like the others."

"That's no reason to disrespect her here," he quips. "Or to abandon her life's work. Now, enough of this damn arguing. This is hardly the place, and it's certainly not the time."

Gloria removes the towel from Mrs. Radcliffe's head, and dips it again in the bucket, the draining water loud in the heavy silence. I remember her telling me that the Radcliffes took her and her brother Tom in when they were both young, raised them like their own. But wasn't it the Radcliffes who killed her family? At least the Park Service killed her family, which makes the Radcliffes responsible for it. I was planning to let things be, to wait for the right time to act, but I'm tired of all these lies.

"Why not now?" I ask. "You worried Gloria will find out that it was you who killed her family? You worried she'll find out that you and Mrs. Radcliffe are the Park Service?"

Gloria drops the wet cloth with a splash, her hands frozen above the bucket. When she looks up, she eyes Dr. Radcliffe and cocks her head, her face scrunched up in confusion.

"That's what you people do down there?" she says. "You run those evil machines? You hunt people?"

"That's an oversimplification," Dr. Radcliffe says, blinking.

"I guess murder is too simple a term for you," I say.

Gloria shakes her head sadly, mumbling to herself.

"It's not possible. Mrs. Radcliffe? It's just not possible. Is it?" Then she reaches back into the bucket, wrings out the towel, drops it again. "Dr. Radcliffe," she implores, looking up, "is it true?"

"I'm leaving," he says.

I cross my arms, blocking the door.

"Nobody's going anywhere until we settle some things."

Dr. Radcliffe turns to me, his fists balled, his face red.

"You little bastard," he slurs. "I bring you up here out of that grimy anthill home of yours. I show you our paradise, offer you the world to protect. I give you my beautiful daughter. And you're gonna tell me when and where I'll go in my own home?"

"I'm not yours to give to anybody, Daddy," Hannah says.

"You know what I mean," he dismisses, waving her off.

"No," she says, crossing her arms. "I don't."

A strange but welcome confidence rises in me. I remember Jimmy's mother talking about the butterflies. About needing to let part of ourselves die so another part could live. I decide to let my fear die and my hope live.

"I know this much," I say, feeling bolder by the sentence, "we're setting the people trapped in that grimy anthill free."

"Excuse me?"

"You heard me," I say. "We're opening up Holocene II."

"We most certainly are not."

"Sorry," I say. "You're not in charge here anymore."

Dr. Radcliffe stands there shaking with rage, wide-eyed and lip twitching. A vein in his forehead swells, snaking its way across his temple. He looks from me to Hannah, as if wanting her to say something, to deny what I've just said. She doesn't—she just looks down. Dr. Radcliffe lifts his chin and looks at the ceiling, as if asking some god above to intervene. Then, with the swiftness of a much younger man, he strides to the bureau, slides the drawer open, pulls out a pistol, and points it at me.

Hannah's hand leaps to her mouth, Gloria drops the towel again. I stand alone in front of Dr. Radcliffe, staring at the gun.

It's old, really old. The barrel is blued steel with delicate floral engravings that look cheerfully out of place on a weapon, and the wooden handle is stained black so that Dr. Radcliffe's knuckles look as white as bone clenched upon the grips.

"Whoa, wait just a minute," I say, holding up my hands. "There's no need for a gun here."

"So it was you, you little turncoat bastard."

"What was me?"

Dr. Radcliffe waves the pistol at my raised palms, the dark potassium stains there plain as day.

"You plan to shoot me?" I say, trying to act unimpressed. "Really? You've stooped to this? I thought you were a pacifist?"

"Oh, I am a pacifist," he says, "but sometimes a peaceful outcome requires violence. I'll be damned if I'll let you undo my work because of a lousy sentimentality towards humans."

"You're insane," I say, shrugging and looking to Hannah and Gloria for support, but they stand mute with blank faces and fear for me in their eyes, so I turn back to Dr. Radcliffe. "Whatever. That old thing probably doesn't even work."

He cocks the hammer back with an audible click.

"Oh, it works," he says. "I restored this myself. It's from the American Civil War, you know. It was good enough for killing traitors then, and it'll be plenty good enough for killing traitors now. So move out of my way. I've got work to do."

I look at the gun, my guts growling with fear, and I almost step aside. But then I think about Jimmy's slaughtered family. I think about my dad murdered in that chair. And I think about all those people trapped down in Holocene II. A strange feeling comes over me, maybe courage, maybe something else, but I know I won't be able to live if I let him kill any more people.

I spread my arms, blocking the door.

"I'm not letting you leave here with that key."

"What key?" he asks.

"I know what you're going to do," I say. "You're going to flood Holocene II. I won't let you."

He shakes his head and lets out a laugh.

"Why is courage wasted on the young?"

Then he steps forward, leading with the pistol pointed at my chest. I stand firm. He pauses just feet from me.

"I'm giving you five seconds to step aside and then I'm shooting you dead."

"I'm not surprised," I say, "you're nothing but a murderer anyway. Don't even bother counting because I'm not moving."

I look him in the eyes and hold his stare. He frowns, blinks three times. The room is silent. His fingers tighten on the grip, his wrist muscles tense. Then Mrs. Radcliffe lets out a moan. And not just any moan, but a sick bellowing moan that fills the room and fades away, leaving all heads turned toward the bed.

Hannah thinks faster than I do—

She rushes up and grabs her father's arm, pushing the gun down toward the floor. He jerks free, whipping her face with the barrel, and she lurches back with a bloody gash on her chin.

I jump to her side and catch her in my arms.

Dr. Radcliffe steps toward the open door, but not before Gloria grabs his belt from behind.

He wheels around with the pistol and fires.

Gloria falls to her knees, her hand caught in Dr. Radcliffe's belt, her arm wrapped around his waist.

Kneeling there in the fatal silence following the shot, she has the appearance of some shamed subject hugging her king's legs and begging for his forgiveness. But it's he who should be begging for hers. A red hole appears in the back of her yellow dress, growing as the fabric wicks the gushing blood.

The gun barrel smokes.

Hannah screams.

Dr. Radcliffe staggers backwards, Gloria's head slumping limply against his legs. Then he turns to rush from the room and drags her body several feet, her hand clutched in a death grip around his belt. He panics, making little choking sounds as he waves the pistol at Hannah and me, struggling to loosen his belt buckle with his free hand. I move toward him, but Hannah pulls me back, tears welling already in her eyes. He steps into the hall, his belt slipping free of its loops and falling to the floor with a soft thud where it lays gripped by Gloria's corpse.

Hannah releases me and rushes to Gloria, sinking to the floor and gathering her head in her lap.

I race after Dr. Radcliffe.

The house is shadowed now, the sun behind the roofline, but the grounds outside are washed in bright light, and I have an odd feeling of running past windows to some other world.

I plunge downstairs and into the dark basement just as the safe room door is closing, the wedge of light shrinking on the tile floor. Reaching out as I run, I snatch Hannah's microscope from the table and dive for the safe room, sliding across the tile floor and thrusting out the scope and wedging it in the door.

"Damn stupid kid," Dr. Radcliffe mumbles from inside.

He kicks at the microscope, attempting to dislodge it, but it doesn't budge, and he stubs his toe and curses with pain, his shadowed silhouette hopping on one foot in the thin sliver of light leaking out onto the tile floor.

"Son of a bitch!" he shouts.

Noticing a fire extinguisher on the lab wall, I jerk it free and stick the nozzle in the crack of the door and blast the panic room full of white smoke. Then I hook my arm through the crack and slap blindly at the wall, feeling for the green button. I hit it and the door swings open.

I rush inside the smoke-filled room toward the sound of Dr. Radcliffe's coughing, catching him just as he's reaching into the panel that hides the doomsday switches. I smash his head with the fire extinguisher, a hollow ping echoing in the small room. Then I grip his collar, walk him to the door, and toss him out into the lab. I smash the keypad off the wall with the extinguisher, and chuck the extinguisher at Dr. Radcliffe where he lies bellowing on the floor. Then I kick the microscope free from the floor and palm the red button that closes the door.

It all happens so fast. I lean against the wall breathing hard and coughing myself. The smoke swirls, clears some. The key is in the switch panel, its chain dangling over the desk edge. The panel lid is open. Did he do it? I look to the monitors—

The lake is peaceful and calm. The Foundation cavern is hazy red in the smoke of Eden's fire. The Holocene II Transfer Station is awake and working, loaders moving across the floor carrying pallets, men stacking supplies into open elevators.

I lean forward and look down. Both toggles are untouched with the safety covers in place. I let out my breath and laugh.

"You're dead, you punk!" He pounds on the door.

I slap the red button again, just in case. Then I search the safe room floor. No gun here. That means he still has it.

The pounding intensifies.

"You're all dead, you got that?" he screams. "You punk! You think I don't have other ways to flood you parasites out? You think I'm that stupid?"

Then he stops. Then he's gone.

CHAPTER 41
The Wave

Smoke sucking through the ceiling vent.

My hammering heart slows, my breathing relaxes.

I look back at the monitors and see a terrible sight—

The boat speeds across the lake toward the dam, piloted by Gloria's brother Tom, Dr. Radcliffe sitting behind him with the gun trained on his head. I replay his parting words:

"You think I don't have other ways to flood you parasites out? You think I'm that stupid?"

He's going down to the Foundation to flood Holocene II. The moment that it hits me, I know what I need to do. My eyes jump to the toggles, remembering his doomsday directions: Phase 1 floods Holocene II, Phase 2 floods the Foundation and triggers the explosion that sets off the tsunami. The only way to stop Dr. Radcliffe from getting to the Foundation and flooding Holocene II, is to trip the Phase 2 toggle, detonating the wave. That must be why he brought Tom along. It's another moral dilemma from the doctor of doom himself.

Tap-tap-tap—

Someone's knocking on the safe room door.

"Aubrey? Are you in there?"

Oh, no, Hannah! How had I forgotten about Hannah? And Jimmy, too. I palm the green button, opening the door. Hannah rushes into my arms. When I pull her away and look into her eyes, they're red from crying, but determined.

"Daddy's on the boat," she says. "We have to stop him."

"I know," I say, nodding to the monitor where the boat speeds toward the dam. "You have any ideas?"

She looks past me to the switches.

"There's only one way."

"You know about the wave?"

"Of course I know," she says. "My mother didn't raise me to be a dummy."

"What about your mother?"

Hannah's face drops. "She'll be dead soon either way."

"What about Tom?"

She frowns.

"Collateral damage."

"That's sounds like something your dad would say."

"I know," she says. "But we don't have a choice."

Looking at the monitor, I watch the boat speed toward the dam, skipping across the lake, getting smaller by the minute. I look back to Hannah and cup her beautiful face in my hands, wiping blood away from the gash on her chin.

"Are you sure?"

"We need to hurry," she says.

"Okay, we'll do it. But here's the deal. You run to Gloria's and get Jimmy. Have him take you up to the bluff where I first saw you. Don't tell him why or he'll want to come down here."

"No way," she says, shaking her head. "You go get Jimmy, I'll stay here and pull the switch."

"No deal. These are my people down there, Hannah. And I need to stay behind and do it."

"What if you can't get out in time?"

"I'll get out in time."

"You promise."

"I promise. Now please hurry. Find Jimmy, and get to high ground. I'll meet you there."

"I don't want to leave you."

I take her in my arms and kiss her.

"Don't worry," I say, pulling free. "I'll see you in a few minutes on the bluff."

She wipes a tear from my cheek.

"Not if I see you first."

I watch her run across the dark lab, her silhouette rising against the rectangle of light coming down the stairs. She stops, hesitates, and turns.

"Aubrey . . ."

"You don't have to say it."

"You don't even know what I'm gonna say."

"Yes, I do. Now go on and get my friend to safety."

She laughs, shaking her red hair and flashing me a smile, then she turns and disappears up the stairs.

The minutes crawl by, the boat crawls across the monitor toward the dam. I have no way of knowing when Hannah and Jimmy are safe, so I wait. I wait and I watch the screens.

Hazy red smoke fills the Foundation cavern, and I know the scientists are down there still struggling to put out the fire Jimmy and I set. The Holocene II Transfer Station is dimmed for rest hours now, the machines parked, the men gone back to their living quarters. On the third screen, the sun glints off the lacquered boat approaching the dam, the monolith of stone hanging precariously above it to the right.

I look at the toggles tucked away in their panel, violent in their simplicity, only their clear-plastic safety covers between fatal disasters for all three of these separate screens.

I plan to leave Phase 1 untouched, protecting Holocene II. I'll toggle Phase 2, flooding the Foundation and setting off the blast that will free the landslide and raise the wave. I'll twist the key free, deactivating the panel, and race for the bluff.

I just hope I can make it in time.

Lifting the safety cover, I slide my trembling finger over the Phase 2 toggle, the plastic smooth and cold. I look in the monitor at the receding boat, an outline of Tom's torso barely visible at the wheel.

"I'm really sorry Tom."

I look in the other monitor at the hazy Foundation cavern where two white-coated scientists stand on the path observing the smoke rising from Eden.

"I'm sorry for you guys, too. Even though you deserve it."

I close my eyes, preparing to pull the switch. I'm reminded of the last question on my Foundation test, seemingly so very long ago now—an impossible choice between sealing off a lower level to save Holocene II, or letting fate take its course by doing nothing. I remember closing my eyes and making a blind choice, a choice I now know was the wrong one. I think about Mrs. Radcliffe lying in her bed, dying but not dead yet. I think about the scientists down in their cavern. I think about Tom driving that boat with a gun to his head. I open my eyes.

The steps are steep, my feet heavy as lead.

I cross the living room and step out onto the terrace. The water is calm, not a ripple on its surface. Far across the lake, the boat is just a distant speck of color against the gray face of the dam. I'm numb and unsure. I'm sad. I don't know whether I made the right choice or not. I doubt I'll ever know.

Just as I'm turning away, a silent puff of powder bursts from the mountainside. Confused, I stand and watch. Several seconds pass and then a terrible explosion reaches my ears, and the granite monolith slides down the mountain in a mammoth tumble of dust and broken stone.

But I didn't touch anything, I didn't throw the switch!

The boat arcs left, turning away from the landslide.

A gray wall of water rises up—way, way up.

The wooden boat lifts, tossed like a tiny fallen leaf riding the monster surf, and then it disappears forever beneath the crushing white-cap break, rolling and thundering as it rises into the sky high enough to hide the entire dam from my view.

I'm mesmerized by its magnificence, frozen by its horror, and in the sheer gray face of the advancing wave, I see a mirrored silhouette of the bluff behind me, the tips of pine trees, the mountains beyond, as if the wave itself were a canvas upon which the setting sun is painting the landscape ahead, recording it there one final time before the wall of water rolls on and devours it forever.

You fool, I think. No man could outrun this wave.

Holocene II! The thought smashes into my consciousness, waking me from my trance. I have to know if Holocene II was saved. I have to know or my last thought will be a thought of failure. I have to know if I've died for any reason at all.

I turn from the wave, run inside the house, sprint across the living room, and race down the stairs to find her in the safe room, pale as a corpse, looking into the monitor, staring at the wave. Stepping up beside her, I look at the toggles—

The key is removed, the panel closed.

I look at the third monitor—the Transfer Station lights are

still dim, the machines still quiet, nothing looks disturbed.

She speaks without looking away from the wave:

"The water will drain from the Foundation. When it does, you and Hannah will need to begin again. The right way."

Me and Hannah? Does she not see the wave, I wonder.

She grabs my hand, pressing something cold into my palm. I look down and see a clear-plastic case filled with syringes of red serum, the same syringes that Dr. Radcliffe showed me. I look over and see the open refrigerator. When I look back, the safe room door is closing, sealing, the loud metallic click of the electromagnetic locks, and Mrs. Radcliffe is gone.

My eyes dart to the monitors, the transmissions dead, the screens completely black. Air rushes in from the ceiling vent, the walls vibrate, something slams against the metal door. My ears pop from the increased pressure. Then the water comes. It streams up from the toilet, leaks down from the ceiling, gushes through the cracks in the locked door. It pours in, covering my feet, swirling in a whirlpool on the floor. I stuff the syringes in my pocket and jump onto the desk. The water keeps coming. The walls vibrate again, harder. The ceiling vent breaks open, funneling a wide stream of water into the safe room, rising to cover the chair, the desk, the controls.

I'm surprisingly calm—maybe because I've drowned already once before. As the water rises to my chest, I stretch up and breathe in the shrinking pocket of air. Then I'm swept off my feet and pulled into the pool, paddling to stay afloat. The LED lights go dark; the safe room turns as black as any grave. I tread water, bumping into walls, kicking submerged supplies, listening to the water pour in from the blown-out ceiling vent. Then the flow of water slows to a trickle and stops.

I slow my paddling and float, listening . . .

Heavy silence punctuated by my breath. Dripping water echoing off the walls. Floating blind, I paddle around the room feeling for the door. I find it. I stretch my foot down into the depths and kick the wall, aiming for the Door Open button. I'm not sure it will even work, but I'm betting the battery's still functioning or the electromagnetic locks shouldn't be holding at all. I feel something—yes, there it is. I tap it with my toe, but nothing happens. Then I remember there are two buttons, left one green, right one red. I move my toe left and kick again. The door springs open and the water rushes out, carrying me with it into the flooded daylight of the basement, or what would be the basement if there were any house left at all.

The ceiling is gone, the walls too. Just a gray open-air pool cut into the ground, the remaining lake house foundation encircling it above like jagged teeth made of stone. The water comes only to my waist, though the lip of the pool is far above my head. I turn and look at the steel safe room, stripped of its coverings, standing exposed against the barren concrete wall.

It held—the damn thing held after all.

CHAPTER 42
One Last Night

Washed clean.

Everything.

I can't imagine the brute force of a wave that sweeps away an entire house and everything in it. I think of Mrs. Radcliffe locking me in the safe room and stepping out to meet her fate, and I remember our conversation about suicide in the kitchen that day. I guess she chose to end it herself after all.

Reaching the edge of the pool, I climb a set of crude stone steps that must have led to some ancient cellar long before the Radcliffes rebuilt. I step onto the peninsula and stand dripping on the bare rock where the lake house had been.

Other than the few foundation stones, nothing remains.

No floors, no walls. Not a blade of grass, not a flower. The dock and the boathouse are gone. The red-clay tennis court is stripped to just a smooth pad of concrete. The garden wall is erased, a shallow trench where it once stood. I look up to the bluff and gape at the destruction. The hillside stripped bare, the raw clay and exposed rock dripping. It looks like the wave ran several hundred meters up the slope, snapping pine trees like twigs and carrying them away in its retreat. All around the lake, an enormous ring of destruction rises up the banks. I look back at the water, strangely calm. A few floating trees, a few bobbing boathouse timbers.

A sparrow circles then swoops down, looking for its nest.

It lands not far from where I stand, jerks its curious head left and right, and then it accepts the new surroundings and dabs its beak in a puddle and begins cleaning itself.

Life goes on, I guess.

I walk to where the garden wall had been. I remember Jimmy boosting me to look over, I remember Hannah standing there with her hands on her hips and telling me that the door wasn't locked. There's no door now. I step across the narrow trench and head up the bluff to look for Hannah and Jimmy.

It feels like climbing a mountain on Mars, everything a wasteland, even the topsoil gone. As the bluff levels off, I pass splintered stumps of enormous pine trees and craters where others were ripped right out from the ground, roots and all.

Arriving at the edge of the wave's reach, I hop over a few trees left lying in my path, and scramble up the steep rise that leads the last several yards to the top. I look around.

Then I see Hannah running toward me through the trees, her red hair bouncing around her shoulders. We come together in a wild tangle of arms and tears and kisses, and we stand meshed together in a tight embrace, turning a slow circle on the edge of the bluff, kissing and caressing one another.

"I was sure you were dead," she says.

"Yeah, me too," I say. "Where were you?"

"We ran," she says, nodding behind her. "I wanted to stay and wait for you, but Jimmy made me run. We're just working our way back now. I'm so glad you're alive."

I feel something brush against my leg, look down, and see Junior jumping with excitement. When I look up again, Jimmy is walking toward us, a wide grin stretched across his face.

We sit together on the edge of the bluff looking out over

the lake. The sun has dropped behind the mountains at our backs, and I know it must be setting over the ocean now, setting on that cove of so long ago. I look at Jimmy, idly petting Junior beside him. His eye is swollen shut from the explosion at Eden, his ear still caked with dried blood. I look at Hannah, her green eyes staring off across the water. The cut her father gave her is sure to leave a scar on her chin. I think about everything that we've been through, everything that we've lost—especially the people we each loved. I think about our adventures, and about the strange events that brought us all together.

Hannah lays her head in my lap, I lean down and kiss the cut on her chin. A long time passes without a word between us. The coming night drops a blue blanket of stars down in the east, the dark mountains cutting a black outline against it. The lake holds the last of the day's light and gives it back in silvery purples—hues that reflect the mood.

By and by, I hear a click and catch a spark. Turning, I see Jimmy lighting a fire made of broken limbs that he's gathered. He blows it lit, builds it up, and soon the flames are licking at the dark, popping and shooting red sparks rising into the night.

I reach to my neck and remove my father's pipe. Then I dip in my pocket for the tobacco canister, unseal it, and stuff the pipe full. Leaning over, I grab a stick and stretch it into the fire, being careful not to wake Hannah sleeping in my lap. Then I draw the flaming tip slowly to the pipe and puff the pipe lit.

I cradle the pipe in my palm, just like my father used to do, and I roll the sweet smoke around my mouth, then blow it out and watch it coil away and disappear into the night.

Hannah sits up and rubs her eyes.

"That stinks," she says, scrunching up her nose.

Jimmy stirs the fire.

"Give 'em a break. It was his father's."

"I know it," Hannah snaps back. "I'm not stupid."

And here I was worried about them and they're back to their old selves and fighting again already. Jimmy stretches out on his back, resting his head in his hands, and Junior lies down beside him, resting his head on his paws.

"We'd better get us some sleep," Jimmy says, after several minutes. "Gotta get up early and hunt up somethin' to eat."

"I hope you don't think I'm eating meat," Hannah says.

"Ya hearin' this over here, Aubrey?" Jimmy calls, laughing. "Yer little princess wants pancakes fer breakfast."

"You're a jerk," she says.

"Yeah, well you's spoiled rotten."

Hannah turns to me.

"You're not going to let him talk to me like that, are you?"

"I'm not getting involved," I say, puffing my pipe.

Hannah crosses her arms and turns her head away.

Several quiet minutes pass. I think about what Hannah's mother said, about us starting over and doing things right this time. I only wish I knew what the right thing was.

I reach into my pocket and feel the case of syringes there. Do I even want to live for a thousand years? And what about Mrs. Radcliffe's warning? Can you really love someone for that long? What about Holocene II? She said the water will recede, and I know we need to get down to the Foundation before the next train arrives for Eden, but I have no idea what to do then. Can you just free thousands of people who've been used to living a certain way for centuries? And if we do, how will we prevent them from destroying the world again?

Then I think about the drones, the submarines, the ships. I've no idea how to stop their targeting of humans, or if I even should. What am I thinking? Of course I should. I must. But what about violent people? Enemies? What about the rest of the world out there? What about all those curious other places that Dr. Radcliffe never got to tell me about?

I'm tempted to tell Hannah and Jimmy about the forever serum in my pocket, to inject ourselves with it right here, right now. To put our three heads together and make a plan for the Park Service, a plan for Holocene II.

I pull the pipe from my mouth to tell them, but before I can say anything, Hannah huffs at Jimmy over her shoulder.

"Savage," she says.

"Snob," Jimmy shoots back.

I clamp the pipe between my teeth again, look into the fire and laugh to myself. I wonder if they'd argue like this for a thousand years. I decide our planning can wait until morning.

For just one last night, I want to be a kid.

THE END *of* BOOK ONE

About the Author

Ryan Winfield is the *New York Times* best-selling author of *Jane's Melody*, *South of Bixby Bridge*, and *The Park Service* trilogy.

For more information go to:
www.RyanWinfield.com

Made in the USA
San Bernardino, CA
27 May 2014